Book One of the 'S

THE UNFORGIVEN SPY

By

Gavin Stone

Masses of Secret Spy Tradecraft Revealed!

First Edition 2022

ISBN: 9798361876198

Message page

Message page

This book is dedicated to all who serve or have served in silence. Those who work in **all** areas of the Intelligence Community and give it everything they have on a daily basis, without recognition.
Your tireless efforts to keep us safe as you remain out of sight are truly appreciated. May your amazing efforts to allow us to continue our daily lives without fear be praised and recognized.
From the bottom of my heart,
THANK YOU!

Message page

blank

Blank

Glossary

AOI – Area Of Interest.
Basha – Army shelter. (Large piece of waterproof material to make a sleeping shelter).
Castle – A secure base of operations/outpost. (CIA)
COS – Chief Of Station (CIA).
Cuds – British army terminology for the rural countryside.
Derog – A derogatory report. An intelligence operative's version of high school detention.
DGSE – Directorate-General of External Security (French Intelligence).
EOD – Entry On Duty. CIA terminology for a new starter at Langley (Usually for Analysts).
ERV – Emergency Rendezvous Point (A backup meeting point in the event of your original RV becoming compromised).
FOB – Forward Operating Base.
Fort Monkton – Codenamed No.1 Military Training Establishment, Fort Monkton is the facility used to train MI6 Recruits and also acts as a liaison center between intelligence staff and Special Forces.
ICBM – Instant Calm Breath Method. Also can be used for Intercontinental Ballistic Missile.
IED – Improvised Explosive Device.
KIA – Killed In Action.
Marine Drill Sergeant – An extremely friendly military officer who will answer all your questions and help you overcome any military issue you're finding difficulties in. Lovely guys.
MICE – Stands for Money, Ideology, Compromise & Ego. This is the system used for recruiting assets by Intelligence Officers.
NLP – Neuro-linguistic Programming. An almost hypnotic method of persuasion is used on a subject

when they're wide awake to develop a connection through social engineering, making the subject more likely to comply with your requests.
OP – Observation Post/Point (sometimes also used for Operational Procedures).
PMC - Private Military Company.
PSD - Personal Security Detail.
Recce – Reconnaissance.
RPG – Rocket Propelled Grenade.
RV – Rendezvous Point.
SCIF - Sensitive Compartmented Information Facility.
SDR – Surveillance Detection Route. A pre-planned journey through particular areas to expose surveillance. Also; Cleaning run. A route used to become surveillance-free.
Shreddies – British army-issue underwear (shorts).
Strap2 File – A secrecy classification level of a file within the British Intelligence community. (Most people authorized to the level of working with a Strap1 File aren't even aware that a Strap2 File exists).
TAB – Tactical Advance to Battle. Used frequently in place of running/jogging. (It's a two-mile TAB to the shops)
Taliwagon – Toyota pickup truck.
TQ – Tactical Questioning.
VDM's - Visually Distinguishing Marks. (Logos on clothing/scars on skin/stickers on cars etc.).
Wheel Artist – An operative highly trained in tactical/defensive/evasive driving techniques.
100MPH/Sniper Tape – Extra strong military fabric duct tape.

blank

Blank

Chapter 1

A feeling of being watched. That's how it started.

Sandy pulled the rear door to the office closed behind her until it clicked shut. The last to leave, she hadn't realized how late it was. It seemed eerily quiet as she locked the door and slipped the keys into her pocket. An uneasy feeling of someone's presence caused the hairs on the back of her neck to stand on end.

She strode along the service road behind the block of shops and offices.

A sound—the scrape of a footstep behind her.

She looked back but saw nothing—just shadows.

She picked up her pace, silently cursing her heels and wishing she could run in them. The noise alone seemed to get louder as she clicked deeper into the narrowing alley.

There it was again. Another shuffle in the shadows.

She was sure someone was there, she coughed, a futile attempt to cover her discomfort and fear. Pulse quickened, heart rate increased, she pulled her purse closer to her side and walked faster, her shoulders raised, her head lowered like a turtle. Rigid arm swings at the side of her body were quick and sharp as she hustled along.

Footsteps drew closer from behind—confirmation. There was definitely somebody there, and they were closing in. Her head felt light as fear intensified, giving her tunnel vision. Yet, she could see the end of the road. It seemed to be taking longer to get there than it should.

Two more minutes until I get to my car.

The denial of danger in one part of her mind was battling with the growing fear in another. She was marching now. She'd gone cold, and her mouth was dry. She hadn't noticed that she'd begun to tremble. The movements of her purposeful, brisk walking covered it well.

Nearly there. She could see her car. The glow from the streetlights in the distance seemed to comfort her as she got closer.

Sandy reached into her purse, fumbling for the keys.

"Don't drop them, don't drop them," she whispered to herself. She fished them from her bag, hands shaking, then attempted to pick the right key.

The footsteps grew louder. Closer. Quicker.

"Don't look back," she mumbled.

She ran the last few yards to her car. The keys jingled as she lost her grip, dropping them on the pavement where they slid under the car.

She cursed herself as she knelt, sweeping her hand left and right under the car. Panicked, she thought of all the movies where this type of thing happened, and the killer got to the victim before they could get the key into the lock.

"Got them." She clambered to her feet and attempted to unlock the car door.

Footsteps were still behind her, getting closer. Her breathing became quicker and more shallow, the steam from her breath visible. She finally got the key in the lock, and the door unlocked.

They were right behind her now.

She dropped into the driver's seat, slamming the door shut. She quickly locked the door and looked up.

Nobody was there.

She took another deep breath. Tried to calm herself. Feeling silly but also relieved, still shaking, she inserted the key into the ignition.

A white panel van skidded to a halt behind her, blocking her car in. The side window smashed inward.

Sandy screamed.

A figure reached in and pulled up the lock.

She froze as her door was yanked open. The man pulled her out of the car, his hand wrapped around her mouth now, muffling her screams. She kicked and thrashed as he dragged her backward.

The side door of the van slid open. Sandy was shoved inside. Men inside the van held her down. She couldn't move, frozen with fear and physically restrained.

The door slid shut, then the van raced away.

The street was quiet again. Stillness in the air. The keys still swinging in the ignition of her car, the door slowly swung closed. Shattered glass peppered both the inside and the outside of her car.

Three years earlier, somewhere near the Syrian border

The black cotton pillowcase over his head let in sufficient light for Jensen to know he was still outside but provided no clue as to where he was or what was happening around him. He gulped for air, trying to get oxygen to his body. His rebel captors fired random bursts from their AKs, yelling and cheering, as they steered him roughly toward a pickup truck. He could only assume that his comrades, Marshall and James, were somewhere nearby and undergoing the same treatment. Several men grabbed him, hauling his six-foot solid, muscular frame onto the bed of the pickup truck. As he was bundled onto the deck, Jensen braced himself and was pulled backward, the momentum sending him crashing into the bulkhead. The bumps and bangs confirmed that his colleagues were equally helpless and close at hand. The duct tape binding Jensen's wrists caused a sweat build-up and stung. He was forcefully held to the bulkhead as the yelling and gunfire continued.

"Breathe," he whispered, trying to calm himself with the knowledge that his captors didn't want him dead. If they did, they'd have just shot all three of them on sight. Instead, they decided to take them prisoner. This was standard procedure. The captives were made to feel disorientated and fearful in order to subdue them mentally and dash any hopes of an escape. Even though he'd been through the process many times before in training and knew each step intimately, his heart still raced. Adrenaline coursed through his body and his throat dried as he gasped for more air. The next stage of the protocol would be to display them as trophies, driving them through an angry crowd, who would happily cut their organs out with a rusty knife, given half a chance. The theory was that the fear engendered by the threat of physical violence at the hands of the rabid crowd would bring about a feeling of dependency on their captors. If successful, the hostages would feel they needed protection from the crowds, and that added strength to the strange but newly forming bond between them and their captors and outweighed the desire for escape.

The gunfire ceased as the drive to a primary holding area got underway. In line with the process, the route was, as usual, over rough terrain and followed an obscure trail to confuse the captives' sense of direction. A dust cloud billowed behind the two-truck convoy as it sped across the arid landscape, the heat from the sun causing the pillowcase to stick to Jensen's face uncomfortably. Their weapons, of course, had been confiscated upon their capture, with the day sacks following shortly afterward. Now the blindfolded Jensen felt tugs at his wrist and realized his watch was about to be a souvenir. After peeling the duct tape back from the watch, the rebel guard also decided he wanted the personalized braided Paracord bracelet, too. An argument in Arabic ensued as another of the rebels rummaged through Jensen's pockets to see what he could find. Jensen's boots caught the second man's attention and ignoring the long zipper that ran the length of the inside of the boot, which would have made the whole task a lot easier, the idiot unlaced and tugged hard to get them off.

All three of them lay stock still, stripped down to just jeans, T-shirts, and socks. None of them tried to communicate for fear of getting the business end of a rifle butt impolitely, telling them to be quiet.

Unbeknown to the hooded hostages, the trucks pulled into what appeared to be an industrial area with a large warehouse and scattered outbuildings, which were slightly sheltered by a cinderblock perimeter wall.

The yelling started again as the three men were dragged into the warehouse. All three were shouted at in Arabic as they were shoved and pulled, not knowing where they were being taken. Each of them tried to keep their footing as they were forced along a corridor and into a dim room. A steel barred door was slammed shut behind them as they were shoved to the floor. Jensen was conscious of the sound of a padlock snapping shut and the footsteps of their new guard as he retreated down the corridor. Jensen pulled the damp pillowcase off his head and let his eyes adjust to the faint light from the small, barred window. The air was humid and stale. The room, now coming into focus, allowed him to see the other two pulling the covers from their heads and the figure of a more mature but equally disheveled-looking man sitting on a chair, hands cuffed behind his back. The stench of stagnant sewage and body sweat filled the air as all three men scanned the room. The rotten plaster was falling off the walls, and the paint only seemed to stay for lack of better places to go. The concrete floor was peppered with litter and blood splashes. The man on the chair looked bemused at the reactions of the threesome.

"You took your time!" he shouted.

"Love what you've done with the place, sir!" Jensen chirped in a cheerful English accent as he got up to look for a right angle in the wall's brickwork. At the barred window, there was a perfect corner for his purpose. He rubbed his wrists up and down to fray the duct tape and free his hands. "I'm trained for this," Jensen muttered to himself.

"Get me out of here," their newly reunited friend groaned. Harrison was Marshall's former department head from when Marshall came over from the States to work for the Brits. Marshall may have been working as a contractor now, but Harrison still commanded the kind of respect he expected when working for him in the past. All three of them worked freelance and had been hired to complete a Target Acquisition job by a PMC. Either way, Marshall still addressed Harrison as "sir" and still kept a good level of professional conduct. A good level for Marshall anyway.

"Yes, sir." Marshall stood and pulled down his jeans.

"Gonna ask Harrison to do you a favor first?" James asked in jest, his American accent somewhat stronger than Marshall's

"Oh, please, I'm not that desperate!" Marshall dug into his groin to peel off a strip of tape. The banter between them had become second nature and was how Jensen and Marshall took the edge off serious situations. James had occasionally worked with them in the past, but it didn't take him long to get into the same mode of thought. Marshall finished peeling the tape away, securing a button compass and a plastic handcuff key stuck to its underside.

The one area rarely checked on captives is the bridge between a man's genitals and his anus. In almost every country in the world and even amongst the most hardened of soldiers, it's a place frequently overlooked as not many men want to go through the invasive procedure of checking there and feel extremely uncomfortable doing so.

With this knowledge, the three-man team had all smuggled in a few separate bits of an Escape and Evasion kit. Marshall freed Harrison while Jensen retrieved a ceramic razor blade concealed in the same fashion.

It's amazing what you can do with a bit of skin-colored sniper tape, he thought.

***

Tension grew as everyone held their positions after they'd got into place. This was the pivotal part of the plan. If this part went wrong, it would make future escape attempts infinitely harder. Jensen silently prayed, controlling his breathing, poised to take action.

Harrison lay on the floor with James and Marshall kneeling beside him.

With a deep intake of breath, Jensen shouted to get the guard's attention. Footsteps clapped along the corridor until the guard was in sight. He ran to the caged door, peering through the bars.

Inside, the chair had toppled to the floor, and one of his prisoners appeared to be suffering some sort of seizure. With a sense of urgency, he opened the cell door and rushed inside toward Harrison. He prodded James with the barrel of his weapon and motioned for both men to move aside, failing to notice that the duct tape no longer bound their hands.

As he knelt to examine the stricken prisoner, Jensen approached from behind. Before the guard was aware of his presence, Jensen pulled the guard's forehead back with his left hand and reached around the front of him with his right hand. He sliced the man's throat with the ceramic razor and, stepping back, lay the guard down slowly onto the floor.

Tradecraft: *The trick is to cut straight, continuing at the same depth from one side to the other, and not to move outward with the shape of the neck. Moving along the natural shape of the neckline will result in only slicing the skin. The damage will be horrendous, but death is not inevitable and will take much longer. Thus giving the subject the chance to react or retaliate in a desperate attempt of defense. Starting from one side and cutting straight across at the same depth will result in the blade going deeper into the curve of the neck. Ultimately cutting the windpipe, muscles, and arteries. Death is much quicker, and the chance of retaliation much lower.*

Blood pumped out over Harrison as the guard grabbed at his throat. Neck scarf soaked, panic in his eyes, the guard struggled as he grasped the front of his neck. There was a gargling noise as he lay there spitting and coughing. Blood seeped through his fingers as it bubbled in his futile attempts to cling to life. His final breaths became shallower as Jensen looked into his eyes. The pupils dilated, then nothing. Like a light switching off, the life was drained from him, the only remaining motion the expanding pool of blood.

The three of them rapidly distributed the guard's possessions between them. It was decided that James would have the boots, as he was a size nine. Because he got the boots, Marshall and Jensen got the toys. Marshall performed the standard checks on his new AK47, and Jensen pulled back the top slide of the Colt 1911.

"Can you get me out of here now?" Harrison grumbled impatiently.

"Yes, sir," Jensen replied. "Marshall will be running point, you stay between James and me, and I'll be at the rear."

"Okay, just get on with it." Anxiety laced Harrison's voice.

It seemed to Jensen that the operation was going to plan—so far at least. Knowing they'd be outgunned and outnumbered, the odds seriously stacked against them, the team had previously set up an observation post to assess the situation. Having identified where their high-priority target was being held, they concluded that the extraction would be much easier if they got themselves captured and driven straight through the front door rather than attempt a pre-dawn raid with all guns blazing. After all, it would be much quicker to shoot your way out if you didn't have to shoot your way in first. It was a risky plan at best, but there wasn't much else in the form of options. Not to mention they weren't one hundred percent sure exactly which part of the compound their target was actually in. They would have had to use up more time and ammunition to find him, lowering the chances of success even more. However, the uncertainty of the situation required that they act quickly before their target was moved to another location. Acquiring the target was only half of the equation, and of necessity, the exit strategy was somewhat crude. Any hope of success required planning. For this, James had cached some useful kits and weapons in various strategic locations around the perimeter wall.

Marshall exited the room into the corridor holding his new AK at the ready. Jensen moved out and over to the other side of the corridor, pistol in hand. Their socks dampened their footsteps on the stone floor, allowing them to move quickly and quietly as they inched along.

They neared the end of the corridor that opened to the right into a large guard room. One man sat on a shabby sofa in the middle of the floor, watching an outdated television. An AK was propped beside him.

Controlling his breathing, Jensen moved as slowly as he could. His socks left momentary moisture marks on the floor with each step. Not having his boots on might have given him a slight feeling of vulnerability, but it definitely gave him a tactical advantage. Aware of Marshall's movements to his left, he inched closer.

Three other doors on the other side of the room allowed access, but only one was open. The open one revealed sunlight from the outside courtyard. Jensen saw Harrison and James making their way silently up the corridor in his peripheral vision. He looked back at the guard as he eased forward.

When Marshall gave a signal to Jensen, he moved into the room. His movements were slight to avoid the noise of his clothes rubbing, the tension of the task increasing the closer he got to the guard.

Marshall eased stealthily to the left, AK raised, ready to give the guard the good news if it went noisy. The guard was deeply engrossed in whatever TV show he was watching.

Jensen eased up behind the guard until he was only inches away. He drew back his fist and snapped forward with a rapid strike to the back of the guard's head. The potentially deadly blow knocked him out instantly while Jensen swooped in and swiftly scooped up the AK47 that sat beside the tumbling guard.

Tradecraft: *The trick is to punch the back of the head at the soft spot where the base of the skull meets the neck. Hitting the bottom right corner with the punch aimed diagonally up in the direction of the left eye has a devastating effect. Equally hitting the bottom left corner with a punch aimed diagonally up toward the right eye has the same result. The blow will incapacitate; a single blow can even prove fatal. The strike will usually knock a person unconscious but can kill if enough force is used.*

James came into the room with Harrison, and Jensen handed him the pistol while making the necessary checks on the AK. Marshall moved to cover the doors in case anyone came through after hearing the thud of the guard hitting the floor, but before he was halfway there, the door on the left rattled.

Their window of relief was only momentary.

The door burst open. Two rebels stormed into the room, brandishing AKs and yelling in Arabic.

Jensen watched as James raised the pistol with his right hand, shoving Harrison behind him and into the corridor with his left hand.

One rebel let out a burst of shots. Jensen dove to the floor, returning fire. A burst of three rounds pierced straight through the rebel to the left. Marshall fired at the one on the right. A tight group of holes had gone through the center of his chest and through the wall behind him, too. Both men dropped to the floor. Without thinking, Jensen's training kicked in. He rushed forward and turned the first body over, kicking the man's weapon toward the corridor. James didn't need to wait for an invite. He snatched it up and handed the pistol to Harrison.

Moving quickly, Jensen repeated the procedure, ejecting the magazine from the AK and stuffing it into his back pocket. Before they had time to move, shouting was heard from the courtyard.

"Shit! We have to get out of here before this becomes a gang fuck!" Marshall moved toward the open door, weapon raised. The gate was about a hundred meters away, with only a couple of trucks for cover. "I'll take James and run for the trucks. You lay down suppressing fire as we move out, and then we'll return the favor as you join us."

Marshall waved in a calling motion at James as he leaned against the doorframe, preparing himself for the run. "Three, two, one, go!"

Letting off a couple of short bursts from his rifle, Marshall ran toward the trucks, sand being kicked up by his socks as he ran, James a second behind him.

Jensen sprang into the doorway. Spraying bursts of fire in the direction of the noise. Rebels fired from crevices around the compound. The familiar cracks of 7.62 rounds sounded all around him.

Jensen continued with his bursts of suppressing fire randomly, then paused and looked over to see if Marshall and James had made it to the cover of the engine blocks of the trucks. A crack of shots hit the doorway and caused him to jump backward. The bullets splintered the wood, peppering plaster and powder into the air. Jensen dropped farther back inside for cover.

His heart raced, and sweat covered his face. Adrenaline surged through him as he took a deep breath again.

Another burst of shots cracked into the walls around the doorway. A few pierced through the guard room and hit the wall behind him. The TV screen shattered.

Jensen ran over and shoved the chair at the two doors that allowed entry to the room, slamming one shut with the action. Then he propped the chair in place and shoved a table in front to stop it from sliding back, blocking both doors. At least no one would get in through either of those doors in a rush.

Marshall and James had gotten into position and were returning fire.

It was now or never.

Jensen grabbed Harrison by the scruff of the neck and ran out of the doorway. Bursts of fire hit the floor around them. He gave it all he had, sprinting toward the trucks, practically dragging Harrison behind him.

Marshall and James were firing at anything that moved, but the number of rebels were increasing. The return fire was becoming more intense. Jensen tucked in as rapidly as he could behind the cover of the trucks. His chest heaved as he gasped to catch a breath.

There wasn't enough time or ammunition for another two-part run. They'd all have to make a dash for the gate together. Being nearly out of ammo wouldn't stop them from shooting as they went, with probably just enough to get them to the other side of the gate that marked the only opening in the cinderblock walls.

They all knew the score. Nobody said anything. They all knew what each other was thinking. A look was all it took.

In unison, all four of them broke cover for the gate.

Bullets thudded into the ground around them as they ran. Their small target was about twenty meters away, but it took ages to get there. They all fired off shots as they ran toward the gate with everything they had.

Nearly there—almost through.

Marshall had his weapon about waist height as a rebel came from the other side of the gate just as Marshall got there.

Time stopped as the rebel stood there, weapon aimed at Marshall.

Marshall had his aimed at the rebel as he continued to run.

The cracks of weapons firing around them seemed to dampen. Everyone was moving but somehow still seemed frozen to the spot.

Marshall's weapon spit several bullets and the rebel dropped as Marshall ran into him and through the gate. Then he checked himself. "Phew! No new holes!" He gulped for air and tried to catch his breath as relief flooded through him.

Jensen kneeled to grab the magazine from the rebel's rifle, relieved his friend was okay. His leg muscles felt like they were on fire while sprinting in the heat, and his pulse throbbed away as he tried to catch his breath. Two more mags were in an ammo pouch on the rebel's belt. He distributed them not a moment too soon. The next wave of rebels rounded the corner of the cinderblock wall. Marshall and James spun on the spot to fire toward them.

Another group was heading toward the gate from the inside. Jensen fired into the compound, taking down three of the rebel guards. The small group on the outside had been neutralized. It was time to move out.

As the four ran from the area toward their cache, they scored another Kalashnikov and an antique, NATO-issue, Browning HP from a couple of rebels on the wrong end of a bad day. With all four now armed, they were marginally better equipped to shoot their way out to the exfil point. It was fortunate that the compound had proved only lightly guarded, with most of the rebels away, no doubt engaged in some nefarious enterprise.

But in the ensuing fire-fight, at least ten more rebels got slotted as the results of the group's exit strategy. The return fire from the compound continued sporadically as they battled their way out of the area, with a few rebel troops in close pursuit. The group reached one of James's hidden caches and punched out a get-me-home signal on a sat phone buried there, with a couple of loaded Gen4 Glock 17s and some extra and much-needed ammunition.

They were all close to exhausted and gasping for breath as they held their position at the exfil point for the chopper. Time ticked away, and ammo was limited. They did everything they could to hold down their position. Fueled on adrenaline, pulses racing, they returned as much fire as they dared while still trying to use the ammunition sparingly.

There was no sign of the helicopter and no way they could hold their position for long. Marshall was beginning to fear the worst. Jensen had already concluded that this might be their last stand. How the hell could they get out of this one if the chopper didn't show up?

Rebels were closing in, and their ammo was running out.

***

The sounds of the rotor blades coming in from above, accompanied by the roar of the chopper's engine, filled Jensen with hope. Marshall fired his last few rounds off from his AK before switching to his sidearm, then looked up, still firing as the helicopter descended. The downdraft pounding the floor kicked up a wall of sand around them. The smell of spent fuel filled the air, and they could feel the heat from the helicopter's engine being pushed by the rotor's downdraft. Jensen spent his last couple of rounds firing toward the enemy as the chopper closed in.

The helicopter gunner rattled away a "mass of brass" to keep the rebels at bay, and not a moment too soon as the team was pretty much out of ammo. While Jensen and Marshall gave the older Harrison a boost, James turned to lay down more covering fire with his last few rounds. With all the noise and commotion, nobody noticed he'd taken a hit until he dropped his weapon and toppled face down in the sand. Jensen and Marshall grabbed an arm and unceremoniously hauled him aboard the chopper as it began to rise.

Marshall and Jensen knelt on either side of James. Only his top half was moving, his chest heaving rapidly up and down and his head going slightly side to side with eyes wide as he looked around in desperation. Marshall used his knife to cut away the clothing from the wound. Jensen grabbed Kwik Clot from the onboard trauma pack as they battled to save James's life.

"Hold on, pal," Marshall yelled over the deafening roar of the engine as the chopper gained altitude. The pleading look in his eyes spoke volumes to Jensen, who was doing all he could. James's breathing became increasingly rapid and more shallow. Then the quick succession of shallow breaths slowed until the life drained from his eyes. Jensen watched as yet again he witnessed the life of another human being extinguished. Marshall attempted CPR, but Jensen knew that their companion was gone. He brushed his fingers over James's face closing his eyes. Nobody spoke further.

All three men buckled themselves into their seats and looked down at their lost companion. The ride in the helicopter seemed to take forever as Jensen sat with sobering thoughts of mortality. James's leg moved from side to side under the motion of the rotor blades, one recently liberated boot swaying back and forth. You could almost think he was merely catching some well-deserved sleep if not for the hole in his torso covered in blood.

The dead guard's boots dragged Jensen's mind back to the haunting look in the eyes of the man as he died. Jensen spared no thought for the others he had killed in the fire-fight, but when you cut a man's throat and look into his eyes, it becomes personal. That pitiful look, screaming for help before the light was extinguished and the life drained away, was exactly the same as that in the eyes of his friend. James had dedicated his life to working in the shadows of a covert world and would now be nothing other than a black star, a name in a book, and another wall decoration. His accomplishments were never recognized, and his service was never rewarded. This was exactly the type of stuff he wanted to keep his baby girl away from.

Chapter 2

The cuckoo clock on the wall would normally have been alerting the world that it was nine o'clock in the evening, but a few weeks after bringing it home, the novelty of its call had worn off, and it was decided to leave it in silent mode. The wooden contraption looked somewhat incongruous amongst the modern interior and designer furnishings, but it was a souvenir of a trip to Switzerland before they'd actually moved into the house and decided upon the décor. Most of the pictures and canvases in the room were portraits of Jensen and his wife MJ or photos of their precious baby girl Elena, all except one.

A picture in a silver frame of his late comrade, James, out of his combat gear, standing beside MJ in front of Big Ben.

Jensen relaxed on the couch in the dimly lit room, nursing a large glass of Russian vodka. He placed his glass on the coffee table, showing his replacement paracord bracelet. A carbon copy of the one he'd lost. MJ was lying across him in a blue satin negligee with an oversized but well-deserved glass of white wine, her long blond hair still slightly damp from her long soak in the bath. With Elena finally asleep, the two of them were getting cozy, ready for a little Netflix and chill. As any full-time parent of a toddler will tell you, "Netflix and chill" translates to "sit and dribble" until you drag your sorry ass off to bed and sleep. Elena was the cutest little girl they could ever ask for, Jensen thought, but she was also one hell of an effective contraceptive. A subtle smirk and mischievous glint in MJ's big blue eyes indicated to Jensen that she was silently teasing him.

"What?" Jensen asked in profane innocence.

"Nothing," MJ replied innocently as she unbuttoned Jensen's shirt. "I was just thinking about the day we met."

"And thinking what might have happened if we hadn't?" Jensen asked. "You'd probably have married that accountant. What's his name? Fred? Ted?"

"It was Jed."

"Whatever. A dutiful housewife meeting the other moms for lunch and to talk plastic surgeons."

"Would not." MJ gave him a playful slap across the chest. "I'd have retrained, taken that law degree I was thinking about and been fast-tracked to partner."

"But instead, you're half a world away, collapsed on the sofa on top of your stay-at-home husband after a long day in the world of corporate recruitment."

"And I wouldn't have it any other way," she said as she undid another button of Jensen's shirt and slipped her soft hand through the gap, probing the rock-hard torso. "You remember the barbecue?"

"Are you kidding me?" Jensen replied. "I couldn't stop drooling, and it wasn't the steaks." He'd always be grateful that six years earlier, he'd accepted an assignment as an "off the books" contractor from an acquaintance named Max, who was working from a C.I.A. outpost in a particularly nasty part of the world. When the contract was satisfactorily concluded, Max had invited him to stay in California for a while.

"I think it was your accent," MJ said. "You looked okay, but when you opened your mouth ..."

"My accent? Maybe I shouldn't have brought my gorgeous American missus back to merry old England where it's full of blokes with English accents."

"Maybe it's a little more than the accent. Burgess Hill isn't exactly teeming with charming trained killers."

"Perhaps not the most useful skill for a quiet life in the commuter belt," he said.

"Do you miss it?" she asked, pulling her head back slightly and displaying genuine concern in her eyes.

"We've been through this," he said after a long inward breath. "It's not just about me anymore. It's not even about you and me. I'm not flying around the world leaving you looking after Elena on your own, wondering if I'm coming back." He couldn't help himself looking at the photograph of James and MJ on the side.

The turning point had come the evening when MJ joyfully announced that the "perfect two" were soon to become three. Over the next few months, Jensen unconsciously reduced his workload, sidestepping contracts as MJ's pregnancy progressed. Eventually, he became unavailable and took a job working locally in the security industry as a temporary measure. It meant he could be working while staying close to home for when the baby was born. After Elena made her appearance, Jensen quit the security work and went back to what he knew best, and for what he had been so intensively trained, taking on a few short-term contracts. At first, the familiarity of being back on the job was invigorating after the dull routine of security work. But somehow, it was different now.

MJ turned his head back from the photograph and kissed him. “When I was pregnant, and you started doing that local security stuff, you were so bored. I hated it.”

“Not as much as me,” Jensen said.

“I know you had to get back to work properly after, but I am glad you’ve stopped. I didn’t think you could be any more amazing when I first saw you at that barbecue, but you’re an amazing stay-at-home dad.”

“You think?” Jensen took a glug of his vodka.

“Yes, I do think.” MJ finished her white wine and set the glass on the coffee table. “And I also think it’s time you had your reward.”

Jensen put his glass down without finishing it and let MJ’s lips meet his again.

Then the doorbell rang.

“At this time?” MJ muttered.

“I’ll go.” Jensen re-buttoned his shirt as he made his way out of the living room toward the front door, shouting “Coming!” to their mystery visitor who had by now rung the bell three times.

Jensen opened the door and Marshall shoved his way inside. “We need to talk. Now!”

Jensen had no idea why Marshall was so rattled. Whatever it was had to be important for him to come at this time of night. He skipped the pleasantries and ushered Marshall in.

The three of them gathered around the dining table as Marshall played a video on his phone. It showed Sandy, Marshall’s recently estranged ex-girlfriend, sitting in a chair with tape over her mouth; she looked scared witless. She was obviously bound to the chair, but the restraints couldn't be seen. Her forehead was covered in sweat, her hair soaked, and she was breathing heavily. Fear showed in her eyes as she screamed, the muffled noise held in by the tape. Her head was jerked back violently, and an arm came around her neck, the rest of the person out of view. Her attempts to scream increased, and the fear in her eyes peaked as the hand revealed a ceramic razor. The skin was pierced, the razor dug in deep, and the cut was deliberate and slow. Sandy obviously felt every second of it, every ounce of pain displayed in her eyes. The struggle continued as panic rose to the surface. She was terrified. She knew this was the end. Finally, her head dropped forward, and the tension stopped. She was gone. Blood poured down the front of her lifeless body, then the video stopped abruptly.

The battle-hardened Marshall put on a brave face, but Jensen knew he was hurting and felt his pain. MJ's hands covered her mouth, as she sat in shock at what she'd just seen.

Tears in the corners of his eyes threatened to flow, but Marshall held them back.

"Where's it from?" Jensen asked, watching Marshall, who was still struggling to maintain his composure.

"I don't know. It was sent to my phone earlier. No demands, no speech, nothing."

"Does anyone else know?" Jensen asked. Subconsciously he was aware of a shift in MJ's posture, but it didn't alert him just yet. He dismissed it as her feeling uneasy after viewing such horrific footage.

"I'm going in to report it, but I wanted to show you first. Just in case … you know." Marshall looked pointedly at MJ, then back at Jensen.

"Do you want me to come with you?" Jensen was concerned for his colleague's state of mind, but Marshall seemed to have regained a measure of self-control.

"No, I'll be fine. Just watch your six."

Jensen stood and clasped his friend's shoulder. "You too, mate. Let me know how it goes, and if you need me for anything, I'm here."

Marshall left without another word.

Jensen closed the door behind him and downed his vodka before pouring another large one. He sat at the dining table opposite MJ, who had remained silent since watching the video. Something didn't seem right.

"Are you okay?" he asked.

Of course, he knew it was a futile question, but he had a feeling that something was off and wanted to try and work out what it was. "Is it Sandy?"

"Yes. Well, no, I just feel for Marshall is all," she said. "Seeing her killed that way." MJ sat facing him with her words, belying what her body was telling him.

Tradecraft: *TSA agents working at the airport are trained to watch a person's feet as they stand at passport control. If they stand straight, everything is usually okay. Still, if their body is straight and their feet are facing the exit, it's a sign of their being extremely uncomfortable and wanting to get away as quickly as possible.*

MJ's feet were pointed toward the door.

"Was it something you saw in the video?" He kept his voice soft, gentle.

MJ's hand went up and twiddled with her Tiffany necklace, a first-anniversary present that Jensen had bought for her when they were visiting America. Jensen recognized the discomfort in her body language; he was sure she'd seen something.

"No, I told you. I'm just upset about what happened." He observed the position of her arms, covering particular areas, one arm flat on the table shielding her torso, the other fiddling with the necklace in front of her throat. It was the limbic brain's way of protecting herself. Subconsciously she was guarding her throat and vital organs, a reaction a person inadvertently performed in times of discomfort or deceit.

"What was it? What did you see?" he pushed.

"How do you do this to me? How do you always know what I'm thinking?" she asked.

"Come on, MJ, it's important." he said.

"I know who was in the video. I know who cut her throat." Her voice wavered as she spoke. Her face displayed fear and confusion.

"Who? Who was it?" he asked. "How do you know them?"

She seemed to be weighing her options, working out what to say and do. MJ had turned her body slightly away from Jensen, her feet now fully pointing toward the door. She displayed signs of being cold and hugged her shoulders.

Jensen was becoming tense. "Come on, MJ, who was in the video?" His voice had raised, and she met his gaze. Her hands were now spread as she leaned onto the table.

“YOU!” she yelled. “It was you!”

Chapter 3

Jensen stepped back, his head spinning, trying to figure out how she'd come to this conclusion. She looked him in the eye, waiting for a response.

"What?" His hands grasped either side of his head above his ears, elbows pointing out, still not able to comprehend her accusation.

"I saw it when you cut her throat. Only for a second, but I saw it."

"Saw what?" Jensen was dumbfounded.

"Your paracord bracelet. You always have it on your wrist. You never go anywhere without it, and now it's showing on a video of you cutting a girl's throat."

Jensen's head was swimming with information. Then it all clicked into place. He spent the next few minutes reassuring MJ that it wasn't him in the video and that he'd never do such a thing. MJ had calmed a little at the reassurance that the man she loved wasn't the cold-blooded murderer of her family friend's ex-partner. He grabbed his phone and quickly dialed a number. As the phone was ringing, Jensen looked over at MJ.

"It wasn't me, baby. That I promise you. I think I know who it could be, though, and that's thanks to you."

Marshall's cellphone was redirected to voicemail. Jensen swore and waited for the tone before excitedly shouting his message. "Marshall, it's me, when you get this, call me! I think I might have a lead on Sandy's killer." Jensen hung up and turned to MJ.

"I need you to trust me, MJ. Get some things packed, and you and Elena go and stay in a hotel for a couple of nights. Pay cash and leave your phone here." Jensen went into the sideboard and pulled out a Go Bag. "Here, there's a phone inside this that I can reach you on. It's untraceable as long as I call you and you don't ring out on it." Jensen had set up what's called a "Break phone."

Tradecraft: *A break phone is when you buy two disposable pre-pay phones and divert the calls from phone one to phone two. Then you smash up phone one and drop it in the river. To get in touch, you simply dial the number of phone one, and the call goes to the second phone. Anybody trying to triangulate the signal of phone one won't be able to because the call has been diverted to the second phone and can't be traced.*

"Here's the address of the best hotel to use. "Don't let anyone know you're there, and do not use your bank cards at all." Their conversation was interrupted by a soft and tired voice from the living room doorway where Elena stood, rubbing her eyes and yawning.

"What's happening, Daddy?" she murmured.

Jensen went over and bent his knees to bring him lower and talk to her at eye level.

"Nothing; it's okay, sweetie. Mommy's going to take you on a little adventure. You can stay in a hotel with a big television and a swimming pool. Doesn't that sound good?"

"Can I take blankie?" Even a two-year-old has her priorities, Jensen thought.

"Yes, darling, of course, you can," he assured her. He looked back at MJ but remained at Elena's level. "One last thing, go and get your little 9mm ACP your dad bought you before we left the States."

MJ looked alarmed. "But if I shoot someone in England, they don't have the same laws here."

"I know that," Jensen said. "But I'd rather have you alive and figure out what to tell a jury than have you dead, and I have to figure out what to tell our daughter. If you need to shoot, don't hesitate. I'll sort everything out afterward."

Jensen grabbed his Glock 17 and two spare magazines, all neatly held in a holster that slotted inside the back of his jeans.

Tradecraft: *Some people would argue that this was unconventional, but in his line of work, most of the time, he had to carry concealed as opposed to open carry, so he'd grown accustomed to drawing it from his back. It offered the tactical advantage of being in the same place of carrying pretty much all outfits and attire. Let's face it, you can hardly go to a black tie event at the embassy with a leg holster halfway down your thigh on the outside of your black trousers and matching tux. Whether you're in a suit or shorts, jeans or tracksuit, you can always conceal a pistol at the small of your back inside the waistband, even if it's in a belly band and not a traditional holster. Changing the location of where you carry with each outfit is also a big no. In an unexpected contact, your brain has little time to think and reacts instinctively. Reaching your leg for a sidearm to find it's not there can be disastrous, and you lose valuable seconds. Always keep your pistol in the same place, and the repetition from training will have you acting automatically in the event of an unexpected attack. Of course, you can draw quicker from the hip, but as a C.I.A. instructor had once told him, "Speed is everything, but accuracy is final!"* And Jensen was pretty sharp with a pistol.

MJ put on a coat that was just long enough to cover the top half of her thighs with some black leather knee-high boots, she still had her negligee hidden underneath. She grabbed the go bag and took hold of Elena's changing bag, too.

"I need the bathroom," Elena asked more than she told them.

"That girl could pee for England!" Jensen laughed, kissed his wife and daughter, and pulled on his coat. "I've got to go. Are you going to be okay?"

"Yes, just go. I'll take care of Elena and get to the hotel. Where are you going?"

"To try and catch Marshall. I'll call you from a payphone when I'm done. I love you."

"I love you, too. Go."

MJ dropped the bags on the sofa, ready to take Elena back up the stairs to the bathroom as Jensen closed the front door. He squeezed past MJ's black Astra Sport to get to the Mondeo, his mind working overtime as he considered the facts leading to the horrific scenario he had just witnessed. Remotely unlocking the doors to the Mondeo, something niggled at him about his current situation. Something wasn't right with his surroundings. He wasn't sure what it was as he rushed to get going, overriding his gut feeling to stop and take a second to figure it out. Against his better judgment, he drove off into the night with haste, hoping he wouldn't be too late.

Chapter 4

The Mondeo's dashboard clock showed that it was approaching ten as Jensen hurtled down the highway trying to catch up with Marshall, the screaming of the engine almost drowning the insistent ringing of his cell phone.

"Marshall, where are you?" he yelled into the phone.

"I went in, but Harrison's not there," Marshall replied.

"Okay, meet me at his house. I think I know who's behind this."

"Really?" The phone cut in and out, the signal patchy. Then it cut off completely as the signal dropped.

Jensen threw the phone onto the passenger seat, wondering why he couldn't get a signal in the middle of the city. Yet, some Taliban asshole can upload a video on his mobile phone from a cave in Afghanistan. Still troubled, he tried to work out what was niggling at him as he left the house. What was it he'd spotted but not registered?

Harrison's house was in a secluded area outside the city at the end of a long private driveway bordered by trees. The house was in darkness, the gray granite façade illuminated only by the moonlight. Harrison's Jaguar sat in the driveway out front, the only car visible—there was no sign of Marshall.

Jensen pulled aside some distance from the house and killed the lights. He shut off the Mondeo's engine and took a few minutes for his vision to adjust and to familiarize himself with the layout of his new surroundings. Jensen took the Glock from its holster and pulled the top slide back just enough to see the brass, then released it again, safe in the knowledge that there was a round in the chamber. Making sure the vehicle's interior lights remained off, he opened the car's door. He got out slowly with his mouth slightly open to increase the sensitivity of his hearing, then clicked the door of the Mondeo shut and moved away from it. He worked his way around to the other side of the car and dropped down the bank slightly amongst the bushes. He knew from experience that cars could give you a false sense of security.

Tradecraft: *Contrary to popular myth, cars actually provide minimal protection, and there are few places on a vehicle that would stop a bullet. You are better moving away from them completely, especially if you don't know from which direction shots might be fired.*

Jensen stopped. Looked and listened. Keeping still and waiting for anything that might indicate a potential problem.

Breathing steadily and using a Special Forces method, Jensen slowly made his way to Harrison's house.

Tradecraft: *Special Forces move in a particular manner, bending both knees and keeping the majority of their body weight to the rear and their back straight. They hold their weight on one leg while the other moves in front, the balance transfer doesn't begin until after the heel of the soldier's foot is on the floor. Then, when the heel is down, the rest of the foot slowly starts to roll forward, and the weight is shifted from one leg to the other. It takes a bit of practice, but this process allows the operative to walk silently without stones crunching loudly or twigs snapping underfoot. Most importantly, his head moves at the same level, not bobbing as he walks. Any up and down motion on a horizon would be caught by the eye immediately; the slow movement is smooth and doesn't attract attention.*

"I'm trained for this!" Jensen muttered to himself.

After stopping frequently to orient and observe, he neared the front of the huge country home where the front door sat ajar. Instead of kicking it open and running inside as they do in the movies, he took the time to get up nice and close to take a look through the windows. Starting on one side, he glanced into the room and slowly moved around in a semi-circle, pie-ing the room, listening closely, moving slowly and carefully, scanning and clearing each section of the pie as he went. He cleared another room and continued to work his way around the whole of the house. Satisfied those downstairs rooms contained no threat, he pushed the front door open slowly. Stopping to listen and make observations again before moving closer, he got as close to the edge of the door as he could without exposing himself in the open doorway. Rapidly performing a button-hook maneuver through the doorway, he sidestepped into the room to avoid the area known as the "fatal funnel" and continued to clear the room.

Tradecraft: *The fatal funnel is the name for the immediate area of the doorway. It's where one is most vulnerable and most likely to get shot. Silhouetted in a doorway, you pose the perfect target for your enemy. The trick is to spend as little time as possible in the fatal funnel and get to cover or concealment as fast as you can. The two frequently get confused.* Cover *means you have some tangible protection from fire;* Concealment *is where you cannot be seen or easily seen but have little or no physical defense.*

Satisfied he was in no danger, he edged his way around the room to the door on the opposite wall, then stopped and listened. Lowering himself to the bottom of the door and staying to one side, he listened for sounds coming from the next room.

He got a careful grip on the door handle and moved it down slightly. Just a fraction. Then a fraction more a few seconds later. He moved it so slowly that anyone on the other side wouldn't even notice. Movement catches the eye and, unless it is so slight, will instantly attract the attention of anyone in the room. The trick is to make any movement so slow it wouldn't be noticed even if you were facing the door. When the handle was fully depressed, he slowly edged the door open a fraction. Again, extremely slowly so as not to alert anyone with its movement. As soon as the door was open enough and he could clear the room, he entered. Using the same technique as before, Jensen moved into the back room to find Harrison tied to a chair and barely conscious.

"We have to stop meeting like this," Jensen said, lowering his pistol. "Is there anyone else in the house?"

"No, they're gone. I live alone." Harrison grunted.

"It's the rebels from Syria, isn't it?" Jensen asked as he untied him.

"How did you know?" Harrison looked genuinely surprised. Jensen always seemed to be one step ahead of the game. The fact that he constantly appeared to know more than was humanly possible never ceased to amaze Harrison. Jensen was not in small talk mode, however.

"What have you told them?" he growled.

"Nothing." Harrison tugged at the collar of his shirt as if to loosen it. "You know me. I wouldn't give them anything."

His blink rate increased as he spoke, indicating higher levels of stress. Harrison's body language contradicted his words. He brushed the tops of his thighs as if trying to sweep invisible crumbs from his legs. Jensen recognized this as one of Harrison's regular pacifying behaviors, a means by which he attempted to soothe his nerves when he found himself in uncomfortable situations. With these visual indicators and a cluster of verbal tells, Jensen knew Harrison was holding something back.

He glared at the man. "Tell me what you've done."

"You were always so good, Jensen. We really missed out when you quit." Harrison crossed his legs, sitting back in the chair. "You just have an uncanny knack for seeing through people."

Jensen stared at him, waiting for what was to come next.

"You remember the guard whose throat you sliced? His brother wants vengeance." Harrison sat there, his legs swaying slightly from side to side.

"So you gave them Sandy? And who else?" Jensen's voice was hard and even.

Harrison's leg went from a swaying motion to that of a slight kicking action as if he was literally trying to kick the question away. He rubbed hard on the back of his neck. More visual tells that Jensen picked up on immediately.

"Who else?" Jensen roared the question at the seated man, his tone demanding an answer. Harrison appeared to sink into his chair, his shoulders slowly rising and his head seeming to retract like that of a turtle.

"I'm sorry." He mumbled the apology.

"You told them where I live?" Jensen was incredulous.

"I had no choice, I had to give them something."

"So you put my family at risk and had Sandy killed, for what?" Jensen yelled into the man's face.

The door slammed open and Marshall burst through it, holding out his pistol as he walked toward Harrison. Marshall's voice erupted as he entered the room. He'd gone through the same process as Jensen to work his way into the house before stopping to listen to the conversation from behind the door. Marshall had been waiting for the timing to be right before he entered.

"What was so important that Sandy had to die by the hand of a Syrian rebel?" Marshall kept his pistol trained on Harrison, waiting for his explanation.

"Don't kill him yet," Jensen called over his shoulder as he frantically dialed the break phone. There was no answer—the phone just kept ringing until it went to voicemail.

"I've got to get home!" Jensen said, looking at Marshall.

"You go, leave this to me. I'll get what I can from this piece of shit." Marshall re-holstered his pistol and rolled up his shirt sleeves as Jensen left the house in a hurry. Harrison tilted his head slightly in an almost sarcastic manner.

"I've already been tortured. It's not like you can do anything—"

Harrison's sentence was cut off as Marshall's fist collided with his face, knocking him and the chair backward onto the floor. The impact was so powerful the chair slid back a couple of feet.

"You didn't ask me anything yet!" Harrison roared through the pain.

"That was just to make me feel better before we get started," Marshall growled.

"And did it?" Harrison's inquiry was more about finding out whether or not Marshall had finished than his emotional satisfaction.

"Hmm yeah, it did a little. Maybe you're right, though, maybe I should keep going to make sure."

***

Later, Jensen would not recall much of the gut-wrenching race back home with his heart pounding and a sick feeling in his stomach that increased unbearably with every mile he got closer to his house. The Mondeo entered the street, tires screeching as it rounded the corner. MJ's black Astra sport was still in the driveway.

"Oh no!" Jensen's eyes filled up. "Oh no, please no!"

Jensen was almost jumping from the car before it had come to a full stop. Although, his first impulse was to burst into the house to look for his family, his training ran deep, and his self-discipline asserted a measure of control. He noted that the front door was open, and the lights were on inside. That sickening feeling returned to his stomach. He instinctively performed a somewhat cursory mental scan of the possible vantage points for an attacker, but now, knowing the identity and purpose of his enemy, he was confident that the trap would be much more subtle; it would not be sprung here. Nevertheless, he approached the door in a habitual manner, then stopped and glanced inside.

The bags were still sitting on the couch.

They had been so close to safety, and I left them alone, Jensen thought.

He entered into the room, looking around. Nobody.

I should have stayed with them.

With this admission, his composure broke, and he mounted the stairs two at a time, frantically moving from room to room, hoping against the odds that some miracle had happened and they were somehow safe.

"MJ, MJ, are you here? Elena?" he called desperately through the empty house.

Dripping in sweat, gasping for breath, his heart racing, Jensen felt sick and ran into the bathroom. He bent over the toilet bowl, retching.

"Daddy, do you need a doctor?" The little voice came from the gap between the cupboard doors of the vanity unit under the bathroom sink.

"Elena! Oh baby. Come here!" Jensen grasped his daughter in his arms and held her tight. "Where's Mommy?"

"Gone. The man was shouting, Daddy," came the muffled reply.

"What man? Where did they go, honey?" He quizzed her in a gentle voice, hoping that she may have seen or heard something that would offer even the smallest clues.

"I don't know." Elena was starting to tear up.

"What did he look like?" Jensen persisted.

"Two mans. They were shouting. Mommy told me to hide. I cried for you, Daddy!"

"I'm here now, baby. You're safe. Daddy's here." Jensen held her even tighter, his head still spinning. The tears trickled down his face, half from the relief of Elena being alive and safe and half because MJ was still missing. He prayed she was okay. The fear of being confronted with a video such as Marshall had received petrified him.

"Daddy, I lost blankie." Elena had her own priorities.

Jensen let out an involuntary laugh as he looked at his baby girl. "Don't worry. Daddy will find it for you," he said as he held her close.

***

Marshall gripped Harrison's shirt tightly to stop the chair from toppling backward as his right fist repeatedly pounded into the man's face. Marshall was releasing all of the pent-up grief as his emotions exploded physically in the form of a brutal beating.

"Okay, okay!" Harrison muttered through mashed lips. "Enough! I'll tell you everything." Harrison's face was a mess.

Marshall paused to catch his breath, his fists and shirt covered in blood and sweat.

"What I'm about to tell you is straight out of a Strap 2 file, so you know the severity of what I'm telling you and how much trouble I'll be in when they find out." Harrison spat out blood and went on to tell Marshall the details of Sandy's killer.

"Where can I find him?" Marshall growled.

"That's the thing, you can't. He's gone to ground, and nobody knows where he is." Harrison shook his head slightly, looking down.

Marshall was far from satisfied. He grabbed his shirt, yet again drawing back his fist.

"Wait, I can tell you how you get to him, though!" Harrison flinched, wincing at the imminent strike, but Marshall paused.

"Go on."

"He has a son, a much doted upon son. He's at a boarding school just outside the city. If you grab his son, he's bound to expose himself to get him back." Harrison went on to reveal the boy's name and the school's location in as much detail as possible. "Can you let me go now?" Harrison asked.

Marshall swung around so fast it would have made the Flash look slow. His right hook hit Harrison hard enough that the chair lifted clean off the floor before falling sideways, complete with Harrison still tied to it. His head collided with the floor, leaving him unconscious and covered in blood. Marshall strode out of the room and was just leaving as he spotted the keys to Harrison's pride and joy. He smiled as he scooped up the keys to the shiny new Jag, throwing them in the air and catching them in the same hand.

Once inside, Marshall switched off the classical music CD and altered the driving position of the Jaguar's lush leather seat. Before driving off, he caught a glimpse of himself as he adjusted the car's rearview mirror. His bloodshot eyes were accentuated by the sweaty sheen of his skin and the bags beginning to form around his eyes. He'd unleashed all of his rage on Harrison, and even though he felt much better, he looked much worse.

He decided a quick stop at a friend's inner city apartment to get cleaned up was the best option. His place was in the opposite direction, but his friend Darius lived en route to the boarding school. Darius was ex Lithuanian army. The two of them had worked together several times in the past on joint operations. Darius had moved to London a couple of years ago to work in the private sector and was continually calling on Marshall for favors as well as asking him to be a reference. The time had come for Marshall to call in a favor.

He drove toward the city, then pulled over momentarily as he was trembling too much to drive. His hair stood on end, and a cold chill shuddered his spine. His arms shook as the adrenaline that had been fuelling him wore off. Without warning, his emotions burst to the surface, and he sobbed uncontrollably. His grief flowed, and he released all of his feelings as tears poured down his face. Everything hit him at once, and the realization that Sandy was gone forever caused pain like he'd never experienced. The chance of patching it up was now extinguished, and now he'd never be in a position to get closure. He would never know if he could rekindle the feelings with the love of his life and have one last attempt to make a real and honest relationship work with her.

As his head lowered, he spotted Harrison's leather-bound hip flask in the door panel of the Jag. Without thinking, he unscrewed the lid and took a small swig. The taste of the expensive malt whiskey somehow took the edge off the psychological pain, just briefly, but it was just what Marshall needed at that moment.

He struggled to compose himself and wiped away the tears with the back of his hand. Cutting away from his feelings, he forced himself back into work mode, and as if someone had flicked a switch inside him, he focused on the job at hand.

He clicked the turn signal upward, checked the mirror, and drove off into the night.

Chapter 5

Carrying Elena back downstairs, Jensen looked around, mentally processing the scene. The door hadn't been forced open, meaning the assailants must have knocked. That would explain MJ having time to hide Elena. His wife and child must have still been in the bathroom when the door knocked, meaning that it happened only a few moments after he had left the house.

Jensen cursed himself again for his haste in leaving them without completely ensuring their security. He'd never forgive himself if something happened to MJ—it didn't bear thinking about.

There were slight signs of a struggle in the family room, but nothing solid would allow him to picture the circumstances of the scenario as it unfolded. Jensen had calmed sufficiently for his control to reassert itself, and he paced around the other ground floor rooms, his analytical mind checking for any small clue that would give him more of an idea of what had taken place. He realized that Elena had drifted off to sleep in his arms so he laid her on the couch. As he moved a cushion to place it under his daughter's head, Jensen noticed that the phone he'd given to MJ lay hidden under it. It was still in record mode.

"Clever girl," he whispered to himself, stopping the video and hitting the playback button.

The recording confirmed she'd let them in. There seemed to be a bit of a scuffle as men piled into the room, pushing MJ around, possibly onto the floor, but Jensen could only speculate from the sounds.

“We’re looking for your husband. Where can we find him?” The man’s voice was muffled slightly, but Jensen could tell that the accent was Middle Eastern.

“I don’t know.” MJ had answered forcefully.

The sharp crack of a resounding slap across the face preceded MJ’s short scream of pain.

“Where is he?” The question was louder and angrier this time.

“I told you I don’t know.” Not quite so boldly this time; the fear in MJ’s voice obvious. A lump came to Jensen’s throat, and he prayed again that she was okay.

“Take her back to the foundry. We’ll deal with her there.” The disembodied authoritarian voice appeared to be giving the orders to at least two more men. A few more small cries and scuffling noises were heard before the distant slamming of car doors, then silence.

Jensen went into his study and fired up his laptop. A quick search revealed there were only three foundries within a thirty-mile radius. Two were still in use, but one had been closed for around eight or nine years. That was the one Jensen had his money on. According to the map, in good traffic, it was twenty-seven minutes from his house.

Over the years, Jensen had picked up a few handy tricks to help him out in his chosen line of work. Government agencies have access to satellites pretty much on demand. Still, when you take on work in the private sector, like a close protection assignment for example, those luxuries are less readily available. He was fortunate enough to know about spymesat.com, an extremely useful website where it’s possible to re-task a satellite and receive live imagery streamed directly to an android phone, laptop or tablet. It was worth every penny to have this on demand whenever he needed it. It made reconnaissance work a lot easier and gave him insight into the target area before he got there.

Within five minutes, he'd managed to locate the site. He studied the area, then sent the GPS coordinates to Marshall. He grabbed some essential kit from around the house and chucked it into a day sack. It was getting close to midnight, and the temperature was dropping fast. With the day sack over his shoulder, he scooped up Elena and her travel bags. As he turned, he spotted blankie, which had been under the bags all that time. He picked it up, too, and walked to the front door.

Once Elena was wrapped in a thick furry winter coat and placed in the rear car seat, he stowed the bags in the foot well and covered Elena's legs with a travel blanket, placing her blankie on top. She was still half asleep and remained motionless while he fastened her safety belt.

He stepped back to close the door of the Mondeo when something struck the back of his head, making everything go dark.

Chapter 6

The illuminated clock on the Jag's dashboard went dark as Marshall shut the engine off, barely catching sight of the time. The working class of the quiet suburb slept soundly as Marshall remotely locked the Jag and walked away from it. His shadow faded for a second, with the lights illuminating the street as they flashed. The cool air of the night ensured he was wide awake as he lumbered toward the low-rise apartment block where Darius lived.

Even though he'd just seen it was twenty minutes to midnight, he checked the time again on his Traser wristwatch. Not that it mattered—Darius would let him in no matter what time it was.

The security door had never worked since Darius had lived there. Marshall pulled it open, ascended the stairs to the first floor, turned to face the front door, and knocked. On the third attempt, Darius finally unlocked and opened the door. A smile formed on his face as he looked Marshall up and down, noting his state.

"Don't tell me, life as a stunt man just isn't working out for you." Darius stepped aside, and Marshall walked in without a smile, glad to get out of sight.

"I need to get cleaned up. Can I use your shower?" Marshall grunted with a gravelly voice. The night was beginning to tell on him.

"Sure, through there." Darius pointed at a door at the far end of the hall. "I'll get you some towels. And a clean shirt." Even though Darius was pretty broad, at a haircut short of five foot eight, even in his combat boots, he looked even broader than he actually was. An all-over golden tan highlighted his piercing light blue eyes, making him a hit with the ladies and earning him the title of the Lithuanian lover man. He grabbed one of his designer T-shirts from a hanger and a couple of towels, then looked for the longest pair of cargo pants he owned. Although Marshall was about the same build, he was a bit taller, and his waistline was less toned than the gym-addicted Darius. The water spray hitting the bath tub and sloshing sounds informed Darius that Marshall was already in the shower. Easing the door slightly open, he dropped the garments and towels on top of the closed toilet seat and pulled the door shut again. Resigning himself to the fact that he more than likely wasn't going back to bed anytime soon, he decided a strong coffee was in order and grabbed a couple of mugs from the cupboard.

Feeling a lot more awake and refreshed, Marshall emerged from the bathroom in his borrowed clobber. Darius sat on his sofa, sipping his coffee and gesturing toward the one he'd made for Marshall.

"Cheers." He picked up the coffee and took a sip. "I need your help."

"With what?"

"We need to kidnap a kid." Marshall sipped his coffee again.

"Okay." Darius shrugged and stood, sipping at the last of his drink. "I'll get my coat."

Seemingly unfazed by Marshall's statement, he wrapped his jacket around him and looked over like an eager apprentice ready to go. A slight smile formed on Marshall's face for the first time that day. Darius's charisma and boyish charms always brought the best out in him, and he instantly knew he'd made the right choice knocking on his door.

"Grab your bino's," Marshall said into his cup as he took another gulp.

"Sure." Darius went to his bedroom and slid open the top drawer. He paused for a moment, looking down at the pistol, flashlight, binoculars, and a few other bits of kit that furnished his top drawer. Weighing up the circumstances and deciding the chances of a drama were pretty high, he tucked his Tokarev pistol into his waistband. He grabbed some bits of kit along with the binoculars Marshall had requested.

Chapter 7

The grimy smell of industrial machinery filled the air. MJ caught a glimpse of one of her captors as he pulled away her black jacket that had been ripped away from her and placed over her head. He shoved her into a dark and filthy room, pushing her so hard she fell to the floor. Her heart had been racing most of the journey, but she thought back to what Jensen had told her in the past.

Over the years, he'd picked apart movies and plots that had been dramatized for the big screen. At first, she didn't take too much notice as he tutted and rolled his eyes at TV fiction, but being the kind of person she was, she wanted to know what would actually be done in the type of scenarios Hollywood gets wrong. She started asking questions and found it truly interesting how it all worked. In effect, she'd been having a kind of theoretical training for this sort of eventuality.

She'd surprised herself with how much she'd actually remembered. That, mixed with faith and confidence that deep down she knew Jensen was coming for her, almost gave her a sense of resilience.

As MJ's eyes adjusted to the dim light, she scanned the room. Jensen had spoken so many times about "Conduct of Capture" and the processes used by kidnappers. She knew time was limited and that right now, keeping herself occupied rather than worrying was best. Being a physical prisoner was one thing, they may have your body, but don't let them into your mind. So she scanned the room for anything useful.

"Perfect," she whispered to herself, spotting a small nail protruding from the edge of the door frame. She moved closer and hooked the front of her negligée over it. Yanking it back, it tore, leaving a small triangle of dark blue satin behind. Not much but a definite sign she'd been there.

Tradecraft: *In the case of being moved from the primary holding area, leaving evidence of your presence can be essential. It will let anyone trying to find you know they're on the right path and not chasing dead-end leads. The more you can do to leave evidence that you were definitely there, the better. One may be found, but the more there is, the more chance of one of them being missed by your captors but found by anyone from forensic investigators to law enforcement.*

On the far side of the room, a telephone socket had a small white cord trailing from it to a hole in the corner of the room. MJ managed to pull at the lead enough to rip out a couple of the plastic clips tacked to the wall holding the wire in place. After pulling one of the tacks out, she headed for an old wooden table shoved into the corner of the room. It was time to help in any way she could. She used the tiny nail to scratch: *Black Mercedes 4 up* and the registration plate of the car she'd been taken away in. She'd spotted it moments before they covered her head with her jacket. She had repeated the license plate to herself for the entire journey.

Keeping the tack in her hand, she gritted her teeth as she used it to pierce the skin outside of her little finger. She pushed hard and winced as she finally got it to bleed. Moving swiftly to the room's opposite corner, she squeezed out as much blood as she could onto the skirting board behind a large steel cabinet. This would be DNA proof that she'd been there and could potentially be a huge help in finding her if she was moved before Jensen got there. A little more blood subtly smeared in less obvious places as backup, and she tossed the tack away.

"What next?" The tear at the front of her negligée was probably a little higher and more central than she would have liked if she'd put more thought into it, but time was of the essence, and modesty was among the lowest of her priorities. Her eyes then focused on her black knee-high boots. "Yes! Jensen knew I had these on." She moved to the door and scraped her heel down the murky, white wooden panels. Black lines marked the entrance where she'd run her foot down a few times to show she'd been in the room and left marks behind.

Tradecraft: *These procedures are productive in many ways. Aside from the obvious fact that it leaves physical evidence of physical presence, more importantly, it keeps the captive's mind occupied, doing something constructive rather than allowing fear to creep in. Kidnappers depend on certain elements in order to keep you compliant. By locking you in solitude for a while, it permits all sorts of thoughts to spin around inside your head. What are they going to do with me? Are they going to kill me? Is my daughter okay? Will anyone find me? They can then play on these fears that have actually been developed and cultivated by your imagination.*

She heard someone approaching. Her heart skipped as she stepped away from the door and waited. Her pupils dilated, her mouth dried, and her pulse raised as adrenaline coursed through her.

The door clunked and clicked as the lock was undone and two men entered the room. They seemed surprised to see her standing and not weeping on the floor in fear. That didn't stop them from doing what they went there for, though. MJ's adrenaline surged as the larger one of the two stormed toward her. Her confidence shrank with his approach. He moved his hand over his body and backhanded her across the face so hard it sent her flying across the room. She couldn't help but let out a screech as she landed on the floor. Fear gripped her as the two came forward again, slapping and kicking her.

"English slut!" one man growled. "We're going to show you!" He grabbed her by her hair and dragged her across to the center of the room again.

"No! Please don't!" she begged as the smaller one of the two followed, unzipping his trousers. A rabid look filled his eyes. She kicked at him, trying to stop him from coming any closer, but he just slapped her and pushed her down. The big one was still holding her in place by her hair.

"No, please, no." Her bottom lip whimpered as she sobbed the words out, knowing full well what was about to happen.

The smaller guy just pulled his trousers down and was almost foaming at the mouth when he spread her legs and forced himself on top of her.

"Please—" she begged.

Her resistance was of no use. She was in such a state that she hadn't even noticed the other men at the door waiting their turn. Five more of them patiently waited for their go as MJ's tears flowed and her sobs became one continual groan. This was going to be the most horrific experience of her life.

* * *

Jensen slipped in and out of consciousness, muffled voices around him as his eyes struggled to come into focus. He felt himself being handled and moved around. The muffled voices argued until they morphed into that of his parents fighting when he was a child. He watched his mom and dad shouting at each other from the crack of the closet door. His mother was screeching and threw dishes that smashed against the wall. His dad was shouting and pointing aggressively. His mind wouldn't allow him to recall what they were actually fighting about, and he couldn't make out the words. He just remembered jumping at the door slamming as his dad stormed out.

His thoughts drifted, and he told himself how he would be a better parent and do everything he could as a father. Then his heart lunged forward, and his eyes shot open with the fear awakening him as his mind told him of the danger—not just the danger he was in, but Elena, too. Panic forced him awake.

The light blinded him as he looked up at the men dragging him along the floor. An exchange of aggressive shouts was followed by one of them pulling back and whacking Jensen on the head again.

Everything went black once more.

Chapter 8

MJ had braced herself for the inevitable. She couldn't escape the smell of the man's stale breath as he lay on top of her, pinning her down. He forced his weight onto her, restricting her breathing and making her feel physically helpless. She cried silently, tears running down her cheek as she entered a state of submission. She was almost trance-like as she tried to block out what was going to happen to her. She was so subdued she didn't even hear the banging of the door being flung back against the wall.

"Not yet!" The one who seemed to be giving the orders had entered the room and stopped them from going any further. "I want to talk to her first."

The guy on top of her let out a groan of annoyance as he lifted himself off her.

"I'll be coming back for you, bitch. Me and all of my friends. We're all going to have you. And then we're going to make your husband watch as we rape and kill you and your daughter right in front of him!" He re-fastened his trousers and moved out of her line of sight.

The guy in charge stepped forward. His pristine suit clashed with the surroundings. He watched as she braved a moment of eye contact.

"Don't worry, I'm not going to hurt you." He paused. "They will. When I've finished with you, they're all going to do whatever they want with you." His voice had softened. "You won't fight when they do. You'll wriggle and scream and feel the worst pain in the world when it's happening to your baby girl and you're forced to watch, but after they're done with her and her throat has been slit, you'll have given up the will to fight and will just let us do as we please with you."

MJ's eyes welled up with more tears as horrifying thoughts filled her mind, and her stomach churned with fear.

"I've seen this before. My men and I have done it many times, so we know. After we're done, a little bit of mutilation for when you and your family go to the grave. That way, even your bodies will still bear the scars of your pains." He bent his knees to come down to her height.

MJ's bottom lip quivered, and she tried to talk, to beg, but she was so filled with dread and emotion that she could barely make a noise. She tried, but it was no use. She simply cried and more tears flooded from her eyes.

"Now, you're going to tell me everything I need to know before I take my turn on you." His tone had changed to aggression. His nasty side returned as he grabbed her hair and pulled her face toward him. Fear filled her as she froze, waiting for him to strike her.

Chapter 9

The overweight security guard actively continued raising his cholesterol levels as he shoveled another bite of his pre-packed gas station sandwich into his mouth. Laughing out loud to himself through the sandwich filling that dripped from his chin to the floor, he remained engrossed in the comedy showing on his portable TV set. The low-budget sitcom continued to distract him from the flickering monitors to its right. White digits in the corner of the screen showed it was now twenty-five to one in the morning and displayed the four-way split screen images of the school's CCTV system. A pack of cigarettes and a lighter sat next to a hot coffee. The security room was an outbuilding to the side of the huge school, out of the way enough to not be an eyesore but just about close enough to serve the purpose. Darius watched through his binoculars, peering into the window from a distance as the security guard continued to feed himself. Lying on his stomach, using only a bush for an OP, he talked into the mouthpiece of his phone, which was on loud speaker on the ground just in front of him.

"SG's static," he said.

"Roger that." Marshall made his way over to an area in front of the school that allowed him to be off camera. Pulling a balaclava over his head, he walked toward the main entrance and aimed a high-powered laser pointer directly at the CCTV camera. Keeping it trained on the center, he left it there for a moment. The laser, intensified by the lens, burned out the camera's retina in seconds. The screen in the security office went blank. The more than miffed security guard banged the side of the old monitor a couple of times before finally reaching the height of his irritation and deciding to go and have a look at the camera. Taking a break from his buffet, he forced himself up and through the door to the outside, where he lit up a cigarette.

"Okay, the camera's down, and Sam's on the move," Darius said into the phone.

"Sam?" Marshall asked with a frown.

"Yeah, Sam Witch! 'Cos all I've seen him do since I've been here is eat those things."

"Can you beat him down here?" Marshall's reply was light and almost rhetorical.

"Already on the way," Darius said, scooping up his cell phone and running down toward Marshall, who was walking along a row of multiple sash windows near the front of the school. Layers of flaking, white gloss paint covered the rotting wood underneath. Moving past one, then another, he finally found one that seemed to his liking. As Darius joined him, Marshall pulled out a lock knife and inserted it into the gap between the top and bottom of the vertical sliding window. Marshall's pulse quickened. He could sense the tension from Darius and knew Sam wasn't going to be far away. They could hear the crunch of his footsteps getting louder as they stood at the front of the school. Marshall worked away with his pocket knife.

Sam's footsteps got closer. He would be there any second.

Pushing the catch open and sliding the bottom window up, Marshall clambered inside the dark classroom, with Darius following only a second behind. Sam was about to be in view of them both. Marshall slid the window back down in perfect time as the security guard turned the corner to the front of the school to look at the inoperative camera. The pair of them quickly ducked down inside the darkness. The typical smell shared by all classrooms across the world of pencil shavings and dust filled the air. They held their breath, waiting for the security guard to finish his inspection. They couldn't afford to be compromised at this point, or the whole plan would unravel.

"He's never been swimming," Marshall whispered.

"What?" Darius whispered back with a confused look on his face.

"It's never been thirty minutes since his last meal," Marshall quipped.

Slowly, the penny dropped with Darius. Sam had never gone more than half an hour without shoveling food into his mouth, judging by his size. Darius tried his hardest to stifle his laughter, putting his hand over his mouth. Marshall's joke tickled him more the harder he tried to suppress the laughter.

Sam aimed his flashlight at the camera to see no visible damage, followed by a quick cursory scan of the front of the school sweeping his flashlight the full length before returning to the security office.

A quick scribble in his shift report said, "Camera at the front stopped working at approximately 12:50 a.m." Sam eagerly continued clogging his arteries while returning to the low-budget comedy.

Marshall and Darius controlled their breathing as their pounding hearts calmed. Their eyes had adjusted to the darkness. They remained tucked in tight against the inside wall, motionless and silent.

When they were satisfied that nobody was about, the pair slowly and quietly worked their way toward the classroom door.

Creeping over and making a stable stance, Marshall listened carefully against the door that led to the corridor. He moved the handle down a fraction, continuing to listen. A fraction more until eventually the door was free, and he moved it slightly inward extremely slowly.

Controlling their breathing, the two men inched forward a fraction at a time. The corridor outside was even darker than the classroom they were in as he continued to ease the door open. They both froze to the spot when the plinking noises of the strip lights illuminated the entire corridor. A motion sensor automatically switched on all the lights, and Marshall looked at Darius with a sheepish grin as they stood stooped, looking like a pair of statues.

"I guess we won't need the flashlights then," Marshall stated sarcastically as he straightened himself up. Darius breathed out and straightened his back, too.

"If we get caught, I'm deaf, and you don't speak English," Marshall jested.

"Si!" Darius replied with his best Spanish accent before continuing in English. "Seriously though, shouldn't we put together a back story, just in case?"

"Like what? We lost the dog and thought he ran into the school?" Marshall replied with a tone of sarcasm. "I don't think it would work. I reckon the best option is to run, and if we get cornered, we'll have to fight our way out."

"I'm carrying if it's needed." Darius patted his sidearm.

"Against who? Fat Sam, the security guard? I think we're good."

They walked along the corridor, their boots squeaking on the polished floor. They worked their way toward the main school office to try and get access to the records. At the end of the corridor, a wooden door took them into an open lobby area with the reception to the left and a large staircase just past it that wound around the cavernous circular room. They pulled out their flashlights again to look around, no sensor lit up this area, and they didn't want to start flicking switches. The smell of commercial cleaning polish was doing its best to camouflage the scent of varnished wood and hidden dust. The reception had a sliding window and an unlocked door to the left. They entered quietly and swept their flashlights around, finding the records room at the back of the office area.

Unsurprisingly the records room was locked. A simple three-pin lock in the center of the stainless steel doorknob was all that secured the room. Marshall rooted around the desk drawers until he found two paperclips. Using his Leatherman multi-tool clipped to his belt, he fashioned the paperclips into a Rake and Tension bar to form a makeshift lock pick set. His improvised lock picks were crude, but the simple lock would be an easy job to manipulate. Darius held the flashlight's beam on the doorknob as Marshall knelt and worked his magic to defeat the lock.

"Ha! Jensen's not the only one trained for this stuff," Marshall said to himself, pleased with his little accomplishment when the lock clicked and the knob turned to open the door to the records room. The two-man team slipped inside and searched through the files to try and locate whereabouts in the boarding school the boy they were after would be sleeping.

"Got it!" Darius whispered. "Room 173, fifth floor on the east wing." He slipped the paper back into the file and handed it to Marshall. Marshall stuffed it down the back of his jeans, and Darius closed the drawer as quietly as he could. A quick scan of the basic black and white map on the wall showed them the school's layout. They figured out where to head to and set off as quickly and quietly as they could to locate the room they needed to get to.

Silently, they ascended the round staircase, then turned left on the fifth floor, then crept along the corridor dimly lit by bare skylights.

"Here, 173," Darius whispered over to Marshall. Moving his ear to the door, Marshall put his index finger over his lips. He turned the doorknob slowly and inched into the room, working his way over slowly and silently to the bed. Darius waited just outside the door, ready to move in. Marshall quickly stepped back out and closed the door as rapidly and quietly as he could.

"I think we're in the wrong wing," Marshall mouthed.

"How do you know?"

"Because, unless he's grown his hair, changed color, and had a sex change, that's not the right kid." Marshall replied as Darius stifled a laugh. They moved back down the corridor to the top of the staircase and began the same exploit in the opposite direction. Before long, they were back outside another room 173, this time in the east wing.

Moments later, Marshall's large hand was stifling the screams of the terrified boy being taped up by Darius. His hands and feet were bound in duct tape, then his mouth followed to keep him quiet as the two men lifted him from his bed. Slinging the boy over his shoulder, Marshall moved out along the corridor as rapidly as he could while still trying to remain as quiet as possible.

Darius tailed behind and only moved in front at times when he needed to open doors for Marshall, the boy bouncing around on his shoulder.

Chapter 10

The tingling sensation in the back of Jensen's neck soon turned to a painful ache as he regained some measure of consciousness. Distorted sounds coalesced and slowly revealed themselves to be muffled voices. His eyes flickered, and his blurred vision eventually focused on the dingy room where he lay, at floor level, against a decaying brick wall that smelled of rising dampness. The solid concrete floor felt cold beneath his legs as he attempted to sit up. His hands were cuffed behind his back and attached to an old steel heating pipe just above the skirting board. The pungent odor of grease and oil filled the air in what seemed to be an old industrial building.

Dragging himself up, using the pipe at his back for support, he took in his surroundings. The once white paint, now a decayed yellowy cream color, peeled from the walls in tattered strips, complemented with splashes of oil and grime. Litter was strewn around him, and rusting steel cupboards and filing cabinets were dotted around the other walls.

His throat felt like he had swallowed a cup of dust, and then the sick feeling in his stomach returned with the realization of the seriousness of his predicament. The whole thing flooded back to him, and his heart rate increased.

The sound of footsteps approaching and the muffled voices increasing in volume informed him that someone was on the way. The door opened dramatically, and a well-dressed, short and wiry, Middle Eastern man strolled in. His hands were held behind his back as he strode across the room, in much the same way the royals do, demonstrating his high degree of self-esteem. It was as if he considered himself too good to be touched and was only to be admired. The staccato click-clack sound of the man's highly polished, expensive shoes echoed as he halted, looking down at his captive.

"Sergeant Jensen! Look up at me!" he barked.

Jensen peered up cautiously, trying to judge how far up shit creek he was.

"That's right, Sergeant Jensen, I know all about you." The man's voice was calmer now.

"Where are they?" Jensen asked. His deliberate withholding of identities or statuses was a calculated ploy to elicit further information as to what his assailants knew.

But it was not lost on his refined visitor, who replied, "Oh, Mrs. Michelle Jensen and little Elena Jensen are safe, for the moment. Of course, the initials MJ haven't always stood for Michelle Jensen, have they? They used to stand for Michelle James. Tell me, Sergeant Jensen, does she know how her little brother really died? That because of your carelessness, he bled-out in the back of a helicopter, and you couldn't save him?"

It seems they do know a fair amount. Jensen thought.

Mixed emotions swirled inside him. Relieved that his wife and daughter were okay, the uncertainty of what would happen to his loved ones still scared him beyond words. His fate was of least concern to him; he had faced death many times before. But would the urbane man in the Gucci suit preserve his air of sophistication by taking his revenge solely on Jensen, or would he be forced to witness the production of yet another video, with his wife and child as the stars?

Jensen's mind worked overtime, and his fears became an ever-increasing distraction. He had to cut away. Nothing positive could come out of worry. He had to concentrate on what was happening right here and right now. It took every bit of his training to implement his compartmentalization skills and focus on the immediate threat.

From the tones of the initial muffled voices and the fidgeting movements on the other side of the door, he'd concluded three men were waiting outside the room. In the room, their boss was calm and composed, his hands steepled in front of his chest. This display of comfort and self-assurance revealed more about him and his present state of mind. With the expensive cufflinks, the Jaeger Couture watch, and the relaxed air of confidence and authority, Jensen wondered at Harrison's claim that this man was the brother of the simple rebel prison guard into whose dying eyes he had looked. Gucci was giving nothing away, but Jensen sensed that this man was accustomed to giving orders and expected them to be implicitly obeyed. Jensen didn't want to be so stupid as to reveal how little he knew by asking who the man was, so he kept quiet and waited for the next scrap of intelligence to emerge.

As Jensen sat motionless, considering his next move, one of Gucci's minions appeared in the doorway and engaged his boss in a short, whispered conversation before deferentially backing out. Jensen did not bother to try his lip-reading skills as the exchange was likely conducted in Arabic, however, he thought he detected a subtle change in his captor's demeanor. His first priority was to get free of his restraints, so he executed a Special Forces technique for doing so.

Tradecraft: *Feeling the cuffs, he built a visual picture in his mind. Keeping the left bracelet still and rotating the cuff clasped around his right hand, he spun the chain links around themselves until they locked up. The process continued until the links were entwined so that there was solid leverage between the two shackles. The two sides were brought together in a folding motion, and one of the links, or perhaps the joint at the end of the chain, snapped under the tension. The more expensive the handcuffs, the stronger the metal, the stronger the metal, the more brittle it was, and the easier it would snap. The cheap ones are more pliable and just bend and bend before they finally break.*

He was confident that his impeccably dressed captor would have only the best, perhaps even Gucci handcuffs. Jensen felt the chain go slack as the cuffs gave way but kept his hands in place behind his back. *The element of surprise is everything*, and the proverbial tables were about to be turned. With his wrists free, Jensen's self-reliance returned. Now he just had to wait for the optimum moment that would come soon. He needed to buy time, however, to formulate a plan and, if possible, elicit more information on the exact location of his family.

"I want to see them!" Jensen demanded.

Taken off-guard by the tone of Jensen's voice, the Arab's air of confidence appeared to waver slightly, and for a split second, he involuntarily revealed a chink in his armor. His hands dropped to his sides, and he subtly turned his body a few degrees, no longer directly facing Jensen. The small man struggled to regain control of the situation.

"You don't seem overly concerned about your imminent fate, Sergeant Jensen." The bravado in his voice seemed forced.

"I've been in worse situations." Jensen's relaxed tone appeared to unnerve the man. In an attempt to cover his discomfort, the Syrian tightened his tie, buttoned his blazer, and then fiddled with his shirt cuffs. To anyone else, these small actions would have gone unnoticed, but Jensen recognized them only too well.

Tradecraft: *The subconscious mind reacts to a physical threat by placing the arms in front of the body, whether by buttoning a blazer, intuitively trying to protect the vital organs, or playing with a watch or cufflinks, instinctively placing a physical barrier in front of the torso. The action of covering the area in front of you is a definitive sign of feeling threatened, nervous, or under pressure.*

This sudden drop in confidence spoke volumes, but Jensen was still unsure as to precisely what had precipitated it; something in the guard's message perhaps. Jensen inspected his captor closer. He noted that the left trouser leg of the superbly tailored suit was slightly lower than the right. Working his way up to the waist, Jensen noted the right side of the jacket was tighter to the body than the left side. Jensen's powers of observation told him that the Arab was carrying a concealed weapon, either right or rear right, inside the waistband of his trousers.

A loud metallic screech and a commotion of voices somewhere out in the main part of the building threw the whole scenario into confusion. A familiar clinking sound caused Jensen's ears to prick up.

Then the lights went out.

Jensen quickly covered his ears and closed his eyes, knowing full well what was about to happen.

Chapter 11

The blinding light was still visible through his eyelids. Even though he knew what was coming next, the deafening boom from the flash-bang grenade still made him jump.

Gucci leaped back in fear, surprised upon realizing that Jensen was free. His eyes widened. He inhaled deeply.

Jensen threw himself into a forward dive. He wrapped his arms around the man's waist to feel for a weapon, knocking the Syrian back at the same time. Jensen managed to grab the sidearm; it was his own Glock. His opponent had somehow pivoted to land on his hands and knees, with Jensen landing face down a few feet away.

Bursts of gunfire echoed. There were sounds of panic. Loud shouts in the main part of the building grabbed Jensen's attention, just long enough for Gucci to scramble away.

Jensen quickly heaved himself up, but bullets sprayed the area around the doorframe. He was trapped in the room. His captor had gotten away. All Jensen could do at that time was to take up a defensive position in the room, with his handgun ready to shoot toward the door.

"Jensen?" A familiar voice shouted out to him.

"Marshall? I'm in here."

"Hold your fire. I'm coming in."

Marshall's voice was like music to his ears. Marshall entered the room with pistol raised; he and Jensen only lowered their weapons to their sides upon visual contact. The tension dropped momentarily.

"He got away." Jensen groaned, with an exasperated expression. "Have you found MJ or Elena?"

"They're not here, the place is empty. But don't worry, we've got some leverage. We won't need to find them, they'll come to us." Marshall's cocky streak had returned. He was in work mode again and shut his emotions off as best he could.

The sound of footsteps made Jensen raise his weapon again.

"Jensen," Marshall said. "This is Darius. He's on our side."

The two men acknowledged each other with eye contact and upward flicks of their heads, but neither spoke. Lowering his weapon again, Jensen relaxed a little and tucked it back into his holster.

"We better get out of here." Darius's voice and body language revealed a small trace of nervousness, but he was covering it well, which didn't show on his face.

The three men walked briskly toward the exit, still alert for potential threats. Outside of the building, Marshall and Darius strolled toward the waiting car.

"You took Harrison's Jag?"

"He won't be needing it for a while." Marshall smirked. "At least not until he recovers."

"I'm not even going to ask. So what's this leverage?" Jensen inquired, moving toward the passenger side of the car. Marshall took the driver's seat, and Darius jumped in the back.

"Turns out our Syrian friend's name is Karim al-Salah, and he has a much doted upon son." The smile on Marshall's face grew wider with each word.

"So we just have to grab the son? Where is he?" Jensen asked.

As if on cue, to answer his question, thumping sounds and muffled attempts at screaming drew his attention toward the rear of the car. "He's in the trunk?" Jensen's tone was more of an exclamation than a question.

Darius sat there with a satisfied smile on his face, and Marshall started the engine.

"I've been busy while you were getting your ass kidnapped." Marshall's smile was beaming now. "I conducted a little research. Harrison was quite cooperative after you left us alone. Seems this al-Salah is an importer-exporter here in London, a legit businessman, on the surface, but he's head of the UK operations of a substantial international family of a drug and armaments cabal based in Syria."

So this Karim al-Salah was only an amateur, as Jensen had suspected back at the foundry. Was the news of the snatching of his only child the subject of the conversation which had rattled him so much?

"Maybe you've been out of the game for too long now, Daddy Jensen." Marshall's taunt interrupted his speculation.

"When this is over, remind me to hit you," Jensen retorted.

Marshall laughed as he pulled away. Most people would be emotional and angry, but Marshall used humor to cover his pain. It had been his defense mechanism since way before Jensen had known him. It was his way of feeling secure, so Jensen encouraged it whenever he thought it necessary.

***

The cuckoo clock ticked its way toward three a.m. as Jensen brought coffees into the living room. Darius had spread himself across the couch, where the bags still sat at the other end in silent testimony to the drama unfolding around them. Marshall replaced the photo of James to its place on the plant stand and turned to face Jensen and Darius.

"What hardware have we got?" he asked.

"I've got my Glock, and I have a .38 Special upstairs." Jensen paused and lifted the flap on MJ's bag. "And an ACP." Her compact handgun was still inside. He wondered how she must be feeling right now, but his thoughts were cut short by Marshall's interruption.

"I got my Sig, but I only have three rounds left. What about you, Darius?"

The Lithuanian lifted his Tokarev and ejected the magazine, shrugging. "None," he replied.

"I've got a couple of boxes upstairs," Jensen volunteered.

Darius frowned, giving him a curious glance. "I thought there were no guns in England. How did you guys get all of this?"

"Same way as you probably." Jensen's remark brought a smile to Darius's face, but he refrained from commenting further.

"Do you still have your rifle, Darius?" Marshall's question brought an immediate response. Darius sat up straight, his legs came together, and his arm dropped from the back of the sofa to his lap. Jensen could sense his discomfort. Darius puffed his cheeks out, holding his breath, a slight frown appeared on his face for a second, and he blew the air out with a subtle shake of the head.

"I'm not sure I can get to it," he muttered.

Jensen knew Darius wasn't being truthful but if he called him out on it, Darius would simply get defensive, maintain the fiction and be even less inclined to help. This wasn't the time for a confrontation or to build resistance, he needed a different approach.

Jensen sat on the sofa next to Darius and tilted his head slightly. Mirroring the other man's posture, he leaned his body slightly forward and looked Darius in the eyes, the concern showing in his expression. The exchange between the two men was brief and reserved.

"Do you have kids, Darius?"

"Yes, I have two."

"How old?"

"My son is four, and my daughter is seven."

"A wife?"

"We're separated now, but we were together for nine years."

Jensen built a scenario to explain his situation. "Imagine your wife and children had been taken. Picture them, scared and alone, starving and ill-treated, and you not knowing if they were alive or dead; not knowing if they were being beaten or tortured, and you weren't there to protect them." Jensen built the picture in Darius's head and let the scene play out. "If that was you, wouldn't you be begging for every little bit of help you could get? If you were in my position, how much would you want me to collect that rifle?"

Darius recovered from his reverie, shaking his head to cut away from the horrific thoughts playing out in his mind, and looked straight at Jensen.

"I'll get it for you. I can be back in an hour. Do you have a car I can use?"

"You can take the Astra, meet us back here." Jensen got up and moved to the sideboard. He opened one of the drawers and took out a box about eight inches square.

"Here." He tossed it to Darius, who fielded it neatly. "It's a radio and earpiece, and there's also a cell phone in there just in case."

Darius stood, and Jensen handed him the keys to the Astra.

"No problem," Darius said as he walked away, pulling the front door shut behind him.

Jensen flopped back onto the couch.

"You should have been a full-time case worker instead of a part-time contractor." Marshall laughed. "You could sweet talk a nun into murder."

Jensen dismissed the facetious comment. He knew it wasn't sweet-talking; it was more of a science, an exercise of his psychological skills. He had merely applied a little social engineering to win Darius's cooperation. In his chosen field, Jensen was fully aware that psychology can be a powerful weapon, and he had absorbed the fairly intensive training with enthusiasm. He had implemented it countless times during his career to flip assets or gain access to restricted areas, however, it also came in handy in getting a good price on his car and negotiating the rental price of the house in which they lived.

"I'll get that ammo from the safe." He moved in the direction of the stairway.

"I'll go and check on the kid," Marshall replied, tossing and catching the Jag keys in the same hand as he headed out the front door to the car.

A short time later, Jensen came down the stairs and back into the lounge room with two sets of body armor and a couple of ammunition boxes.

"Nine millimeter hollow poi—" Jensen stopped mid-sentence upon seeing the twelve-year-old boy sitting in the armchair, hands behind his back and duct tape over his mouth. The boy looked petrified, absolutely motionless as if frozen to the spot. His knees were pressed together, his fists tightly clenched, and terror showed in his eyes. Jensen moved over to the boy, peeling the tape from his mouth.

"For fuck's sake, Marshall, we're not animals." Jensen held the boy's arms just below either shoulder and looked him in the eyes.

"You're going to be okay, all right? Don't worry, no one is going to hurt you, and you'll be back home real soon, I promise."

He could appreciate Marshall's disregard for the child whose father had callously murdered Sandy, but the boy had done nothing. Jensen could only hope and pray that someone was giving the same reassurance to his family elsewhere. He went into the kitchen and grabbed a pack of potato chips and a bottle of water from the fridge.

"Here, kid, have these." Jensen handed them to the boy as he cut the tape from his hands, leaving his feet bound. At first, the boy was hesitant, but as soon as he realized that his situation had taken a turn, that someone was actually being kind to him, he tucked into the snacks.

"How long's it been since he's eaten?" Jensen asked.

"I don't know, he was in bed when we snatched him. We just ran it like a standard Target Acquisition Op, we were in and out with him in less than ten minutes. We didn't exactly want to stick around and ask if he'd had supper."

Three loud thumps at the front door caused them all to jump. Jensen's heart raced as he thought of all the possibilities of who it could be. Marshall grabbed the boy, placing a hand over his mouth, and dragged him backward into the kitchen. Jensen pulled out his Glock and moved cautiously toward the front door.

Chapter 12

Doing his best to remain concealed, Jensen flung the front door open. His daughter stood on the doorstep looking terrified. Tape covered her mouth, hands behind her back, and her feet were duct taped. She had wet her pants, and her eyes were raw from tears. She wept continuously, the only thing muting the noise being the silver tape over her mouth.

Elena stood gazing helplessly up at him looking pitiful and distraught. Jensen's heart was beating out of his chest as he grabbed her and brought her inside the house to safety. He looked down the street as he swept her up, but whoever had dropped her off was gone.

"Oh baby, you're safe now. Daddy's got you. You're safe." Jensen brought her into the living room and took the tape from her mouth. Elena wept loudly. The nonstop sobbing continued, and he shook as he removed the tape from her wrists, revealing a disposable cell phone clenched between her hands. As soon as she was free, the child's palms flew together and tucked between her knees as she curled up into the fetal position.

Jensen tried to hold and calm her down, but Elena was inconsolable. He was forced to disregard her weak resistance and her plaintive cries as he began a frantic search of Elena's body, looking for injuries, marks, or, God forbid, even worse, explosive devices. Tears of pain and anguish ran down his face, his hands shaking as he stripped her clothing away. Trembling as he went on, he did all he could to ignore the gut-wrenching feeling in the pit of his stomach. He needed to check her all over, and his fears escalated as he pulled off her clothes. He could barely look as he pulled down her underwear to check for blood or other bodily fluids and finally broke out in a choked gasp of relief when they were clear of everything except urine. He was so consumed with his inspection of his baby girl that he hadn't even noticed Marshall had come back into the room and had sat the boy back down in the chair. He pulled Elena in close and held her tight to his chest.

"You're okay, baby, you're okay. Safe now. Daddy's got you!"

"Is she okay?" Marshall felt like a prick as soon as he asked the question, but he simply didn't know what else to say. He looked down at Jensen; he'd never seen him like this before. He was completely flummoxed, he didn't know what to say or do next.

"I'll run her a bath. You stay here and watch him." Jensen pointed to the boy on the chair. "Keep him safe." The words came out, and he meant them, but the rage boiled up inside him, and he had to prevent himself from unleashing it on the frightened twelve-year-old sitting in his living room. His best option was to take Elena upstairs and keep the boy from his immediate sight.

He scooped his arms under his baby girl, ready to lift her. Marshall still stood looking on, unsure of what he should do. Jensen was normally so cool, calm, and collected but seeing the extent of his concern for his little girl and noting its effect on him left Marshall somewhat perplexed. He grabbed the bottle of vodka left from earlier that night, took a swig, and held it out in front of Jensen. Jensen paused before he could lift Elena and looked at the bottle.

The thought of glugging the lot crossed his mind, the temptation was appealing, but he decided that a clear head would be needed for what was to come.

"Not yet." He lifted Elena and stood to make his way to the bathroom. He was barely at the living room door when the cell phone taped to Elena's hands rang. Jensen's heart came up into his throat, and his eyes widened. His hands trembled with mixed emotions, and his throat went dry.

"Let me." Marshall stepped forward and picking up the phone. "You're not thinking straight. I'm the best one out of the two of us to do this."

Jensen paused. He wanted to speak to the low life that had caused all of this, but deep down, he knew Marshall was right. He stood still as Marshall answered.

There was silence for a second as he put the phone to his ear.

"By now, you would have checked Elena and know she's not harmed." The voice on the other end was that of al-Salah, as they now knew him to be. "I gave her back as a gesture of goodwill. I trust my son is being looked after equally as well?"

"He's alive." Marshall's reply was harsh and abrupt.

"Well, now you have something I want, and I have something you want. I believe exchange is a way forward, do you agree?" The businessman was struggling to control the anxiety in his voice.

"The old quarry at Godstone, six o'clock—"

"No, I say when and where or—"

"That's the time and place," Marshall said, cutting him off. "Or we send him back to you in pieces. It's not negotiable."

"Very well, but I want to talk to him. I sent the girl back. At least let me know my son is alive." al-Salah was pleading now.

"Only when we get proof that Mrs. Jensen is alive," Marshall countered.

"I sent the girl back, surely—"

"This isn't a game, there's no, your turn, my turn. Let me hear her voice, and I'll let you speak to your son."

"I'll call back in five minutes." The tone of voice was somewhat more subdued.

The line died, and Marshall lowered the phone from his ear. Jensen was standing in anticipation, his eyes showing his desperate need to know what was happening.

"He's gone to get MJ. I told him he could speak to his son if he proved she was alive."

Marshall waited for a response, but Jensen was distracted. He was piecing everything together in his mind. He had to step aside from his emotions, he told himself, which was easier said than done after the recent events. But if he were to get through this, he would have to keep his head clear and not let his heart cloud his judgment. Yet again, he summoned up every ounce of will power he possessed to go through the process of compartmentalizing it all. He had blocked out his feelings and turned off his emotions when the phone rang again. This time Jensen's head was clearer.

"Put it on loud speaker," he said.

Marshall complied and placed the phone on the coffee table.

"Jensen, I'm …" MJ's voice was cut short by someone who'd covered her mouth, and the muffled attempts to carry on talking faded away.

"Now you know she's alive. Let me speak to my son." The Syrian's voice had regained some authority.

"He can hear you," Jensen said, giving the nod to the boy to say it was okay to talk.

Karim al-Salah said something in his own language.

"In English," Marshall ordered.

"Are you all right, my son?" al-Salah asked.

"Yes, but I'm scared."

"Do not be frightened, you will be—"

"That's enough!" Marshall cut in again. "You can chat all you want when we all get home. Now we both know each other's position, we can get on with this. Be there at zero six hundred, and don't try anything stupid."

Marshall shut the phone down abruptly. The longer they spoke, there was more chance of giving too much away. Jensen appeared to have regained control, but Marshall sensed that he was unpredictable, and until MJ was safe, they couldn't afford for Jensen to slip up with an irrational choice ruled by his emotions. Elena had cried herself to sleep on the couch, and the boy sat beside her, still frozen to the seat. Jensen was looking intently at the pair. *Two innocents caught up in something they couldn't possibly understand*, he thought.

Marshall watched him. "Are you back with me?"

"Yes, mate, let's get this done!" Jensen nodded as he spoke and took in a deep breath. The silence was broken by a car pulling up outside. Marshall moved toward the boy, and Jensen looked out the window, instinctively drawing the Glock from its holster yet again. It was the Astra.

"Darius." Jensen re-holstered his pistol and opened the front door.

Marshall relaxed, and he, too, put his pistol away.

Now that the three of them were back together, it was time to formulate a plan.

Chapter 13

"You said rifle!" Jensen exclaimed.

"Yeah, beautiful, ain't it?" Marshall was like a kid in a candy shop, looking extremely pleased with himself. The Dragunov sniper rifle sat proudly on the dining room table as Darius and Marshall admired it, a sense of overwhelming appreciation displayed on their faces.

"This is a fifty-caliber ticket to the top of shit creek!" Jensen blurted out, his arms flailing and his posture animated. As much as he didn't like to admit it, he, too, had a bit of a semi-on looking at the Russian work of art.

"It was my father's. He left it for me when he died."

Jensen saw the pride on Darius's face as he spoke. *No wonder the man was nervous about fetching it*, Jensen thought to himself.

"Can you use it?" he asked.

"Of course. My father spent many hours teaching me how to shoot," Darius replied.

Jensen noted the body language again. Darius displayed all the physical signs of confidence in what he was saying. Body front on, looking Jensen directly in the eyes, there wasn't a single show of doubt or second thought even after he'd finished speaking.

"In a perfect world," Darius went on, "we would be able to get there and zero the sights exactly, but I guess on this occasion, you'll have to trust my judgment."

Jensen nodded and gave Marshall a look of approval, which was returned with rapid reassuring nods and a slight squint that indicated he trusted this guy.

"Then let's get a headstart, shall we?" Jensen flipped open the lid of his laptop and pulled up the satellite imagery of the quarry. The three of them put their heads together to formulate a plan that covered all the what ifs as Elena slept on the sofa. The boy hostage had drifted off to the same place and was sleeping deeply, completely unaware of his imminent future, presently being planned out by the newly forged trio.

After much deliberation over a multitude of possible glitches, the biggest issue now was ensuring Elena's safety during the Op. They'd discussed several options and covered as many avenues as they could but to no avail. Finally, the inevitable happened, and Jensen did what any other battle-hardened, highly trained, and exceptionally skilled alpha male would do. He phoned his mom.

He didn't like lying to his mom, but he couldn't exactly tell her the truth at the moment. The others smirked at each other as they imagined the other side of the conversation.

"It's just for a few hours, Mom. Yes, I know … Of course, I know the time. Please? Thanks, Mom." Jensen hung up the phone. "Okay you two, you both have mothers, don't you? Anyway, we're good to go. First, though, give me a swig of that vodka. I've got a throat dryer than a pharaoh's sock!"

When Jensen's parents divorced years ago, his father moved back to the States, and his mom decided to use her mother's maiden name. It was a fresh start for her but also added a layer of protection, distancing her from him enough so that a connection would not be made between them. In his line of work, this was a real help. Having no trail linking him to his mother made life a lot easier.

It was time to start bringing it all together. Darius had taken the liberty of collecting his Ghillie suit when he picked up the Dragunov, which according to the satellite feed, would give him a huge advantage. Jensen and Marshall both donned the body armor under their coats.

"Here, just in case." Jensen handed the .38 Special, still in its ankle holster, to Marshall, as a secondary weapon. He put MJ's ACP in his right jeans pocket and, after making sure all mags were full on his own weapons, handed the box to Darius for his Tokarev. The men put their earpieces and loops in place to do a transmission test, and Jensen handed his tablet to Darius with the sat feed already up. This was it, time to go.

"Hey, kid. Time to wake up." Marshall shook the boy's shoulder, and he woke with a huge intake of breath and a startled look in his eyes which turned again to fear at the realization that the whole thing was real and still happening.

Marshall tried to calm him down. "Don't worry, you'll be home soon. A few miles drive down the road, and this will all be over. You'll be back with your dad and on your way home." Marshall neglected to tell the boy that he would kill his dad for Sandy's murder.

Jensen gently attempted to lift Elena without waking her, but she gasped and started sobbing yet again. It wasn't apparent whether she was awake or still asleep, but she was most definitely not happy.

"It's okay. Daddy's got you. You're okay. You're safe, baby." It was unclear whether or not Jensen's reassuring words were making her feel better or even being heard, but he continued anyway, possibly as much for himself as for Elena.

"Are we all clear on what we're doing?" Jensen addressed his team.

Marshall responded eagerly, spoiling for the coming action. "Crystal. You get Elena to your mom's, Darius will set up, and I'll hole up somewhere out of sight until I get your signal. Now go, and I'll be close to the quarry waiting for you."

All three of them projected an air of confidence in an attempt to reassure themselves, but deep down, they all knew the whole thing was one twitch away from being a disaster. They all prayed that everybody involved got away unscathed, but the risks were high, and the probability of a smooth operation was low. With the odds severely stacked against them, the three men went their different ways to reach the same goal, which was get everyone out alive!

Jensen looked up at the cuckoo clock; twenty past four. He grabbed the changing bags and looked back at Marshall and Darius.

"Just in case I don't make it out of this, I want to say thank you, both of you."

"Hey, I'm sure your mom won't be too rough on you." Marshall's banter lightened the mood, and the tension eased momentarily. Jensen's smile caused a chain reaction that spread to Darius, and all three chuckled.

"Go, get out of here before we all start hugging trees and making daisy chains."

Jensen complied, going back outside to put Elena in the car. This time he was making sure nobody was approaching from any direction. Being extra vigilant and over-cautious, he strapped Elena into her car seat, her whimpers still faintly sounding in her sleep. Jensen's drive to his mom's was filled with unpleasant thoughts as his mind drifted, presenting a slideshow of horrific images of what could happen to MJ. He shook his head in a physical attempt to remove the negative thoughts from his mind. He had to get back on track, but he couldn't help his mind wandering from when he had first met MJ.

Jensen had just completed an assignment as a contractor, hired under the radar by Max at a CIA outpost. Usually, the hiring part was left to the operations officer, and no paperwork was kept on who would actually be conducting the operation. That way, the plausible deniability was always kept in place as a safety net for all parties, that is, all parties except the contractor, of course. This time, however, something unorthodox had occurred.

What was ostensibly viewed as a suicide mission by most involved was flipped by the contractor and turned out to be a successfully completed operation, which had achieved much more than its targeted goal. The seventh floor, where the management resides at Langley, Virginia, were curious as to who exactly the operative was that had pulled off this specialist assignment so smoothly. They requested that Max invite Jensen in for a personal citation for his efforts and achievements on behalf of the agency. Jensen sat with Max in Langley's own Starbucks, which is affectionately referred to as "Store number one." It was the same as any other Starbucks in the world, except that this branch is the only one that doesn't call out your name when your drink order is ready. *If you're a spy or a life-threatened defector, you probably don't want your name being yelled out publicly even if you are in CIA HQ.*

After a satisfying, much-needed cappuccino, Jensen was escorted to an office in the Original Headquarters Building (OHB), commonly incorrectly referred to as the Old Headquarters Building by the staff of the NHB or New Headquarters Building. The meeting had gone well, and Jensen was welcomed into the fold, personally engaged as a contractor of choice by the Director of Central Intelligence (DCI). He was now officially a Floater, an operative occasionally called upon for specialist covert intelligence operations where certain skills were required. Also known as Green-Badgers, due to the color of their ID badge being green, as opposed to the blue badges of the full-time staff. When the meeting had concluded, and the DCI departed, Jensen found himself at a loose end and was grateful for the invitation back to Max's house to attend a family barbecue that evening.

The social occasion was just what was needed to round off what had been a perfect day for Jensen. The grill on the patio sizzled and hissed, and the aroma of meat cooking was mouth-watering. Not even a trace of a breeze disturbed the smoke gently rising upward in the warm evening air. He and Max stood together under a large tree in Max's yard, discussing the events of the day, and knocking back a few well-deserved beers. The conversation had turned to a discussion of future possibilities and opportunities for further training for Jensen if he remained in the US when it was interrupted by a vaguely familiar voice calling from the side of the house.

"Hey Max, I brought beers!" An arm reached over the gate to lift the latch. A young guy came strolling through with a box of beer and a smile. Jensen's attention was immediately drawn to the beautiful blond girl who walked right behind him. He stood there breathless and had to avert his eyes. He could only assume it was the young man's wife and didn't want to appear rude.

"Close your mouth," Max muttered to Jensen before raising his voice in greeting. "James, good to see you. You know Jensen, of course. The two of you have worked together before a few times, right?" James wandered over, extending a friendly hand to Jensen.

"Sure we have. Good to see you again, buddy. And this is my sister, MJ."

"Oh no," Max muttered under his breath, sensing the direction of future engagements.

"Nice to meet you, Mr. Jensen," MJ said with a smile that could not hide her immediate attraction, which increased tenfold when he replied with his British accent, "Very nice to meet you, too, MJ." With a blush and a gush, the relationship began, and the rest, as they say, is history.

The physical attraction was obvious, her toned and tanned body complemented by long waves of blond hair, but there was more than that, MJ had an unshakeable sexy confidence about her. A charismatic charm that allowed her to keep the perfect balance between cute and sexy. She had a way of demonstrating a desire to be treated like a lady. Yet, invisible boundaries seemed to show that despite her desires, she also had an independent personality and did not have a need for anybody, only a want. She intrigued Jensen, and he was hooked.

If it meant getting to know MJ better, Jensen decided that a stay in the US, with Max's offer of future possibilities would not do his career as an operative any harm. It wasn't too much later that Jensen found himself engaged as a black trainee at Camp Peary, the training center better known as the Farm. Further counter terrorism training followed at the Point, also known as Harvey Point in North Carolina. His new 201 file as an operative at the CIA, with all his personal info, training, and operation details, was filling up nicely.

Eventually, he was ready to go and was considered "top choice" for certain black ops (covert operations that are not attributable to the organization performing them) and black bag jobs.

Chapter 14

The chill in the air at his mother's doorstep and the still of the night were emphasized as Jensen clung tightly to his daughter. He had leaned in to pass Elena to her grandmother but couldn't yet bring himself to let her go. The pause seemed to last an eternity as his heart battled with his head; rational thought told him what he had to do, but it was as if his body just wasn't listening. The conflict ended as reason reasserted itself. Too many people depended on him, none more so than Elena's mom, the love of his life.

Jensen released his baby girl into her grandma's arms with a deep intake of breath, the tears rolling down his face as he pulled away. "Love you, baby. Daddy loves you so much."

She was fast asleep still, but he didn't care. His emotions were in turmoil, not knowing if he'd ever see her again. He prayed he'd be back soon and Mommy would be coming home, too.

Jensen's mom knew better than to ask questions. She'd seen this kind of thing all his life, and even though she knew what Jensen did, it was never spoken about. This time, though, she sensed it was closer to home than ever before.

"When you come back to pick her up, I want you to promise me that this will be the last time this girl has to stay here under these circumstances. Do you hear me?" His mom's stern words were spoken softly. She wasn't the demonstrative type as a rule, and affection didn't really flow freely from either of his parents, but the love was there, and fortunately, the whole family doted on Elena in every way.

Jensen tore himself away and strode toward his car. “Back soon,” he called over his shoulder as he got into the car and drove off, not once risking a glance back for fear of changing his mind about leaving her. The clock on the dash showed it was about ten after five and a faint glow in the eastern sky hinted that dawn was rapidly approaching. Jensen’s mind returned to the forthcoming negotiations to get MJ back. He prayed hard that this would all be over soon and they could put it behind them and move on.

***

Godstone quarry is located just off the exit of the M25 for the A22. Surrounded by fields and a golf course, it gave the team a tactical advantage. Not too far away from a housing estate and fire station but out of the way enough to do the exchange, they could do what they had to do and be gone in no time at all. The quarry was only a short spell from the London Orbital and was still in deep shadow.

Tension grew with every mile that Jensen drove, and the closer he got, the worse the sickening feeling in the pit of his stomach became. He had to clear his head. He forced himself to practice all the compartmentalization methods he’d learned in training. The moment of truth was on the horizon, and he needed to think clearly. He went over everything again in his head, playing out all the possible outcomes, and visualizing how he would react to each one should it happen.

Jensen pulled over for a few minutes away from the quarry. Parked at the side of the road, he switched off the headlights and killed the engine. The car was making that familiar ticking noise that they make when they’ve just been turned off and are cooling down. He sat in the driver's seat and put his head into work mode. Using a technique called ICBM, which stands for Instant Calm Breath Method, he psyched himself up for whatever lay ahead.

I'm trained for this, he told himself.

Fishing in his pocket, he pulled out his smart phone and brought up the satellite imagery of the quarry. In the dim predawn light, he saw that the Syrians were already waiting for his arrival. Jensen spotted two cars and a van parked just outside the arc of light cast by the single globe above the door of the site manager's office at the south end of the quarry. Harrison's Jag was parked up not far from the perimeter, but even with the level of HD satellite imagery, he couldn't see Darius. Either he was real good or not there.

Dawn was breaking now, and the big moment was about to get underway. Jensen drove through the quarry gates and down the track leading to where al-Salah's group was parked.

"Radio check. Are you receiving, Marshall?"

A momentary hiss of radio static sounded in Jensen's ear, then Marshall's voice broke the silence, "Loud and clear."

"What about you, Darius?"

Darius looked down the scope of his rifle. Jensen's car moved down the quarry's lane, leaving a dust trail behind. He traced the movements of his car, keeping it in the cross hairs of the scope.

"I can hear you and even see you coming down the track," came the response.

"Try and resist the temptation to pull the trigger, Darius," Marshall quipped to try and relieve the tension.

"Good to know you're there. This is it, guys. Let's get it done!" Jensen used the bravado to camouflage the apprehension in his voice.

"Roger that!" Marshall didn't even bother to make a joke as he normally would.

The tension truly was mounting.

Jensen rounded the bend into the quarry yard to see the two cars forming a T shape, the first parked sideways to act as a block, and he noted that the second, a shiny black Mercedes, had its engine running, obviously in preparation for a quick getaway. The white Toyota van sat at the back, just far enough away to be out of the immediate threat area. Karim al-Salah sat in the back of the Mercedes in the luxury and warmth, with Syria's answer to *Dumb and Dumber* standing on either side, looking like night club bouncers, legs apart and hands clasped in front of them.

Jensen pulled the Mondeo up about sixty meters from the group and slightly left of the center. He shut off the engine, killed the lights, and paused, using the ICBM one last time.

The Syrian emerged from the back of the Mercedes in yet another designer suit. He moved to the rear of the first car and stood, looking like a Middle Eastern version of Mr. Burns from the *Simpsons*. The hired muscle stood on either side of him like a pair of gorillas waiting for a banana. Jensen got out of the Mondeo and closed the door behind him. He stood his ground and looked over at al-Salah.

"Where is my son?" the Arab growled.

"He'll be here, show me my wife first." Jensen's reply was cool and relaxed.

Gucci nodded, and MJ was pushed out into plain view from behind the white Toyota van. The coat had gone, and she stood there in the cool morning air in her blue satin negligee ripped at the front, and black leather, knee-high boots. Tape covered her mouth, and her arms were being held behind her back, presumably taped together as well. She was bent forward with a pistol pushed into the back of her head, and the look of terror in her eyes, visible even from that distance, brought a lump to Jensen's throat. Her captor stood in a position behind the van, ready to pull her back on command.

"Now, my son!" al-Salah's tone had changed, and the tenor of his demand clearly suggested that he meant business. The demeanor of his two bodyguards, however, told a different story. Their wide stance had disappeared, and their feet had drawn together. The one on the left had his thumbs, but not his hands, in his pockets, and the other had joined his hands, his thumbs concealed behind his interlocked fingers, displays which Jensen recognized as a lack of confidence.

"Bring him into play." Marshall heard Jensen's comment on his radio and started driving down the track. The Syrian's hands slowly dropped to his sides, and his mouth opened as the car drew closer. Pushing himself up on the tips of his toes, he stared at the tinted windows of the Jag, eagerly straining to catch a glimpse of his only son as if the extra couple of inches would give him a greater view. Marshall pulled the Jag sideways in front of the Mondeo in the same T configuration as the opposition.

"We got you this time, you slippery son of a bitch." Marshall muttered under his breath, looking directly at al-Salah as he pulled the car up. He got out and walked around the back of the car to open the rear passenger door, keeping the Jag between the boy and his father.

"Okay, let the girl go, and I let your son go. We all stay on our own sides, and when we both have them back, we all drive away!" Marshall shouted out the instructions, and al-Salah gave a nod to the man in the shadows to release MJ. She started walking forward, and Marshall bent to speak into the boy's ear.

"Nice and slow, kid. Walk back toward your dad. No matter what, you don't run. You hear me?" The boy nodded but could only keep looking at his father, Marshall released his grip. "Slowly," he stated again in a firm and low voice. The boy stepped forward nervously, walking toward his father.

MJ's eyes were firmly locked on Jensen's all the way. *Dumb and Dumber* were getting twitchy while al-Salah extended his arms toward his son, his hands beckoning as if to pull him forward as he called encouragement to the boy. His son, not knowing what to do, desperately wanted to speed up and run into his father's outstretched arms but remembered all the weapons he had seen and Marshall's terse instruction, *No matter what, you don't run*, and was too scared to risk it.

MJ's pace increased the closer she got to the Jaguar, and at the vital point, Jensen quickly grabbed her, pulled her behind the car, and held her tight. The Syrian finally got his arms protectively around his son, and, clutching him tightly, he turned rapidly and moved around the back of the first car toward the waiting Merc parked behind.

"Kill them!" al-Salah barked through the side of his mouth. He clambered into the getaway car with his son. The two bodyguards drew their pistols. They let the first shots off.

Jensen instinctively threw MJ to the ground, taking cover and pulling her behind the rear wheel. His actions were controlled enough to be short of injuring her. She curled up in a panic, and Jensen reassured her.

"Stay here. Don't move, no matter what. You'll be fine!" he shouted above the gunfire.

Marshall drew his Sig, instantly returning fire at *Dumb*. Darius took the liberty of sending a 50 caliber present straight through the shadowy figure who had emerged from behind the Toyota. A delayed boom from Darius's shot echoed through the quarry moments after the man's chest erupted. Jensen's pulse raced. Adrenaline kicked in as he drew his Glock. Simultaneously advancing as he fired at the other bodyguard.

Four more men jumped out of the back of the Toyota van, shooting at Jensen and Marshall and spraying bullets everywhere. Another boom of the Dragunov echoed throughout the quarry. Darius had taken another one of them out. Two more armed men came from around the back of the site office, on the opposite side of the fire fight. Jensen turned to shoot at them. Marshall concentrated on the guys from the van. Another man dropped, a huge hole where his chest used to be, followed by the blast of Darius's rifle resounding throughout the quarry.

The dull thuds of bullets hitting the cars caused MJ to flinch and further curl up in fear. Glass from the car windows exploded and sprayed everywhere.

Jensen brought his pistol up and aimed in the direction of the enemy. He hit one of the guys that had emerged from the back of the site office. As the second guy watched his colleague drop, Jensen used the window of opportunity to shoot center mass and take him out, too. He fell back into cover to reload and change the magazine of his Glock.

Another boom filled the air. Darius took out one of the remaining two guys from the van. Marshall managed to shoot the other. Center mass shots, dropping him to the ground. The hired thugs were still shooting, though. Jensen sprang back up and turned toward them to return fire. Marshall changed his magazine and advanced about three paces in front of Jensen. Both of them continuously fired as they paced toward the two gorillas. Pumping them full of hollow points.

The shiny black Mercedes kicked up a cloud of dust as it sped off through the southern exit of the quarry. Shooting through the cloud of dust, Marshall and Jensen fired at the car. The only pause between shots was for a magazine change. The dust settled, and the two men stopped shooting. Marshall threw his fist in the air in rage, his gun still in his hand, cursing that Sandy's killer had gotten away. They stood for a second, catching their breath. Then Marshall bent forward, his hands on his knees, his chest heaving as he gulped for air in an attempt to catch his breath. Jensen stopped, turned, and quickly ran back to his wife.

Jensen pulled MJ up and held her as gently as he could. He pulled the tape from her wrists; she instantly ripped the piece away from her mouth. "Elena?" The anxiety of her question was reflected in her eyes.

"She's safe. She's at my mom's."

MJ fell into Jensen's arms, her head sinking into his chest and her hands reaching up his back, pulling him tight to her body. The sky was lightening with the new day. The post-firefight silence was broken only by the chirping of the dawn chorus from the distant treeline.

"We've got to get out of here." Marshall's tone was urgent. "That gunfire would have been reported by now. We can't afford to hang around." Marshall pushed the pressle on his radio. "Darius?"

"Copy." Came the sharp response.

"Get out. We'll meet you back at Jensen's."

"Okay, Darius, out."

They didn't have time to collect brass, but they did decide to quickly check the bodies for anything that might give them a lead. Marshall did a search through the personal effects of the recently deceased, while Jensen calmed and reassured MJ that everything was going to be okay.

The side of Harrison's Jag was riddled with bullet holes. Glass from the shattered windows peppered the Jag's lush interior.

"You better get out of here. I'll get MJ back home. Harrison will blow a fuse when he sees that." Jensen pointed at Harrison's newly ventilated car while walking his wife to the Mondeo.

Leaving Marshall to dig around, he and MJ got into the car and set off for home. The adrenaline was still pumping inside him, and his mouth was so dry and sticky he could barely talk. MJ sat beside him, her hands shaking and her body quivering beyond control. The goosebumps on her skin became more prominent as the morning sunlight shone through the windscreen.

Jensen looked over at her, relieved she was alive and safe.

Chapter 15

"I'm going to make sure this has ended once and for all." Jensen's words were said with conviction and were quite convincing.

MJ looked around the hotel room. It was a lot nicer than she'd imagined. "And I'm just supposed to stay here until you get back?" It was more a statement than a question.

"It's the safest way. It's paid for in cash, untraceable, security all round—you even need a key card to operate the elevator. Trust me, all that cottage in the country safe house stuff in the movies is bullshit. This is how it really works."

Tradecraft: *Safe house selection has a lot of myths surrounding it, mainly put into place by Hollywood directors for the purposes of budgets and action shots. In reality, a five-star hotel is a top choice. Its sudden occupation doesn't alert nosey neighbors, and it can't be traced back to anyone if you pay in cash. With several layers of security, such as CCTV, security guards, alarms, and even a parking garage that you can access straight from your room if you pick the right hotel, the general rule is the bigger, the better. An easily accessible four-star plus located in the middle of the city is the guide. You can get to it quickly and not be too far away from a secondary option or even a police station if things go pear-shaped.*

Jensen's experience told him that the ill-advised lodge in the countryside would leave you stranded in the middle of nowhere, as vulnerable as you can possibly make yourself, miles away from any secondary option you may have considered. He had provided close protection for foreign defectors at home and abroad in the past, and he had already selected this hotel as the best option for the protection of his family in the event of this kind of emergency.

"Now, you remember the safe word, right?" MJ gave him a sarcastic look for asking the same question yet again.

"Jupiter." She had lowered her voice in a cynical but slightly humorous way.

"I know I keep asking. I'm just making sure."

Tradecraft: *Safe words don't work in the way most people would expect. They are not slipped casually into a conversation to let someone know that you are in danger, it is actually leaving them out that conveys that message. If the safe word is not mentioned by the person on the phone, then an operative knows the person is compromised. As an extra precaution, a danger word can be used. This time, it's the mention of the word which alerts an operative that the subject needs help urgently.*

"And the danger word?" Jensen prompted.

"Neptune." MJ shook her head. "Look, I know all this. What I don't know is where you're going, what you're going to do, or even when you'll be back to pick up Elena and me."

Jensen tried his best to reassure her. "I know it's not what you want to hear, but it's better you don't know. Don't worry, I'll make contact as much as I can, and I'll be back as quick as I can possibly make it. You've got the break phone. Keep it charged, and I'll call you on that. Outgoing calls are barred, so only I can call you."

MJ looked up at Jensen, and tears welled up in her eyes. He wrapped his strong arms protectively around her and held her tight, her face turned sideways into his chest, her one leg moving back and lifting slightly. Elena lay sleeping in the travel cot kindly provided by the hotel. She'd had a traumatic couple of days and kept shuddering in her sleep and letting out the odd moan or whimper.

"It will all be over soon," Jensen whispered to his beloved partner.

He was reluctant to leave the hotel room, but his family was in the safest place they could be for the moment. He bent over the side of the travel cot and kissed Elena on the head.

"Daddy loves you. I'll be back soon, baby. Look after Mommy for me, okay?" Turning back to MJ, he gave her one last kiss and looked her straight in the eyes. "Don't worry. This is what I do. I'm trained for this." He then turned and opened the hotel door, looking back only for a second. "I love you."

She looked like she was going to cry as she watched him leave. "I love you, too." Her voice was shaky as she croaked the reply.

The door closed, and Jensen walked along the corridor. With his family now safe at last, it was time to get his head back into work mode.

Time to bring this to an end.

Chapter 16

On the drive back to his house, Jensen's mind worked overtime with dark thoughts. His temper was boiling over, and he wondered who to hurt to put him on the path to, not only al-Salah but to the one who had ordered this vendetta of revenge. The need to make somebody pay for his pain and what his family had been put through was growing by the minute. He had to calm himself down. He needed a clear head to get this done right; flipping out now wouldn't do anyone any good.

He pulled up outside his house. The Astra was in the driveway, but there was no sign of the Jag. That didn't bother him as much as it would had there been a squad of police cars out in front. That's when things would have gotten messy. At least for now, everything was quiet on that front.

He pulled into the driveway and entered the house, listening carefully for anything that seemed out of place. In the living room, Marshall and Darius were drinking his tea.

"Where's the Jag?" Jensen asked.

"I thought it was best to put it out of the way for the moment. A car full of bullet holes tends to attract attention, which we don't need right now. I hid it and got on the radio for Darius to come and pick me up."

Jensen nodded. "Okay. Did you find anything?"

"The two guys playing PSD were sterile. It wasn't until I got to their colleague behind the van that I found this." Marshall threw a business card onto the table.

Jensen recognized the logo immediately. "Spearhead Security Solutions. I remember this guy. Jack someone or other." Jensen flicked the card onto his hand like it would help him remember.

"Bishop." Marshall's interjection sparked a memory for Jensen.

"Yeah, that's the one. He left the three Tops Security guys to go it alone. He was the one who hired us in the first place to retrieve Harrison."

"Who is Harrison?" Darius asked, feeling out of the loop.

"We'll fill you in on the way," Marshall said. "Come on, let's go see if we can't ruin Bishop's day, shall we?"

The trio piled into Jensen's Mondeo and headed out.

"Do you think we should head to his office and wait?" Marshall asked.

"No." Jensen shook his head. "Let's get to his house and see if we can catch him off guard. It's only seven-thirty. He probably hasn't even left yet. Darius, have you still got my tablet handy?"

"Yes, right here." The Lithuanian produced the machine from his daysack that he had grabbed before leaving.

"Great, see if you can re-task a satellite over the address I'm about to give you."

Jensen reeled off Bishop's address, and Darius got busy on the iPad. The live feed would give them a great heads up as to what was going on before they got there.

"Wife and two kids just leaving in a white Range Rover," Darius said. "Looks like a man going back into the house. There's a black Bentley still outside. No other cars, and no signs of perimeter security."

"What do you think the chances are of a residential security team being there? After all, he owns a security company." Marshall's inquiry seemed to be directed to Jensen.

"No, I doubt it." Jensen glanced in the rearview mirror. "He's tight, and he's complacent. If he had men to spare, they'd be out on jobs, not sitting in his garden listening to the football. The only way he'd have an RST is if they volunteered for extra duty."

"What about weapons in the house?" Marshall asked.

In Jensen's opinion, Bishop was one of those new age metrosexual hipster types, the kind of guy who wears skinny jeans with a lumberjack shirt and sports a well-groomed beard but couldn't change a tire on a car to save his life. All the looks and none of the guts with soft hands to match.

"Nah, not likely," he told Marshall. "As I said, he's complacent. Bishop keeps his distance from the action. He's a broker. He hires idiots like us to do the dirty work."

After checking there were no security cameras, they pulled up in front of the gates to Bishop's large house, which didn't directly face the gates, as it was angled to face the south for better exposure to the sun. The three of them scrutinized the property intently. A stately period house on the outside, no doubt with its heart and soul ripped out to be replaced by a characterless modernized interior. So far, nothing seemed to be ringing any alarm bells that would pose a problem.

“There, the side door, simple cylinder lock, nothing else.” Marshall passed Jensen the binoculars to see for himself.

Satisfied, Jensen said, “Okay, we should be able to get through that with a simple improvised slide. Let’s go do some shopping.”

***

They were happy to find the local convenience store open early. A quick mini market sweep produced a two-liter bottle of lemonade, scissors, and a pack of paper plates. Parked up out of the way, Jensen took a swig of the cool drink before tipping the rest out. He cut the top and bottom from the bottle and then cut it lengthwise from top to bottom. He flattened out the curved sheet of plastic, used the paper plates as a template, and drew a circle with the Sharpie from his car’s trauma kit. Cutting around the circle and throwing the remnants away, he packed his new improvised lock slide in his jacket.

One last check of the satellite imagery to confirm their exit strategy and a backup plan if it all went wrong and they were ready to move.

“Okay, that should do it. Ear pieces in. Let’s go.” Jensen growled, and the well-drilled trio moved off together.

Here we go again, Jensen thought.

Tradecraft: *Unlike what is shown on TV, you don’t stoop as you run around the outskirts of a building, handgun held high and looking like a bunch of wannabe SWAT team members. What you do is look like you actually belong. Three mates casually walking home after a night shift or whatever is unlikely to draw any unwanted attention. Having a credible backstory in place is a must, too. The last thing you want is to be asked a simple question by one of the locals, and all three blurt out a different answer. Comical as it may seem, it can result in a load of unnecessary and unwanted trouble.*

The trio stood chatting at the quietest spot of the perimeter wall where there were no overlooking properties on the other side of the road. They listened for any traffic, and, agreeing that all was clear, they boosted Darius up onto the wall. Jensen gave Marshall a leg up, and the two leaned down to pull up Jensen, then they sat legs on either side momentarily.

"Radio check." Marshall clicked the pressle. Nothing. The radios had stopped working.

"Moscow rule number two, mate," he said. "Technology will always let you down."

Jensen shrugged before dropping to the other side of the wall. This was the last thing they needed right now. They were trained to operate without comms for just this reason but having the use of them would have made life a whole lot easier. Now they would have to rely on each other's intuition and experience rather than signals on the radios.

They quickly made their way to the side door, and Jensen pulled out the lemonade bottle slide. He pushed the top and bottom of the door to see if there was any give; they both moved back just enough to confirm there were no bolts on the other side holding the door firm. He slid the plastic circle between the door frame and the door at the point where the lock was located. The theory was to push working parts of the lock back by feeding the plastic in and creating a wall between the lock and the housing.

TV heroes use a credit card, but in reality, they're far too brittle, and aside from that, who wants to wreck a credit card? Not to mention the possibility of accidentally dropping it and leaving evidence at the scene.

It wasn't long before Jensen had done his stuff, and they were in.

Chapter 17

The three of them worked their way around the house, creeping as silently as they could. Controlling every breath and steadily distributing body weight so as not to creak floor boards, they cleared the house. They moved room to room until they located the office from which Bishop conducted his business. There seemed to be two doors into it, one from the side and the main one from the front. Marshall waited at the side door, and Darius stood ready at the front. Jensen crept closer and listened carefully right outside the front door, the tension growing within him the closer he got. His mouth was becoming drier by the second, and he was beginning to perspire as he pressed his ear up close to the door. Without radio confirmation, he would have to hope Marshall was at the ready.

He leaned in and listened to the faint sounds from the other side of the door, trying to determine if Bishop was alone. The muted one-way conversation came to an abrupt end, and the silence that followed was enough to make Jensen take his chance. He burst into the office where Bishop stood behind a large desk.

"Sit!" Jensen commanded. "Get your hands up!"

A startled and apparently shaken Bishop sat quickly and elevated hands as high as he could get them. His pupils had enlarged, and the hair on his neck bristled.

"We need to talk," Jensen growled, keeping the Glock high as he advanced closer to Bishop.

"Oh, it's you." Bishop lowered his arms and seemed to relax a little.

"Keep them where I can see them," Jensen ordered again, motioning with the weapon.

Bishop raised his hands again, this time with less conviction, only about halfway, bent at the elbows.

"The Syria job, to extract Harrison, who was it that we killed?" Jensen asked.

"It's all in your file over there." Bishop indicated a stack of personnel files on top of a filing cabinet in the corner of the room. Jensen's glance was fleeting, but the distraction was just enough for Bishop to open his desk drawer with his left hand and grab a pistol with his right.

"A Highpoint?" Jensen laughed. "All the military hardware you've got access to, and you pull a Highpoint on me? Well, your reputation is totally out the window now."

Darius moved to the doorway, and Marshall entered through the side door, all with their weapons at the ready. Bishop lowered his pistol, set it on the desk, and put his hands back where they were.

Defiance was present in his voice when he spoke. "Well, bravo, gentlemen, the three of you bursting in here like the three musketeers. All you need is D'Artagnan, and you'd be complete. Ha, what you don't realize is that as soon as you made your dramatic entry, my foot hit a panic button, and a response team will be here within fifteen minutes."

"Oh, we won't need that long," Jensen said. "Darius, keep your weapon on him. Marshall, tie his hands."

"And how did you get mixed up with these two losers, Darius? Did they tell you what happened to their last third wheel?" Bishop's smarmy smile only agitated Jensen further.

"Shut up, asshole!" Marshall growled, moving Bishop's head and snatching his hair back.

Gripping Bishop firm and pulling his arms back, Marshall wrapped a zip tie around his wrists and pulled it tight.

Darius moved sideways to keep his weapon trained on the captive. Jensen pulled out a pocket knife, locking the blade open. His voice sounded almost good-natured, as if sharing a confidence, as he looked directly into Bishop's eyes.

"It takes less than a pound of pressure to pierce the human skin, and then the pain begins as I push it deeper into the top of your thigh, tearing the muscle, slicing through your flesh. The tip of the knife scoring along your thigh bone until the pain hurts so much you beg me to kill you. And then, well, you can't even imagine where I move to next."

Bishop's reaction was both visible and audible as Jensen neared him with the knife.

His eyes widened, and he sucked in a huge gulp of air in his apprehension. Jensen intensified the fear by moving the blade down toward the top of Bishop's thigh and pushing it just deep enough to cut through his fashionable skinny jeans without breaking the skin of the nervous man's leg. The build-up of fear Jensen had created in Bishop's mind was working well.

Tradecraft: *In recent years it's been proven that if you torture a man, he'll say anything just to get the pain to stop. Better results are achieved by engineering a mental surrender. Plant a seed of fear in the subject's mind and watch as he imagines all kinds of scenarios playing out in his head. Say the right words, and his fears will multiply inside his mind. All the hard work is done for you without the actual need to do anything physical. After all, who knows a man's fears better than the man himself? The fear of the pain can sometimes be more effective than the pain itself.*

"It's not my fault." Bishop pleaded, a wet patch appearing at the front of his H&M jeans. Jensen added just enough pressure to draw blood, and now there were two wet patches.

"What do you mean?" He increased the pressure, and Bishop talked.

"When we hired you for a target acquisition job, we didn't think for a minute you'd pull it off. We didn't even know for sure if Harrison was still alive, let alone if he was in the compound we told you he was in."

"That's the reason for a good recce before we do the job." Jensen was getting aggravated but not much wiser. "So?"

"You weren't supposed to succeed. Three freelance private contractors hired through a dodgy broker with no solid checkable work history." Bishop gulped in air, his nerves overwhelming him. "We thought you'd make one big gash of it, and Harrison would be killed for sure. When your call came through on the radio, we couldn't believe it. Of course, we had to send the chopper then because we were being monitored, but we were shocked that three guys could go in and pull it off."

"I still don't understand what this has to do with anything."

"Well, you left a bunch of pissed-off people behind you. I gave them Harrison in the first place to smooth things over as we bartered. You see, the guy whose brother you sliced open is not just a London businessman. He's part of a powerful family which controls a large slice of the border country between Turkey and Syria. A man called Sheikh Aram, the head of the family runs a private army; a rebel group that controls a supply route we use. Companies send their trucks through there to avoid being hit on the main roads, and we have a deal with the rebels that makes sure the route is secure, and the trucks get through. When you pissed off the main man by slitting his kid brother's throat and taking his prize away, he wanted revenge. He got in touch with his brother over here and told him to sort it out, family honor and all that."

"So you gave them me?" Jensen's voice was scornful.

"No, that's the point. It has taken them three years to figure out that we were involved in the extraction. I don't know how they found that out. They obviously thought it had been done through official channels. When I wouldn't give them intel, they got irate. They were threatening to cut the supply route off and ransack the trucks. You have to understand, if they cut off the supply route, it would have cost my company a fortune, as well as my reputation for keeping the route secure. So I gave them some leverage. I gave them Harrison. I figured it was all they had in the first place, and it would keep them happy. I didn't know that you and Harrison were so well acquainted." Bishop unwrapped his legs and tucked them as far under his chair as he could. Jensen knew he was lying, or at least not being entirely truthful.

"Go on." Jensen lifted the knife, making a circular winding motion to direct Bishop to keep talking.

"They weren't happy with that. They wanted you," Bishop continued. "The man who cut the throat of the beloved youngest member of the family. It appears they had high hopes for him, that he was being groomed for a bigger role in the family business, starting at the bottom … you know."

"So for you to keep your conscience clean, you didn't give them my details, you gave them leverage to extract those details from Harrison, all wrapped up with a nice little bow. They kill me, Harrison's in the frame for it, and your supply route stays open. Tell me, what's the cargo?" Jensen was piecing it all together.

"It's trucks of cashew nuts. The manufacturer makes a fortune delivering them to a wholesaler at the end of the supply route, and the wholesaler distributes them locally. The company makes money, the wholesaler makes money, and I make money keeping the trucks flowing. It's a win-win."

"My daughter got kidnapped over cashew nuts!" Jensen had lost his cool, and all the rage from the last twenty-four hours bubbled to the surface, about to explode. He spat as he shouted. "My wife nearly got killed. My friend lost his life. My mate's girlfriend got killed, and we could all be in deep shit so some asshole in the sandpit can chew on a bowl full of nuts. You fucking prick!" Jensen had turned red, the anger and rage making his eyes bulge. "Marshall! Go get me the bluntest instrument you can find from the kitchen. I need to kill this man slowly. Very, very, slowly."

Jensen was livid, and Marshall wasn't actually sure whether or not he meant it.

Bishop was trembling, and his face had gone ashen with fear. It wasn't just the front of his girly jeans that were stained now.

"I'll tell you where to find him." The desperation in Bishop's voice was clearly evident. The man was almost crying, and his eyes were pleading with Jensen not to kill him. His legs were quivering, and every vestige of color had drained from his face.

"Where?" Jensen snapped.

"Aram has a house on the Turkish border. It's where he runs the family business. He monitors everything from there. Runners from a nearby village keep him informed about what's happening locally, usually on motorbikes, but he has sophisticated satellite communication set up as well. The file's over there on top of the cabinet."

Jensen gave him a sideways glance.

"No, it really is, third from the top. I swear." The words tumbled from the desperate man.

Jensen snatched the designated file and folded his knife away. Marshall looked over at Jensen, unsure of the next move.

"What about him?" Marshall asked. "Do we kill him or take him with us?"

"No, please, don't kill me. Please!" Bishop visibly shrunk, his eyes filled with tears, and a look of trepidation spread over his face. Jensen walked up in front of him and drew the Glock out of its holster.

"No, no, I beg you!" Bishop's shriek was piercing.

"Where's your cash? You've got to have a safe in here, where is it?" Jensen watched the stricken man's eyes swing toward a portrait on the wall.

Then, with no warning, Jensen swung a huge blow to the side of Bishop's head, knocking him out. He walked over to the picture of the posing model and pulled it off the wall to reveal a safe on the other side. He handed the picture to Marshall and punched in a six-digit number, and the safe opened.

"Wooop woooh, she's hot!" Marshall said, putting down the picture of the gorgeous brunette that had driven off in the Range Rover earlier that morning. Moving his attention away from Bishop's wife, Marshall looked over to see what Jensen had discovered in the wall safe. Over forty-five thousand pounds, twenty thousand euros, and fifty thousand US dollars, all neatly stacked under several pieces of expensive jewelry, a couple of USB flash drives, and a Fortezza II plus.

Tradecraft: *A Fortezza is a crypto card used by the American government to encrypt digital communications. About the size of a credit card but around three times the thickness, to house the internal circuitry. It's fitted with an NSA microprocessor called Capstone MYK-80, which utilizes the Skipjack encryption algorithm. The original Fortezza card (KOV-8) is a Type 2 product, which means it cannot be used for classified information. The most widely used Type 1 encryption card is the KOV-12 Fortezza card which is used extensively for the Defense*

Message System (DMS). The KOV-12 is cleared up to TOP SECRET. A later version, called KOV-14 or Fortezza Plus, uses a Krypton microprocessor that implements stronger, Type 1 encryption and may be used for information classified up to TOP SECRET. It was discontinued in 2007 and replaced by the newer KSV-21 PC card with more modern algorithms and additional capabilities.

"How did you know the combination?" Marshall looked amazed.

"He's an egotistical prick, so I figured he'd use his own date of birth." Jensen was still cooling down. Darius had lowered his pistol now and looked into the safe with a smile.

Marshall stared at Jensen. "I'm surprised you only hit him over the head. I thought you were going to kill him."

"So did I." Jensen's response wasn't exactly what they expected, and both Marshall and Darius stifled a chuckle.

"Why didn't you?" Darius needed clarity on this one.

"In case I was wrong about the safe combination." Jensen's cool and collected reply was enough for the other two to laugh, which eased the tension somewhat.

"You know, sometime in the future, there's going to be a joke in this story about you bashing the Bishop," Marshall said, laughing heartily at his own joke.

Jensen threw a wedge of around three thousand pounds to Darius and scooped the rest into a bag, then put the flash drives and Fortezza card into his pocket.

"There could be a bit more to come later," he said.

"I love working with you guys!" Darius's smile had gotten bigger.

"We better get out of here before Bishop's response team arrive." Marshall had gone back to being serious again.

Jensen used a handkerchief to pick up the Highpoint and drop it back into the desk drawer.

"Do me a favor, will you guys? If ever I get shot by Highpoint, tell people something less embarrassing, like I was raped to death in a gay brothel or something." Jensen smiled, watching Marshall and Darius chuckle away.

"Time to get out of here," Marshall said, looking out of the window as a couple of black SUVs pulled up to the gates.

"Do you like Turkish delight, Darius?" Jensen asked.

Chapter 18

Jensen was cruising along the highway heading back home, the shiny Bentley following closely behind. Marshall sat in the driver's seat of the prestigious luxury automobile with a grin on his face that Jensen could make out through the Mondeo's rearview mirror. Luckily for Bishop, the trunk on a Bentley is quite spacious, so he had plenty of room to freak out when he woke up in a panic, not sure whether he was alive or dead. The house was no doubt compromised, so they decided to drop the car off in the parking lot of a nearby pub.

Jensen pulled the Mondeo into a parking space, jumped out, and got into the back of the Bentley. The smell of the tooled leather upholstery pervaded the luxurious interior of the car. The immediate feel of quality was apparent from the moment the door was opened. Jensen sat back in the soft leather, and the feel of abundant indulgence was most gratifying.

"I thought you'd be fighting with Darius over the front seat," Marshall said over his shoulder.

"Nah, I think I deserve to be chauffeured for a while. Onward, James," Jensen quipped.

"Where to, me lady?" Marshall's attempt at Parker, the chauffeur from *Thunderbirds*, was a fair imitation and even elicited an audible response from Darius, although the other two weren't entirely sure he understood the joke.

"Weymouth," Jensen stated.

"Weymouth? As in Dorset?" Marshall sounded surprised. "What's in Weymouth?"

"Not what, who. You start driving, and I'll make a call and get us some weapons for when we're on the other side of the Channel."

Darius peered over at Marshall with a look of curiosity on his face.

"Don't ask me, mate." Marshall shrugged. "I haven't got a clue either."

Darius flicked his thumb through the wedge of money that Jensen had tossed him from Bishop's safe. A fleeting thought of asking to be dropped off home evaporated as soon as it had been conceived with just a look in Marshall's direction. His friend, Marshall, was the only person who'd truly been there for him every moment since he came to live in England. And the only person he'd made a point of getting close to and being a part of his world. He wasn't going to let him down now. He needed to be there for him more than ever. Something deep inside Darius told him this is what he was supposed to do. This is what he was there for, to be a friend to Marshall.

Jensen scrolled through the contacts on his phone, working his way down until he found the name he wanted. John, short for Gianluca, an old acquaintance from past exploits.

Jensen hit send and waited for the ringtone. It wasn't long before John answered the phone with an elated tone.

"Jensen, how are you?" John's Italian accent had hardly faded, even after living in Kent now for about five years.

"Gianluca, it's good to hear your voice, my friend." Jensen answered in the same warm manner. "How are you?"

"Ah, you know, same old same old. What can I do for you, mate?" John asked.

"I'm about to go into Europe and need some equipment when I get there." Jensen explained non-committally. "Can you help me out, mate?"

"For you? No problem! What do you need?"

Jensen reeled off a few details of the desired kit using veiled speech to indicate what he wanted so that Gianluca knew what he was on about, but to anyone else listening in, it would have just seemed like an ordinary conversation—or at the very least not reveal anything that would be considered incriminating. After reeling off his wish list, Jensen left his friend to start making calls. As he hung up, the screen saver clock informed him it was now 11:22. He decided it was time to give MJ a call and make sure everything was as it should be.

He dialed the break phone and waited for the connection. It had rung several times, and Jensen was beginning to get concerned. At first, he just thought it might be over the other side of the room, but it was taking way longer to answer than it should. Where was she? The fear built within him that maybe someone had got to them. Why was it taking her so long to answer? His gut churned as unsavory thoughts swirled around in his mind.

The line clicked, and Jensen blurted, "You had me worried there for a moment. What took you so long to answer?"

"Sorry, I was getting Elena out of the bath. And I know what's coming next, by the way, Jupiter," she said, stressing the safe word with a hint of exasperation.

Jensen smiled, knowing his family was fine.

"When are you coming back? We're bored witless trapped in this hotel room, and I'm worried sick about you."
After nearly half an hour on the phone reassuring MJ and making small talk with Elena, Jensen put the phone aside and stretched out, sprawled across the back seat of the lush Bentley. Darius had already passed out in the front passenger seat, leaving Marshall to do the driving. Marshall was not in the least concerned, in fact, he was happy. He'd always wanted to drive something as sumptuous as a Bentley, which kept him distracted from his thoughts and grief. He glanced over his shoulder at Jensen, burned out and exhausted, lying on the back seat. Marshall settled himself comfortably into the driver's seat and returned his attention to the road ahead, he'd be able to get some rest when they stopped. Jensen had been through hell these last few days and thought the man deserved to get some downtime. He needed the rest now more than ever because Marshall surmised that things were going to get real noisy soon, and Jensen needed to be on form when they did. He'd never admit it, even to himself, but he looked up to Jensen and relied on him more than he knew.

Chapter 19

Weymouth is a picturesque little seaside town. It's well worth the journey, but they were not here to simply admire the scenery. Jensen had his own reasons for the choice of location.

"Wakey, wakey eggs, and bakey!" Marshall's tone was so filled with enthusiasm, it was difficult to believe he was the only one who hadn't had any sleep.

"Where are we?" Jensen was coming around, still sprawled across the back seat.

"I can see your training as a squaddie all those years ago wasn't wasted, and you've maintained the ability to sleep anywhere." Marshall chuckled with self-amusement. "We're at the Granby Diner. I just drove through Weymouth until I found an industrial park and looked for the nearest café."

"Great, food, I love food, it's my second favorite thing to eat." Jensen waited for the penny to drop, and soon enough, both Darius and Marshall were laughing heartily on the way into the eatery.

"We should work together all the time," Darius added, enjoying this spy-on-the-run lifestyle enormously.

All three felt like they'd been starved for days. Jensen ordered a full English breakfast with a coffee for each of them, and they took a table by the window, not too far from an exit. Jensen wanted to be able to see exactly who was arriving or if anyone developed an interest in the Bentley parked across the road.

The breakfast was thoroughly welcomed and eaten in true military style, that is, in less than sixty seconds. Even though it was rapidly approaching two o'clock in the afternoon, for these guys it was breakfast.

***

It soon became obvious to the other two that Jensen was quite familiar with the town of Weymouth. They parked the Bentley out of the way on a quiet street and boarded a bus that would take them into the town center.

"Right then, let's get some new threads." Jensen took them into a hiking Outfitters Store, and some twenty minutes and eleven carrier bags later, they emerged with most of the range that Trespass had to offer and some new walking boots.

"Now what?" Marshall was a skilled operative, but he trusted Jensen's ability to formulate a detailed plan that he would see through to a logical conclusion.

Jensen took the lead. "Darius, up by the pavilion are some cheap hotels. Pay cash and book us in under fake names. Oh, and see if you can pick up some wash kit on the way." Jensen pointed up the street leading to the beach. "We can all meet up in Costa Coffee in half an hour. Marshall, Down by Wilko's is an army surplus shop. Go in there and ask for Ricky. Tell him Jensen sent you, and get us some kit to stick in these hiking Bergen's. Nothing overboard, we want to look like hikers traveling through, not Rusty and the boys about to storm an embassy."

"Roger that. Got it." Both men answered readily.

Darius walked off in the direction Jensen had indicated, loaded with all the bags to drop into their new digs, while Marshall set out to find the army surplus store. When both went about their assigned tasks, Jensen turned his attention to the harbor. He was looking for a boat, a particular boat. First, though, he had some shopping to do for some rather unlikely items. He grinned to himself; a couple of meters of plastic tubing, a roll of duct tape, and an umbrella.

Tradecraft: *To access the pontoons where the boats are moored, you need a fob to open the electronic lock on the gate of the marina. If you're coming from outside, that is. Leaving the marina, you simply press a button on a post that releases the lock to enable you to get out. The button faces away from the gate, so you can't simply get a stick and press it or throw something hoping to get lucky and hit it. A small lip covers the top and sides, boxing in the button so you can't even see it from the shore. This simple little security measure works to keep the majority of common thieves at bay from the expensive boats moored within.*

Jensen pushed the pointed end of the golf umbrella down the tight-fitting plastic tube with just the J-shaped handle sticking out of the end. Running the duct tape around it a couple of times ensured that it wasn't going to slide out any time soon. With this new little device, Jensen walked up to the dock gates and quickly slotted the tube through the gate and around the rear of the button post so that when he pulled the tube back slightly, the handle hit the button and released the lock. He opened the gate, walked down the pontoon a little, and dropped the improvised entry device on the side and out of sight.

The pontoons swayed, making the odd sloshing noise as Jensen walked through the array of rich boy's toys, expensive motor cruisers, and ocean-going yachts. Finally, he found the one that he was looking for. Formerly the property of a super wealthy, organized crime lord, "Sin King" sat proudly at the end of a line of luxurious yachts, gleaming with the summer sun reflecting from the water on the rich gloss paintwork. The smell of salt water seemed more prominent, and the noise of the town seemed dampened somehow. Stopping at the edge of the pontoon, Jensen looked up to the immaculate super yacht's rear deck.

"Captain Fordington? Permission to come aboard, sir?" Jensen shouted, waiting for a response.

It wasn't long before a glass panel slid open, and a white-haired, distinguished-looking gentleman peered over the edge of the vessel.

"Jensen," he called out in a friendly tone, extending a welcoming hand. "Don't just stand there, come on up. How did you get—" He stopped midsentence. "Of course, it's you, I don't even need to ask."

Jensen followed him into an impressive seating area, furnished better than most people's homes.

"Captain Fordington," Jensen began.

"John, I've told you so many times. You can call me, John."

"I need to get to France tonight, under the radar. I have cash, but there will be three of us, stowaways, as far as you're concerned. Just one way, and I'll be out of your hair as soon as we hit Cherbourg."

"Sounds pretty urgent." Fordington knew Jensen well enough to know that it was. If it weren't, he wouldn't be asking. Jensen had used Fordington as a broker for contracts before, although this wasn't his usual specialty.

Captain John Fordington's business card read "Marine specialist." He used to act on behalf of large insurance companies to negotiate the return of expensive super yachts from Somali pirates for about ten percent of the vessel's value. The insurance companies would rather pay Fordington three million pounds than have to pay out a thirty million claim on a luxury boat. The word *negotiate* was a rather ambiguous way of saying that Fordington's crew could possibly pull up in ex-navy battleships and scare the pirates so much that most of them would take their chances in the sea before the boys with the AKs boarded and convinced the remainder to follow suit.

This form of operation was Fordington's primary area of expertise, but he occasionally ventured into other areas as well. Jensen had known him for some years now since they got talking about his Rolex watch one day. According to Fordington, it was bought for him as a gesture of thanks when he returned a luxury yacht to a rich Saudi royal, Jensen recalled with a smile. Apparently, he was told to go into town, tell the staff at Rolex just who had sent him, and select whatever he wanted, cost not an issue, with the bill to be added to the prince's account.

"All right, my friend, I will make some arrangements. You go and fetch your two associates, and we will rendezvous back here tonight."

Fordington's cultured voice drew Jensen out of his reverie.

"Thank you, Cap … John." He stammered.

Fordington gave him a sideways smile as the two men stood to shake hands and parted company. At the coffee shop, Darius and Marshall waited patiently, nursing a couple of cappuccinos, until Jensen finally arrived.

"Hey guys, all good?" Jensen sat down, noting Darius's posture was slightly different than normal, and a bashful grin was permanently fixed on his face. "What's with him?" Jensen asked Marshall, jerking his thumb at Darius.

"He's got his eye on Olivia. The barista who served our coffee. He's been chatting her up and smiling at her since we got here."

"Oh, so you wanna make Olivia spread?" Even Darius laughed at Jensen's remark as he sat there looking down, shaking his head like an embarrassed schoolboy. Marshall stifled his chuckle and looked over at Jensen.

"On a serious note, did you manage to sort the transport?" he asked.

"We leave tonight, so we've got enough time to get to the digs and get cleaned up, changed, and sort the kit before we go." Jensen shifted his focus back to Darius. "Did you get the hotel rooms sorted?"

"Yes, three rooms, all booked in different names." Darius fished three sets of keys from his pocket and distributed them. "Room number four, David Porthos, room number five, Paul Aramis, and mine, room number six John …"

"Don't tell me, John Athos?" Jensen interrupted.

"No, Johnny Depp!" Darius blurted out with a smug laugh.

"Okay, you got me. Before we go, we'll have to get our weapons cached. Passports too. We're going in sterile." Normally Jensen would have gone to what's known in the trade as a *Cobbler* to get false passports (known, predictably as *Shoes*) for all three of them, but there just hadn't been time. He could have retrieved one of his own he had stashed in the name of one of several legends.

Tradecraft: *A legend is the term used for a false identity set up by an organization or operative. Usually complete with backgrounds, social media presence, an education, and other layers making the identity of the legend credible.*

Jensen had several he'd previously set up, but that wouldn't help Darius any, and they had enough to sort out without running all over for passports. "All personal effects and stuff we don't need, we can bag up and leave with a good friend of mine, Adam."

"Can he be trusted?" Marshall wasn't sure about leaving his valuables with a stranger.

Jensen nodded. "He's one of the few people I trust."

"Me being one of the others, right?" Marshall asked, sounding concerned about the possible answer. Jensen spotted a perfect opportunity to taunt Marshall.

"How's the coffee?" Jensen asked, ignoring the question and trying his best to disguise the trace of a smirk that slighted his face.

Marshall was unsure whether or not Jensen's jesting was simply part of the banter.

“Don’t change the subject, am I one of the others?” he persisted, taking the bait that Jensen had set out to wind him up.

Jensen smiled without answering, slid his chair back, and stood. “Right, let’s get going.” He knew full well his jestful taunts were working on Marshall.

Darius looked over at his crush, who was reciprocating his bashful smiles.

“I’ll be right behind you.” He said the words to the other two but was looking at Olivia as he walked over to the counter. Jensen turned and walked to the door. Marshall, tagging along inches behind, still kept at him. “Seriously, am I one of the others? Do you trust me?”

Jensen maintained the smile as he walked out of the coffee shop.

Chapter 20

The summer sun had set, but without the slightest of breezes, there was still warmth in the night air. Jensen paced through the town in his new hiking attire to meet a friend at a bar ironically called, Rendezvous. His stomach sent him a gentle reminder that he hadn't eaten since his late breakfast several hours ago. The man he was set to meet was a former Kurdish militant now living in Weymouth and currently working as a car wash attendant instead of living the life of a freedom fighter.

The sound of seagulls surrounded him as he walked past small crowds of tourists, the smell of fish and chips wafting through the air as he approached the entrance he wanted to use to gain access to Rendezvous.

Occupying three floors, with two levels of exits and entry points, Rendezvous had a good view of the harbor. Serving food and beer by the day and blasting out modern music by night, it was an ideal, all-around meeting place. The lighting was low but not yet at nightclub level. This was the lull period when the dregs of the daytime drinkers had diminished before the next shift of revelers arrived and the nightlife erupted. The flowery smell of industrial cleaning fluid clashed with the scent of stale spilled beer, all losing the battle to the ground fresh coffee from the machine behind the bar.

Enjoying the calm before the storm of eighteen to thirty-year-olds, Jensen spotted his friend, who sat with what appeared to be only a glass of water in front of him. Jensen didn't bother to order a drink. He quickly scanned his surroundings, scrutinizing every detail of the premises, from the nearest exits and CCTV cameras to the other clientele in the room and even the staff. His final assessment was complete, he was satisfied that any potential threats were minimal and strolled over to start his meeting.

"How are you, my friend?" Jensen extended a warm hand as the Kurd turned to greet him.

Ako leaned in toward Jensen, in an almost bowing position, as he shook his hand.

Conscious of the use of body language, Jensen took a barely noticeable, small step back at the end of the handshake. Whether Ako stepped forward or remained on the spot would indicate his comfort level. If he stepped back, it would inform Jensen that he needed more space and allow him to adjust the proximity accordingly. This would prevent Jensen from invading Ako's comfort zone.

The Kurd stepped forward and clasped his hands in front of himself, revealing to Jensen that he was comfortable but still cautious about what was about to unfold.

"I'm good, Jensen, but tell me, what is so urgent that brings you here to meet with me?" Ako's eyes projected concern. Jensen tilted his head and offered a friendly smile to put Ako at ease.

"Do you mind if we sit here?" Jensen asked, gesturing at the seat a few tables back from where his friend was originally sitting. Jensen gave Ako a visual invitation to sit down, selecting for himself a seat at the rear of the table, which ran along the back wall and allowed the best surveillance of the room.

"Ah, you spies and your habits." Ako joked with a smile as he relaxed a little and sat down next to Jensen.

"I need a favor," Jensen began. "I've parked a Bentley a few blocks away. I need you to go down to it early in the morning and let a man out of the trunk."

"What?" Ako's eyebrows raised in surprise, the levels of concern growing once again.

"He won't be too happy but don't answer any questions just let him out and go."

"I couldn't answer any questions if I wanted to." Ako was dubious but didn't reject the proposal. Below the tabletop level, Jensen handed him a wedge of cash and a note. "Text me on this number when it's done. The car's location is written on there, too, and here's a few quid for helping me out."

The Kurd's acceptance of the payment had been automatic. He had grabbed it without even thinking, as most people do when something is passed to them, and now he protested. "You don't need to pay me for this, my friend." He was a proud man to whom friendship meant more than money.

"I know," Jensen replied. "But I'd feel better if I know you've had some cash out of the deal at least. Go and locate it tonight but don't let him out until the early morning hours. I need to be out of the area by the time he's released. Keep yourself out of harm's way and get out of there as soon as it's done."

"Thank you, my friend. I will do it first thing tomorrow," Ako said with sincerity. His body language showed Jensen that, while he may have been uncertain about the whole thing, he was both sincere and trustworthy and would go through with what was asked of him. His actions had always spoken louder than his words since Jensen had known him.

The two men left the bar and parted company, Ako set off to find the Bentley so he knew exactly where it would be in the morning.

Jensen walked farther along Saint Thomas Street to yet another bar called The Slug and Lettuce. It wasn't far, and Jensen's stomach was now insisting that it needed Mcfeeding. He walked through the doors into the midtown establishment where the charts were being played in the background, just low enough for people to still hear each other talk. A large table in the slightly elevated area against the back wall offered the ability to observe the room, as well as being not too far from an exit. A faint smile formed on his face as he made his way over to the table, not surprised to find Darius and Marshall waiting there nursing two drinks, with two empty glasses on the table in front of them. Another drink sat untouched beside them, obviously in anticipation of his arrival.

"See, I told you he'd pick here to sit," Marshall said, nudging Darius with a cocky look.

"Good, now can we order something to eat?" Darius seemed more concerned with satisfying his appetite than anything else, and Jensen conceded that an evening meal was well overdue.

Waiting for their food, Darius sat with a big cheesy grin as he exchanged messages with Olivia. Marshall restlessly fidgeted with the table napkins, went to the bar, ordered another drink, and paced around examining the prints on the wall. Jensen simply sat, deep in thought, going over the fine details of his plan again. The weapons cache had been organized, the goody bag had been stashed with

Adam, Bishop's release had been fixed, and when they were finished eating, the trio was almost ready to set sail to France. Checking the other occupants of the room before he spoke, Jensen brought the other two up to speed.

"Right, when we get dropped in Cherbourg, it's the train from there. We pay in cash, and the train will take us from Paris to Geneva, and then we'll have to change and jump on another train to Italy. When we cross the Italian border, we'll have to get off the train and hop on the tube to central Milan. Gianluca's contact will meet us there with a car, kit, and weapons. Then our road trip begins." Jensen's words sounded more like a briefing than anything else but the other two paid close attention. The arrival of the waitress with their meals brought all further discussion to an end and all three of them tucked in without a second thought.

Clearing the plate of every last morsel, Jensen pushed it away and sat back in his seat, rubbing his stomach in satisfaction and washing it down with a swig of his drink. The others, too, had finished their meals, and Darius was back to pursuing his romance via the cell phone. Marshall appeared to be unsettled. Watching him closely, it was obvious something was troubling him.

"What's up, mate?" Jensen's question shook Marshall out of his preoccupation.

"Ah, it's nothing," he replied. "I just hate being without a sidearm. I'd just got used to carrying again, and now I feel naked without it. In fact, we don't have any weapons at all, and I don't feel comfortable."

"I'm the same." Darius lifted his head from his phone just long enough to agree with Marshall.

It would make no sense to take weapons out of the country when they're so easy to obtain in Europe. Gun runners earn a fortune on the black market bringing weapons into England, nobody takes weapons out. As the saying goes, you don't take sand to the beach.

"Okay, I know it's not much, but as soon as we get to France, we'll pick up some pepper spray and pocket knives. They're legal there, and it'll be something at least until we get to Italy. Good enough?" Jensen's reassurance sounded somewhat unconvincing, even to himself. After all, he felt the same. Like being incomplete, the way most people feel when they go out without their cell phone.

Marshall and Darius nodded, but it still didn't seem to dispel the feeling of vulnerability entirely.

Jensen decided to attempt to bring the mood back up a level or two. "Then let's get back to the digs, grab our Bergen's, and get to the boat." Filled with enthusiasm, Jensen slid his chair out, poised to stand, when his cell phone rang. He didn't recognize the number, but answered and waited.

"Jensen?" Ako's voice on the other end of the line was hesitant. He sounded rattled.

Jensen's trained senses picked up on the stress. "Ako, everything okay, mate? Did you find it?"

"I got to the Bentley, but the trunk was already open," the Kurd replied.

Jensen breathed a sigh of relief. "Ha, the slippery son of a bitch got away already, did he?"

"No, he didn't. He's lying in the back with a nine-millimeter hole in his forehead."

Jensen's heart skipped a beat as Ako's words hit home. "Ako, I need another favor, mate. Get to the shops and buy a shit load of WD40. Take it back to the Bentley, and drench it with the stuff."

"WD40? The lubricant spray?" The Kurd sounded confused now.

"Yes. No time to explain. Just drown it in the stuff and don't miss an inch. I'll make sure you get rewarded when I get back, mate."

"Okay, last favor like this, though, Jensen. Only because it's you." Ako sounded reluctant but agreed. Jensen just hoped there were no more problems with this little disaster.

The WD40 should do the trick, he thought to himself.

Tradecraft: *Most people tend to think that setting fire to a vehicle is the best way to get rid of DNA evidence. However, in some instances, it helps preserve it, and forensic investigators can get a lot of information from a burned-out shell of a car. If you really want to get rid of DNA, then WD40 is the stuff. Fingerprints are not actually marks from the lines on your fingers, as most people would believe, but rather a stain from the grease built up in the gap between the lines in your fingers. When the pad of your finger touches a surface, the grease gets left behind, and the dusting powder that crime scene investigators use sticks to the grease and reveals the pattern most people think is their actual print. WD40 disperses that grease and most DNA you could leave behind, making it almost impossible for forensics to get anything worth logging. Most people would just try and wipe the handles etc., but that doesn't always work. You can easily miss an area, and sometimes, a quick wipe with a cloth will only smear a fingerprint, leaving behind a partial print. To make sure it's completely sterile, WD40 is the stuff.*

Marshall could see the concern on Jensen's face as he sat back at the table.

"What is it?" he asked.

"Bishop's been slotted. His body's still in the back of the Bentley, leaking the red stuff from his forehead."

Chapter 21

"Fuck me! That won't be an open casket. How? I mean, who?" Marshall was trying to figure out how the hell anyone even knew he was there. The gravity of the situation showed all over his face. "We've got to get the guns back."

Darius looked over, putting his phone away for the first time since the coffee shop.

"It's got to be a setup. Maybe he was alive and bribed your friend into making the call or even got the better of him and forced him to say it." Marshall and Jensen took on Darius's suggestion.

"Does your man know what we're planning to do?" Marshall asked Jensen, realizing he should have known better than to ask the moment he finished his sentence. Jensen just gave him a sideways look that spelled sarcasm in a visual way.

"Nothing changes. Nobody knows what we're up to. Whoever offed Bishop is irrelevant. So we get on the boat and finish the job." Jensen wasn't completely sure if Bishop was really dead, but at the moment, he remained certain that nobody else knew about how he was getting into Europe. He decided to carry through with his plan, despite a feeling in the pit of his stomach that something was wrong. Very wrong.

***

Captain Fordington moored his luxurious vessel in Cherbourg Marina, in an area known as Quai d'Artimon. His deckhands tied it securely as he unscrewed the lid from his Mont Blanc pen to scribble the docking time of 18:21 into the log.

Leaving the yacht for a quick ten-minute stroll, he came back and gave the men the all-clear

"All's looking well ashore, boys," Fordington called to the team waiting below.

Fordington poured himself a well-deserved glass of sherry as he sat in the glow of the slowly setting sun. The noises of the sea sloshing up the inside of the vessel soothed him as he relaxed, glass in hand.

A final check and setting of ERVs before clicking their Bergen's into place, and the trio set off. The remaining daylight caused their vision to be a little distorted as they emerged from below deck into the brightness of the evening sun. At this point, their composure needed to remain intact.

"Everybody good to go?" Jensen asked.

"Roger that," Marshall replied.

"Ready when you are," Darius added.

Tradecraft: *Cherbourg has little in the way of port police, and it's usually assumed that the wealthy and respectable owners of super yachts are operating well within the confines of the laws, so passport checks aren't usually top priority once the captain's declaration of who was on board has been submitted. When leaving the luxury liner, the trick is to look like you belong, act as if you have absolutely nothing to hide, and mosey on your way. It's highly unlikely that you'll be approached if your appearance suggests that everything is as normal as it could be. Sneak around like something out of a Tom and Jerry cartoon, and you'll be in cuffs before you can say cheap wine and tobacco.*

Being about two kilometers away, the train station was about a twenty-minute brisk walk, with just enough time to stop off at a local tobacco shop and buy a couple of pepper sprays each. They were far from ideal but, for the moment, gave them just a little bit more of an edge than being completely without any form of defense at all.

Walking inside the train station, Jensen took the lead and headed to the counter.

"Do you speak English?" Jensen asked with an element of hope.

"A little," the young cashier replied, moving her head from side to side, the slightest eyeroll, and a matching smile.

They were happy with the price and bought the tickets in cash at seventy-five euros each, and even though the clerk claimed to be able to speak English, Jensen deduced that "Platformay Twa" meant "Platform 3." The ticket departure time was 19:09.

They sat patiently waiting, currently low in confidence. This was the mere beginning, and the last thing they wanted was drama at this point. The platform clock showed it was 18:56. Not long now, they would soon have this stage over, and the jitters would ease some.

Tension was growing on the platform as a small crowd formed. Jensen was wondering if this amount of commuters was normal for this time in the evening. It was 19:08 and still no sign of the train showing up, yet a platform of passengers bustled about, every one of them looking like they could be a part of a surveillance team.

Jensen sat on one of the platform benches, Marshall stood slightly to the left behind him, and

Darius stretched out the other end and relaxed as he cocked a leg up onto the bench.

"I hate this part," Marshall grumbled, looking around and attempting to soak up as many possible escape routes as he could in the event of drama. Jensen, on the other hand, remained calm. Even though he had the same feelings as Marshall, he had mathematically deduced the escape route he would use with the lowest percentage chance of being compromised if he needed to run.

Tradecraft: *In an adrenaline-fueled situation, choices need to be minimalized. Too many options overload the brain's decision-making process and cause delays or even a freeze. This fatal hesitation as you weigh up your options can ultimately result in you being killed or captured. Whereas if you've already worked out the route that your hunters are more likely to enter the area from, giving you the answers as to where your hunters are less likely to enter the area from, you are already on your way to deciding your escape route. As soon as you've figured out the place your hunters have the lowest chance of having any presence, your escape route presents itself. The timing for the decision process is minimalized if you don't actually have to make the decision and can simply make your escape. If you only have one option, then that time is cut to practically zero, increasing the chances of your plan succeeding. On the other hand, if the plan fails, then you simply have your backup plan to commence moments after capture.*

"Just keep your cool, and we'll be fine," Jensen muttered. "You're clear on the ERV?"

"Yep, if the reality TV hits the fan, I'll see you there," Marshall quipped.

"And you, Darius?"

"Yeah, the café you told me about by the Eiffel Tower." He made eye contact before looking around the platform once more.

"Hey, heads up. Here comes the train," Marshall said.

Jensen breathed out a small sigh of relief as the train neared the station. The squeal of brakes as the train slowed at the platform seemed to indicate to most commuters to edge toward the doors of the carriages. All three remained stationary until the masses alit from the train, and the crowds on the platform boarded.

Darius seemed extremely familiar with spy tradecraft, considering he was only Lithuanian army, but Jensen was glad of that fact right now.

One man in jeans and a gray jacket stood motionless beside one of the advertising boards. He just stood there looking down slightly, with minimal movement. Plain walking boots and a baseball cap with no logo.

Tradecraft: *When in training, it's drilled into surveillance operatives always to take note of a person's footwear. When in the field, it's easy to swap a top or shirt, add or remove a cap or hat, jackets can be reversible, and even trousers can have Velcro seams at the rear so they can be ripped off quickly to reveal jeans or shorts underneath, but a person's footwear is not so easily changed. It takes time, it's awkward, plus, it's not exactly like you can carry a spare pair of Doc Martins around in your pocket to switch when nobody's looking. So even though all the other garments can be changed or covered reasonably quickly, whatever shoes or boots a person wears generally remain the same. Hence the reasons they're trained to pay close attention to what's on a person's feet.*

The guy on the platform was the typical *gray man*, a quintessential example of a surveillance operative. To anybody else, he would have blended right into the background and remained unseen, but to Jensen, he stood out as it was the exact type of attire he'd pick himself. Other commuters fidgeted and checked their phones, sipped drinks, or read magazines. This guy was almost like a statue until the trio boarded the train. As soon as they were inside the doors of their carriage, the man jumped onto the train, three carriages down, moments before the train pulled away.

"See him?" Jensen asked.

"On it!" Marshall replied. Jensen and Darius stood firm as Marshall walked back to blend into the crowd two carriages down. The man in the gray jacket rapidly marched toward Jensen and Darius. He slowed when he made visual contact with them both through the windows to the next carriage. The whistle blew on the platform. The man paused in the area where the carriages joined to look through the window, and within a second, Marshall's arm slipped around his neck and held him tight. The train crept forward.

The man's hands shot up to his throat, clutching in an attempt to free himself. Noises of aching steel informed Marshall they were in motion as the train gained momentum.

Marshall's mind filled with questions. Who was this guy? What were they going to do with him after he was knocked out? The risks were high of being caught if they let him go, but how were they going to restrain him? Then he realized he'd been squeezing a little too long. The two of them swayed as the train continued to speed up. Marshall needed to let go, but for some reason, he was having trouble stopping himself. He knew he should, but it felt like he was easing his own pain by passing it on to someone else. The man thrashed in a futile effort to save himself but was lifeless by the time the train had reached full speed. The rhythmic motion seemed soothing as the man fell to Marshall's feet, and the train continued slicing through the continental countryside.

What had he done? He never meant to kill him, he just wanted to stop him. A flash of fear ran through Marshall's body. *No time for panicking.* Marshall needed to get back on the clock and sort his mental mess out later.

After dragging the body into the toilet area, Marshall checked him for any sign of who he was or where he came from.

***

Jensen stood listening to Marshall give him all the details he had on the man who had been following them.

"Nothing." Marshall said. "He was sterile. No passport, no ID, nothing."

"What about tattoos?" Jensen asked.

"Nope. No VDMs, not even a branded item of clothing."

"Damn, he's good. Wristwatch? Cell phone?"

"No cell phone, digital wristwatch set to local time. Even the train ticket was paid in cash. All he had on him was another 235 Euros in cash, not even a wallet." Marshall seemed impressed by this guy, yet they had no idea if this guy was assigned to watch them, but it was a huge coincidence, and Jensen didn't believe in coincidences.

"What have you done with him?" Jensen asked.

"I accidentally killed him," Marshall replied sheepishly.

"Marshall? What the fuck? How did you kill him?" Jensen leaned back in disbelief.

"I didn't mean to. I was just going to knock him out and search him, but he struggled, and it got out of hand."

"We'll have to assume he wasn't operating alone and that he was monitoring us." Jensen shook his head and weighed the trouble they were in. "We continue with the assumption we're still under surveillance right up until we're able to confirm we're surveillance-free." For now, all they could do was press forward and remain extra vigilant.

Marshall had sat the man in a corner seat, looking like he was taking a nap. He'd be discovered sooner or later, but it should buy them enough time to make their next move without too much to worry about.

"Okay, well." Jensen snapped his fingers. "We're all exhausted from a sleepless crossing, so how about we get a bit of downtime? We've got just over three hours until the next change in Saint Lazare, so we'll go on stag. You two get your head down first, and I'll keep watch. Then you two can draw straws from there to Paris." Marshall and Darius needed no second invitations and were unclipping their Bergen's and sprawling out in no time.

Jensen sat a few tables down with them in full view, observing as they snoozed, using their luggage as pillows. Keeping an eye and an ear on both doors, he wondered who the man surveilling them could be. Was he alone? Who else knew what they were up to? Or was it just coincidence? Years in the job had Jensen believing there was no such thing as coincidence.

Tradecraft: *It could be argued that moving to the last carriage would give a tactical advantage. When you're in the last carriage, there's only one way a hostile can come from, which would cut down the need to look and listen out for two doors. On the flip side, it also cuts down your chances of survival because there's only one way you can go, too. If your only escape route is blocked, then your means of evading death or capture are halved as well.*

Even if moving down a cart only buys you a few valuable seconds, it might just be enough to give you the edge when it comes to escaping. So the middle of the train is the favorite. Once again, if it happens that hostiles approach from both directions, then go to plan B and escape after capture. Although avoidance of capture is always a favorite primary plan.

The same drills on the train station platform as in Paris suggested that nobody else was following them, although the inevitable doubts crept into Jensen's mind. Were they actually surveillance-free, or were the people performing surveillance on them this time just better at their job?

Darius drew the short straw and sat four tables down, keeping a watchful eye on the de-energized duo. Darius was glad it was only a mere ten minutes before the next change, where Marshall would take over and have his turn on lookout. The clock on the platform informed them it was 22:42 as they alighted the train to change for Gare de Lyon. A four-and-a-half-hour journey to Geneva, which wasn't due to depart until 05:50. Jensen sat there like a zombie, struggling to stay awake until the time came when he dropped into a seat and seemed almost comatose. Darius sat opposite, cuddling his Bergen. Marshall had moved down the train to the last seat facing them, right by the carriage door.

Jensen had no idea how much time had passed when he was rudely awoken by the commotion of two uniformed men holding up a highly intoxicated Marshall. He had no idea what they were saying, but they were clearly not happy. Fears manifested deep in Jensen's mind. Had they found the sleeping surveillance guy who was in a sleep he'd never awaken from? Had Marshall been spotted by someone? Had he blabbed off to someone in a drunken stupor about the dead guy propped up in one of the carriages? How had the guards even connected Marshall to him and the now stirring Darius?

Marshall had decided to make full use of the buffet car and invest in some liquid entertainment to ease the dull drag of the journey. He slurred some incoherent dribble as the two guards started gobbing off in French while prodding Jensen, who'd never been much of a morning person at the best of times.

Piercing brown eyes on either side of a long nose that sat above an Inspector Clouseau style mustache seemed to be awaiting some kind of response. Darius stirred after a subtle under-table kick. Waffling away in French again, the tone became increasingly hostile as the train decelerated. The decrease in speed warned Jensen that things could possibly get noisy pretty quickly if they didn't defuse the situation rapidly.

Jensen was fluent in German and Spanish, his Russian was a little rusty, but the only French he knew was words that consisted of four letters: rendezvous, ménage a trios, and cul-de-sac. Using an open posture and non-aggressive body language, he attempted to calm the two irate guards. The train slowed further, and Jensen implored the guards before glancing over at Darius discreetly.

"Get ready to grab Marshall and hoof it out of here," Jensen grunted through the side of his mouth to Darius.

The train's brakes squealed as they got applied close to the station. Jensen caught a glimpse of a group of armed, uniformed officers crowding the platform, ready to storm the train. Darius stood and held Marshall upright, swaying and staggering as the guards released his body weight for Darius to prop up.

"I'm not sure we're going to be able to run," Darius said with a look of desperation in his eyes. Marshall's arm flung around Darius's shoulder, and the pair of them looked a sight as they struggled to stay upright under the heavy braking of the train.

Pulling onto the platform, there was a commotion among the officers, desperate to scramble onto the train.

"Okay, sit him down. We're all in this together." Darius dropped the inebriated Marshall into the window seat before sitting next to him. The two guards dissipated into the background as the train finally halted.

Jensen awaited his fate as the armed police rushed onto the train shouting in French, and a sense of panic filled the air.

Chapter 22

Police officers marched up the aisle toward the trio. They surrounded a man in the seat behind them. Jacques Durand was swiftly arrested on multiple charges. Jensen had no idea what Jacques had done, but it seemed pretty serious. Everyone watched as he was cuffed, and the French police frog-marched him off the train.

Breathing out a sigh of relief, the trio relaxed, only to find the tension mounting once more as soon as the officers had exited the train. The two guards closed back in and stood staring at Jensen and his friends. The train remained stationary with the carriage doors open.

Jensen raised his hands in animated mock surrender. "Okay, we get the picture."

He placed his hands on his knees, then pushed up and out of his seat. Darius and Jensen hauled Marshall to his feet and dragged him off the train and through the station to the nearest bench. The whistle finally blew, and the train crept forward, accelerating away, leaving the trio alone on the platform at Gare de Lyon Part Dieu.

"What do we do now?" Darius asked.

Marshall was propped up against him, dribbling on his shoulder and snoring like a lion with hay fever in spring. The clock on the platform display showed it was 08:37.

"We get breakfast," Jensen said, feeling somewhat relieved about being in the situation that he would have been furious about being in only minutes earlier. As much as he hated to admit it, and bad as their current dilemma was, it was certainly much better than being dragged away by French authorities before their task had even really begun.

"Pan-Gakes!" Marshall slurred at some volume out of nowhere. All accompanied by a floppy hand gesture that slapped right back onto his leg.

"Let's go and see what we can find, shall we?" Jensen lifted Marshall to a standing position Negotiating the footbridge with the slowly sobering Marshall returning to the land of the living was a task in and of itself, but when they finally got to the other side, they soon found that they were only seven or eight hundred yards from a McDonald's. The translation of the directions left a lot to be desired, but they weren't too far away.

"At least we'll be able to use the WiFi and have a look on the tablet at the satellite imagery to get an idea of the terrain and what to do next," Jensen told Darius as they continued to steer Marshall toward the golden arches.

***

Marshall sat eating his sausage and egg McMuffin and sipping at a large black coffee while Jensen studied the tablet closely to decide the next best route. Darius sat smirking at Marshall as he groaned with the onset of his hangover.

"My head's banging like a hooker's headboard." Marshall moaned, rubbing his temple before taking another sip of coffee.

"It could have been a lot worse. At least we're in McDonald's and not in custody." Jensen shook his head. "Darius and I have looked at the map, and the best bet is to get a taxi from here to the Swiss border. There's a sleepy little village where we can get the taxi to drop us off, and we can sneak over the border from there."

"Sounds easy enough," Marshall said, taking another sip of coffee. Jensen decided to leave out a vital detail at this moment for Marshall to find out later when they finally got to the village.

"It's about a two-hour drive to the border, roughly about one hundred and thirty kilometers, so finish your breakfast, and we'll go and see if we can smooth talk a cab driver into taking us up there," Jensen said, mainly because Marshall's second coffee had encouraged Darius to join him for one and a chocolate donut to boot. "Oh, and we'll need some crocs?"

"Crocs? As in the horrible plastic sandal type things?" Marshall asked with a frown.

"Yep, come on, let's go do some more shopping." Jensen stood with Marshall and Darius following suit.

"Do you think they've found the dead guy on the train yet?" Darius asked.

"Hopefully not yet," Marshall replied. "But let's not be here hanging around to find out when they do." He picked up the pace as they headed to the exit.

"Who do you think he was?" Marshall's question seemed to be aimed at Jensen.

"At this stage, I haven't got a clue. I'm hoping to get the job done before we find out." The trio walked along the backstreets of town. The owner of a local tourist gift shop was pulling out his displays to stand outside the front of his store. "Ah, just what we need."

After a quick excursion in the gift shop, they were kitted out with a couple of extra bits that Jensen insisted they buy. He still held back on the one factor that would add a little difficulty to their final stage of the border crossing. Marshall wasn't firing on all cylinders, so he hadn't quite pieced it together yet, but Darius was beginning to suspect what awaited them where France ends and Switzerland begins. A touch of anxiety developed inside him.

They'd each managed to get about a half hour's sleep during the two-hour taxi ride. The taxi continued toward Pougny before stopping a few miles short of a little village on the D76. The quaint and quiet village was home to the bridge that acted as the border control. As soon as you cross the bridge, a small veranda-type structure housed a checkpoint. There was a high chance they could have driven straight through it without being stopped, but it was better to be safe than sorry.

Jensen told the taxi driver they would walk the rest of the way and asked about bars and amenities in a different village in the opposite direction of where they were heading. It was only a thin veil as a decoy but might buy them a little time if they needed it. The hands of the clock on the taxi's dashboard showed it was nearly a quarter past eleven when they were dropped off. They walked one way until the taxi was well out of sight, then turned and walked back in the direction they actually wanted to travel until they could get out of sight of the main road.

The trio walked through the picturesque village with Jensen a pace or so ahead. It had taken over an hour before they'd reached the other side of the village and were leaving the last dots of civilization behind.

The river Rhone acts as the actual border between France and Switzerland, with one side of the river being French and the other side of the river Swiss. You can literally sail up one side of the river and be in France and down the other side in Switzerland.

Once they'd got through the few chateaus dotted around the village, they soon found they were trampling through grass and light foliage. They gathered in a small area with high grass at the riverbank, sheltered from sight as best they could be. The seed of anxiety within Darius beginning to sprout.

"Now I see why you wanted the Crocs," Marshall said as the final puzzle piece clicked into place.

Jensen smirked as he checked his watch. 12:43.

"We don't have to swim in the river, do we?" Darius asked with a deep look of concern on his face.

"Only until we get to the other side," Jensen replied.

"What's the matter, Darius? You can swim, can't you?" Marshall hadn't seen this side of his friend before.

"Yes, in a pool. I don't like rivers and the sea." Darius inserted the knuckle of his index finger into his mouth. He was evidently becoming more anxious, and Jensen spotted signs in his body language that showed he wasn't too far away from freaking out.

"Don't worry. Marshall and I will be on either side of you all the way. We'll cross in formation and make sure you're all right at every moment. Any issues, and we'll come right back and get out." Jensen kept his voice soothing, hoping it would reassure Darius that he'd be okay.

Tradecraft: *Intelligence agencies train their recruits in NLP and social engineering for use when recruiting assets in the field. You can always tell when a new starter, or EOD (Entry On Duty), as they're sometimes known, starts at Langley fresh from the Farm. They walk around overflowing with self-assurance, flashing a smile and displaying a sickly sweet confidence like that of a double-glazing salesman or gameshow host.*

Dishing out compliments and boosting the ego of everybody they converse with. It's where the saying "Don't caseworker me" comes from when a person tries to calm a colleague using a bit of smooth talking. Eventually, it fades to a natural level and doesn't seem as false. One of the most important tools, though, is getting a person to agree with you. When talking to someone in a situation where you want them to concur with you, there are tactics to assist you along the way. Mixed with your social engineering, you can ask questions in a way where the subject is constantly answering "yes." This gets them into a pattern of agreeance and compliance. All the time, looking them in the eye and nodding. If they mirror your action and nod along with you, there's a higher chance of success. Mixed with one or two other social engineering tactics, plus using the right words, you can get most people to agree to almost anything.

"Besides, there's a science behind it. Watch, and I'll show you." By engaging Darius in his checks and making him a part of the test, Jensen helped to ease his mind, even more, all the time talking calmly and reassuringly as he went. "The first and most important thing we do is check that the river isn't in flood."

"How do we do that?" Darius asked as Marshall flashed an all-knowing look at Jensen to indicate he knew what Jensen was up to.

"We look for discoloration, surging water, and debris. If there's none of that, then we know the river isn't in flood." Jensen wrapped his arm around Darius at the edge of the river bank and looked into the flowing water. "Do you see anything?"

"No, I guess," Darius replied, pursing his lips, still not completely sure that his river reading skills were up to any measurable standard.

"Okay then, see, that's a good start. Next, we check the speed of the water." Jensen paced back for a moment to snap a leaf from a nearby plant. Darius watched as Jensen threw it out onto the water, and they watched as it floated away on the surface. "Excellent, it's less than walking pace, so we know it's not rapid running water that will knock us off our feet." He looked at Darius with yet another head nod and a smile.

Darius reciprocated with his head nodding away and a nervous smile flashing across his face. "What next?" Darius asked like he was waiting for more enlightening tricks on the best possible ways to gauge if it was safe to cross a river or not.

"We double-check the color and clarity. If it's extremely muddy and the water isn't clear, then we take extra precautions, but if it's running reasonably clearly, then we're good to go. Looks clear to me, what do you think, Marshall?"

"Looks okay to me," Marshall replied, knowing full well the whole point of his question was simply to reassure Darius.

"Does it look like clear water to you, Darius?" Jensen asked, nodding like a toy dog in the back of a car.

"I guess so," Darius concurred.

Jensen patted him heartedly on the back with a big smile. "Then there you go. We're all good and can cross the river. We just pick an exit point on the other side, and we all make our way toward it slowly and carefully. Okay?"

"Okay." Darius reluctantly agreed, crediting Jensen with a whole lot of trust and having faith in what he'd said that they'd all be okay. Stripping down to nothing other than shorts and Crocs, the team had placed their kit inside a dry sack that lined their Bergen's. Aside from keeping their stuff dry, they also acted as floatation aids. Making the whole of Bergen a large buoyancy device as they crossed the river.

After more than an hour of prepping and planning, Marshall was the first to lower himself into the water, reaching a level just above his knees. Letting out a shudder, he pulled his Bergen down into the water and waded out a little before strapping it on loosely. Jensen helped lower Darius in and dropped into the river just behind him. The crisp and cold flowing water was pushing against him as his feet touched down onto the riverbed. It deepened as they waded out a little farther, coming up to waist level. Resisting the urge to urinate, Jensen pressed on and lowered himself into the water as they edged out farther. He checked his wristwatch one last time. It was just after two in the afternoon.

Even though they'd picked the narrowest point to cross, the river was still about sixty meters wide. Luckily though, the river Rhone is only about three meters deep at its deepest point. Going with the natural flow of the river, the team pushed on diagonally toward the nominated exit point, a little bit at a time. It had taken a while to get there, but they were nearing the middle of the river. Just short of the halfway mark, the water was up to Marshall's shoulders, making it harder for him to walk. He looked back at Darius, who was showing slight signs of panic in his eyes.

"Hey Darius, the more time you spend with Jensen, the more you get used to being in this position." He laughed. "Up to your neck in it."

Darius just gave a quick half nod accompanied by a nervous smile and carried on swishing across, trying his best to keep his composure. Jensen watched him intensely as they neared the center of the river.

Tradecraft: *Drowning doesn't look like drowning. Ask pretty much any Force Recon Marine. Drowning is nearly always a deceptively quiet event. The waving, splashing, and yelling that dramatic television shows us is just that. Drama for television and rarely seen in real life. When a person is drowning, there is minimal splashing and no waving, yelling, or calling for help. Except in rare circumstances, drowning people are physiologically unable to call out for help. The respiratory system's primary function is breathing, speech is secondary. Its primary function (breathing) takes priority and must be fulfilled before speech occurs. When drowning, people's mouths alternately sink below and reappear above the water's surface. Their mouths are not above the surface of the water long enough to exhale and inhale and call out for help. When their mouths are above the surface, they attempt to exhale and inhale quickly before their mouths sink below the surface of the water again.*

People who are drowning cannot wave for help. Nature instinctively forces them to extend their arms laterally and press down on the water's surface. Pressing down on the surface of the water permits drowning people to leverage their bodies so they can lift their mouths out of the water to breathe. Throughout the Instinctive Drowning Response, they cannot voluntarily control their arm movements. Physiologically, when drowning, people who are struggling on the surface of the water cannot stop drowning and perform any voluntary movements, such as waving for help, moving toward a rescuer, reaching out for a floatation device, etc. From beginning to end of the Instinctive Drowning Response, people's bodies remain upright in the water, with no evidence of a supporting kick.

Unless rescued by a trained lifeguard, drowning people can only struggle on the surface of the water from twenty to sixty seconds before submersion occurs. That doesn't mean a person yelling for help and thrashing isn't in real trouble, they are experiencing something known as aquatic distress. Not always present before the instinctive drowning response, aquatic distress doesn't last long, but unlike the actual drowning process, these victims can still assist in their own rescue. They can grab floatation devices, reach lifelines, etc.

In order to spot someone who is drowning when a person's in the water, look for signs like; Head low in the water, mouth at water level. Head tilted back with mouth open. Eyes glassy and empty, unable to focus or closed. Hair over forehead or eyes. Not using their legs and hyperventilating or gasping. Trying to swim in a particular direction but not making headway or trying to roll over onto the back. Finally, a big giveaway is when a person appears to climb an invisible ladder.

Jensen knew Darius was in trouble just after the halfway point. He'd lost his footing, and his head went under the water. It wasn't under long, but when he re-emerged, it was just his face peeping out of the surface of the water. A gasp and a glug before he went back under. This time a little longer.

"Marshall!" Jensen yelled to get his attention as he swam as fast as he could toward Darius.

The tug of Jensen's Bergen reminded Jensen just how powerful the force of the water could be. Darius was still under the water, getting dragged downstream by his Bergen. Jensen went with the flow of the tide and attempted to steer himself toward Darius, who was occasionally bobbing to the surface. Marshall was trying an approach from the other side.

Eventually, they both got to him at pretty much the same time. Tipping him up, they held him above the surface of the water and floated with the tide, still trying to steer themselves toward the bank. All three were being swept downriver and tugged along by the current. Using an arm each to keep Darius afloat and the other arm to try and steer, they neared the far side of the river. A branch sticking out was their savior as Marshall grabbed a hold, swinging them all with the tide and sending them crashing into the riverbank.

Marshall gripped the branch tight with one hand and tried his best to hold Darius above the water as Jensen let go to drag himself up onto the land. He pulled his Bergen off and threw it out of the water, then grabbed the one attached to Darius, too. Clambering out, as soon as he had a good footing, he tried to pull up the dead weight of Darius's body. Even with Marshall pushing from below, he was only able to pull him up so far and hold him there until Marshall got out. Marshall pulled his Bergen up and released it from around him.

Marshall and Jensen got a good grip on Darius and dragged his limp body onto dry land.

Chapter 23

They hauled Darius onto a flat clearing away from the river. Surrounded by trees and foliage, Jensen opened and checked Darius's airway, then gave chest compressions. Marshall stood watching, panic and concern filling him. Jensen tried to remain calm and control his breathing. He recited the technique in his mind as it had been quite some time since he'd last given CPR. He'd also forgotten how exhausting it was. Two more rescue breaths and Jensen started the next set of chest compressions. About five or six in, Darius choked, coughing up a mouth full of river water and foam. He sat up and turned sideways.

Coughing and retching, his eyes filled with water, and he rubbed his chest. He spit and groaned as he came to grips with what had happened. He held one nostril flat as he blew down hard in an attempt to clear the other nostril, then repeated for the next one. Marshall had opened his Bergen and dug a towel out to wrap around him.

"I lost my Crocs." Darius croaked between coughs with a little chuckle. The tension dissolved, and Marshall let out a small sigh of relief.

"Me too," Jensen replied. "But the good news is, we're on the right side of the river. Can you imagine if we're back where we'd started and had to do it again?"

"I think you'd be doing it alone." Darius laughed. He was shaking, and his teeth were chattering. Marshall wrapped a jacket around him from the Bergen while Jensen checked him for signs of hypothermia. Digging into the Bergen, Marshall set up the camping stoves, and mess tins, then opened the rat packs they'd bought from the army surplus store back in Weymouth. After performing a river crossing, whether successful or not, it's important to always have something to eat and a hot drink as soon as possible.

Under normal circumstances, Marshall would have taken the time to fetch water, as well as set up a proper fire. But with everything that had happened, it was just quicker and easier to use their camping stoves and water from their canteens. It meant a decrease in supplies, but time was more important when it came to assisting Darius.

Encapsulated by the visual protection of the trees, the team stood drying themselves off a few yards from the riverbank. The microfiber travel towels seemed to spread the water around the body more than dry them. Creating an even, all-over dampness. They were no longer wet but weren't exactly dry either.

Once Darius was comfortable, Marshall and Jensen served up some food. There's no actual treatment for hypothermia. The best thing you can do is get them comfortable and leave them alone. Obviously, you can still keep an eye on them, but a healthy body will take care of itself. Shivering, however, burns up calories, so a sugar intake of some sort is always a bonus.

Marshall set aside his hot chocolate and started rooting around in the box of the rat pack. He seemed a bit fidgety and a tad irritable.

"Where's the Yorkie bar?" Marshall asked, looking up from the box and picking his drink back up again.

"They don't put them in any more," Jensen said.

"You're kidding? They were the best thing about the British rat packs," Marshall said, sounding like he'd found a dime and lost a dollar.

He sat silently, the sound of a slight breeze between the trees and the subtle background noise of the flowing river. A few minutes of uncomfortable silence passed by. Darius seemed solemn as he sat forward, his hands wrapped around his hot chocolate cup. The sun was setting behind him. Jensen checked the time—it was approaching six p.m.

Where had the time gone? Jensen sat deep in thought about what was awaiting them in the near future.

"Was there ever any doubt in your mind about getting MJ back?" Marshall's sobering question seemed to pause the background noise of rippling water and chirping birds. Jensen was thrust from his thoughts of the near future to his thoughts of the recent past.

"It was the hardest thing I've ever done in my life, Marshall. You know some of the things I've had to do in the past. I'm not afraid to get my hands dirty for the greater good, but I've always been able to compartmentalize it before. Like when I get home, I can switch off work as soon as I sit around the table with my family. Like the horrors just stop as soon as I'm through the front door. Until it's time to go to sleep, at least."

Jensen watched as Marshall gave a distant nod in agreeance. "But when those lines blurred." Jensen shook his head like he couldn't even comprehend his thoughts. "I've never experienced anything like that before, and honestly, I'm not sure how I managed to cope with the doubts and fears that filled my mind. I'm just glad you guys were there to help me through it."

Darius let out a smile as he nodded at Jensen. What he'd done hadn't actually had much impact, and they'd have coped just as well without him, but to Jensen, his being there was immeasurably appreciated.

"I'm sorry I let you down on the train," Marshall said.

Jensen watched as he packed his towel back into his Bergen, barely able to make eye contact.

"We all make mistakes, mate. Just do me a favor and try not to make too many more over the next few days, will you." Jensen's words lightened the mood.

Marshall smirked back at him, and the contagious smile soon infected Darius, too.

"You betcha," Marshall replied as he pulled his top on.

"Good," Jensen said. "Well, we'll set up camp here, seeing as we're halfway to being set up anyways, and move out under the cover of darkness late tonight. You both okay with that?"

"Roger that," Marshall said.

"Sounds good to me." Darius agreed.

"Right then, Marshall, you set up a small fire, and I'll go and replenish our water supplies from the river.

Tradecraft: *Salt water should never be drunk directly from the sea or river. It should always be clarified and purified first. The two frequently get confused. Clarified is when you filter out the dirt and chunks etc., from the water so it looks clear. There are several methods of doing this, like pouring it through a cloth filter or having water in one container (slightly higher than the other), then running a small cotton strip of soaked material from the container with the water and draping it into the empty container next to it. In time the water drips through the cloth and filters out the muck. The majority of the time, water should be clarified before its purified.*

Purified is when all of the pathogens etc., are removed to make the water safe to drink. Again there are several methods like boiling it, drinking it through a Life Straw, or using chemicals such as potassium permanganate sterilizing crystals (which can also be mixed with antifreeze to create a chemical fire) or things like oasis, the army issue water purification tablets that come in the British ration packs.

Once the three Basha's had been set up in a pattern that would have made Mercedes proud, Marshall began the process of setting up an actual campfire in the center rather than just the stoves that were placed into a bit of cut-out ground.

Tradecraft: *When setting up a campfire, sheltering it is also important. Sudden gusts of wind can not only impede you from starting the fire but also make it harder to control. The last thing you want is to get a roaring campfire going, then a gust of wind blows sparks and flames everywhere, burning your whole camp down. You should also be extremely cautious of drying wet clothes by a campfire. They won't catch fire when they are wet, but as soon as they're dry, they can go up in flames pretty quickly.*

Fires should be contained as best as you can, but don't use porous rock. If water trapped inside boils, the rock can explode. So always be aware when setting up a campfire or stove, especially when near water or even snowy or icy conditions.

Darius was cheering up and on the mend while Marshall proceeded to cook the puddings from the rat packs. Jensen had set up a trip wire around the camp's perimeter in something that was as close to resembling a circle as he could get. Running the full circumference of the camp, the trip wire was attached to a mousetrap that was secured to a tree. The mouse trap had a glow stick duct taped to it so that when the wire was tripped, the mouse trap would strike the glow stick, and the glow stick would then light up to alert the team to a possible threat. It wouldn't give them a huge amount of reaction time, but it was better than being woken up by the business end of an officer's or local farmer's gun prodding you and pointing at your mush.

Tradecraft: *When setting up camp, most people would assume it's the optimum choice to utilize a spot close to the water. The opposite is actually true. Tactically it makes no sense at all. As soothing as the babbling water might seem, it acts as a form of white noise and can cancel out noises made by any possible threat that may approach the camp. There's the risk of flooding, the fact that the ground may be muddy, soft, or become waterlogged. Plus, you've halved your escape options by as much as fifty percent. A potential 360 degrees of direction to run if needed has been reduced to 180 degrees, halving your chance of possible escape. Not to mention the fact that as picturesque as it may be, all the bugs and wildlife gather near water.*

"I hope Gianluca comes through with the goods without any problems. Did you tell him I was with you?" Marshall asked.

"Hell no. He can't stand you."

"Me? What did I do?" Marshall's tone was complete innocence.

"What did you do?" Jensen asked rhetorically. "Well, where do I start? First of all, you insulted him on the last job we did together. At the end of it, we went for a few drinks to celebrate a job well done, and when you got drunk, you decided to wind him up by telling him you thought the Italian Special Forces motto was 'Who cares who wins?' Then, after, you took those two Latvian girls back to *his* hotel room, not yours, *his*, to play naked twister." Marshall let a smile slip out as he recalled the memories of that night. "You then left Gianluca and me to deal with Sasha the mad Russian, who proceeded to smash up the bar in anger because *somebody*, not mentioning any names, was practicing their gland to gland combat in his wife."

"Once! I only slept with her once!" Marshall protested in his defense. Darius let out a giggle and covered his mouth with his hand trying not to make his amusement obvious.

"Either way, since that op, he can't stand you, and you didn't even have a twister mat," Jensen said in exasperation.

"Improvise, adapt and overcome, buddy," Marshall said with a smile.

Darius watched closely, idolizing Marshall like he had some kind of bromance going on. After the new revelations, his man crush had Darius seeing Marshall as some kind of hero.

Jensen rolled his eyes as he laid his roll mat out under his Basha and stuffed his sleeping bag inside the waterproof Bivvy bag.

"Now, where have I heard that before?" Jensen asked in jest, looking up at Marshall, who'd wandered over to hand Jensen his portion of his pudding. "Thanks." Jensen gladly took the pudding, knowing the extra calories would soon get used up.

"How did that guy find out someone was sleeping with his wife?" Darius asked. Knowing how good Marshall was at tradecraft and how cautious he'd be, he was genuinely curious.

"Someone sent him a photo of her taking it doggy style, but the picture stopped at the chest so he wouldn't know it was me." Marshall chuckled as he munched away at his pudding from the plastic spoon that came in the pack. Darius swallowed his spoonful of pudding and paused for a second.

"Do you know who sent it?" Darius asked.

"Yeah, me!" Marshall said with a chuckle as he spooned another pile of pudding into his mouth.

"Seriously, Marshall? I sometimes wonder what's wrong with you?" Jensen shook his head as he finished his pudding and lay down, pulling his sleeping bag up to his head.

"Hey, he was an ass! Besides, he drank the last of my whiskey," Marshall replied through a mouthful of pudding.

"You drank *all* of his vodka! Not to mention the little fact that you were hanging twenty toes with his wife!" Jensen shouted back from within his sleeping bag.

"Once! I told you already, I only ever went nuts to guts with her once!"

"Yeah, once too often!" Jensen shouted back.

"Yeah, that was one hell of a puddle cuddle. Them were the good old days, eh?" Marshall replied, reminiscing at a slightly lower volume, while Jensen was still mid-rant.

"And then you sent the evidence to her husband. A giant, crazy, six-foot-eight Russian Spetznaz soldier, with a torso like an olympic bodybuilder and a temper shorter than a dwarfs washing line." Jensen went on. "An actual printed photo of yourself mid clunge plunge in his wife. Why the hell would you do that anyway? In fact, I don't even want to know. I'm getting my head down before we move out." Jensen rearranged his position in the sleeping bag to get comfortable, his back facing Marshall.

Marshall and Darius just looked at each other with a silent chuckle.

Jensen decided against calling MJ this early on. Especially when the only thing he could tell her was that things weren't going as smoothly as he'd hoped. He lay there thinking about Elena and MJ, it wasn't long before his mind wandered to the other side of the pond to America. He thought about Dakota and his dad. He promised himself as soon as this was over, a trip to the States was definitely overdue. Making a mental list of plans, he drifted to sleep with his thoughts.

* * *

The snap of the mouse trap woke Jensen with a start. His eyes were taking their time adjusting as he came around. He had no idea how long he'd been asleep, but it was still pitch black. A tad disorientated, he slowly moved up out of his bedding and tried to compose himself. The chemical glow illuminated the immediate area, and Jensen quickly covered it with a shemagh. The smell of the extinguished campfire filled the air. Marshall had poured water on it earlier to make sure it was completely out before they went to sleep. Rustling noises from their sleeping bags informed him Marshall and Darius were awake, too. Faint noises of them preparing to react to a threat was mildly comforting.

Jensen's mind worked overtime. How did anyone know they were there? Had intelligence services somehow tracked their movements and picked them up on satellite or with thermal imagery? Maybe the taxi driver had been questioned by local authorities, or was it just some local farmer who'd spotted the smoke from the fire earlier that evening. Surely they wouldn't be out investigating it this time of night? Maybe they'd called the police, and the local law enforcement had only just got there. Had they found the dead man on the train? This was the last thing they needed. He cleared his thoughts and focused on the immediate threat that was getting closer by the second.

The rippling water in the background made it harder to single out noises and ascertain the distance of the threat.

He pulled out the pepper spray and moved to cover behind a wide tree trunk. Not-so-distant noises of rustling and breathing drew closer. He heard the crunching of branches and twigs as the intruder crept closer to the camp. His eyes still hadn't completely adjusted to the darkness. He opened his mouth and listened intensely, controlling his breathing and waiting for the intruder. His heart raced, and his pulse quickened.

They were almost upon the camp.

Chapter 24

Jensen braced himself, the tension mounted as the noises intensified. They were inches away. Jensen sensed the movement more than saw it as Marshall jumped out toward the threat. Darius moved out and skirted round, ready to dive in and attack from the side.

At first, Jensen saw nothing. Then a movement in his peripheral vision caught his eye. The shadows moved as Marshall closed in. The movement was low to the ground, and Jensen was just in time to catch a glimpse of the badger turning to scurry away rapidly into the darkness.

Jensen breathed deeply as the team relaxed.

"Damn thing nearly give me a heart attack," Marshall gasped.

"Time to pack up and move out, I think," Jensen muttered to Marshall.

"Oh yes." Marshall agreed.

Darius closed in and joined the other two. Their eyes had now fully adjusted to the dark, and they could make out the shapes and silhouettes of their camp clearly.

"We've got one hell of a TAB over a lot of farmland in the dark to do before we get anywhere near civilization, so let's get sorted and hoof it out of here," Jensen instructed.

He hadn't even finished his sentence before Marshall and Darius were shoving their sleeping bags into their sacks. A rapid pack up and a final check of the camp and their Bergens were back on. In turn, they each jumped up and down on the spot to do a noise discipline check, and when they were satisfied they weren't going to rattle or clang, they were good to go. A final check was that all parties knew the ERV and then they were moving out over the Swiss countryside.

The first few drops of rain indicated to the trio what the rest of the night was going to be like. Hours went by of traipsing through the countryside in the rain, leaving them aching, breathless, and exhausted by the time the sun had risen. They marched into a small town unshaven and a tad disheveled.

"Looks like we might be able to get a bus from here to the center of Geneva," Marshall said.

"Yeah, but we can't go looking like this," Jensen added. "Let's see if we can get checked into a small hotel and cleaned up before going much farther."

"Guys, I need to stop," Darius called out as he sat at the edge of the road.

Marshall and Jensen turned to see him taking his boot and sock off to reveal a large blister on the rear of his heel.

"Ouch, looks painful, buddy," Marshall said. "Here, let me get my sewing kit for you." Marshall rummaged in his Bergen until he found it and passed it over to Darius. Cutting a short length of white cotton and threading it through the eye of the needle, Darius pierced it into one end of the blister and out the other until a piece of the thread was hanging on either side. He removed the needle and passed the kit back to Marshall.

Tradecraft: *Fluids from a blister should be drained to relieve the pain. This method achieves that by soaking through the thread and leaking out, at the same time as leaving the blister sealed and not exposing raw skin and running the risk of making it even sorer or getting infected.*

"Thanks," Darius said as he handed the kit back.

"No worries." Marshall turned his attention to Jensen. "Yeah, I think you're right. The last thing we want is to rock up in central Geneva looking like a bunch of escaped convicts. One of the richest cities in the world, and we look like we've just come back from the bush. Let's see if we can get booked in somewhere."

Darius padded his heel with some dressing and pulled his boot back on. It was time for the team to make themselves presentable. Cargo pants and rucksack might have been okay normally (just about), but with the rough couple of days they'd had, they were a little unkempt, to say the least. Not even close to the baseline needed to blend in once they got to Geneva.

Tradecraft: *Hiding masses of diplomatic and commercial secrets and being home to several UN secretaries as well as accommodating the HQs of multinational companies, Geneva is probably the world's largest hub for spies and has been for many years. A multi-lingual culture (a third of its residents being foreign) with the added bonus of the country remaining neutral, Geneva acts like a perfect home for spy rings. Home to most of the world's humanitarian organizations, the CIA has also spent a lot of time and resources in Geneva because of its banking facilities. Let's face it, there are huge advantages of having a peek into a secret bank account whenever you need to.*

In the recruiting of spies, MI6 looks for three things. One; access. Does the potential recruit have access to secrets? Two; motivation. What will motivate them to share those secrets with you? And three; security. Is there a high-security risk to any of the parties involved?

In recent years the acronym MICE has been used as the summary of recruiting assets. Which stands for Money, Ideology, Compromise (sometimes alternatively Coercion), and Ego. (Rice is sometimes used in its place with money simply being replaced with the word reward. The concept, however, remains the same.)

Of course, in the likes of Geneva, the MICE system has to lose the M straight away. The very concept of trying to financially bribe a Swiss banker is a complete waste of time. I mean, they're not exactly struggling, are they? Next to go is the I. The world in which Swiss bankers are accustomed doesn't leave much scope for selling them any form of ideology. So most of the time, C is the way forward. CIA officers act under diplomatic cover, and they have quite a powerful influence in Geneva. So they tend to use dirty tricks in order to recruit assets from the Swiss banking network.

For example, on one occasion, a CIA officer under diplomatic cover made friends with a Swiss banker and got him drunk. When he was completely intoxicated, the officer encouraged him to drive home. The banker did so and not only crashed his car but got arrested, too. The CIA officer (who was the one who'd actually called the police) used his influence to get the banker released without charge in order to get him owing a favor and in his pocket.

Methods like this are used frequently to gain favors from and recruit Swiss bankers.

US intelligence agencies CIA and NSA maintain some eighty data collection centers worldwide, including one in Geneva's US Mission to the United Nations. Referred to as Special Collection Service (SCS). By scanning the airwaves for cellular signals, intersecting wireless data packets, and sucking in satellite transmissions, masses of data analysts have access to any and all communication in the area.

Due to the amount of spy activity in Geneva, there are more intelligence officers needed to spy on the spies. So Geneva is pretty much spy central.

The hotel owner had reluctantly checked the team into three single rooms, with them looking like a rough bunch of muddy hikers. The distaste was clearly visible on his face as he handed over the keys to each room and told them not to leave any mess. It was finally time to call MJ and bring her up to speed as well as check how she and Elena were coping. Jensen pulled the sat phone from his Bergen along with the charger and foreign plug adapter. Once it was plugged into the wall, he left it tucked inside the signal-blocking bag. He could hear the showers from Darius and Marshall's room on either side of him as he walked over to the dressing table to boil the small kettle that sat next to complimentary tea, coffee, and sugar sachets.

After a hot drink and a shower, shave, and shine, the sat phone was fully charged. Time for a walk. He unplugged the charger at the phone end and folded the flap of the signal-blocking bag. Jensen grabbed his room key and walked for about twenty minutes until he found a hotel fitting similar criteria to the one he was actually in. Sitting outside the hotel entrance, he pulled the sat phone from the bag and dialed the number of the break phone. After a long pause, he finally got a ringtone.

It was unlikely the sat phone was being tracked, but his actions acted as an extra layer of precaution. If somebody were tracking the number, then it would ping as being used at the hotel he was sitting outside and not the actual one he was staying in. It wouldn't buy him a huge amount of time but would hopefully cover his tracks long enough for him to make a getaway if needed. As soon as he finished the call, he would put it back in the signal blocking bag, and it wouldn't ping again until the next time he used it.

"Hello?"

"Hey MJ, it's me. How are you holding up?" Jensen asked gently.

"Oh baby, it's you. Is everything okay?" MJ was relieved at the sound of Jensen's voice.

"Yes, sweetie, it's fine. You have a word for me?" He needed to get the important things out of the way first. Upon hearing the safe word, Jensen breathed a small internal sigh of relief. At least things were okay on one end. "I haven't got long to talk. How's Elena?"

"She's missing her daddy, we both are. She still cries in her sleep and is very emotional, but she's getting better. I think it'll be much better when you come home. I need you, I'm having nightmares when I'm asleep and going stir crazy when I'm awake. How much longer will you be?"

"I'm not sure. We've got quite a way to go yet, but I promise I'll be home as soon as I can."

"How are you, Marshall, and Darius getting along?" MJ was trying to lighten the mood.

"Marshall caused some drama and nearly got us all arrested getting drunk on the train and got us kicked off in the middle of France. Darius nearly died when he almost drowned in the river Rhone, and a badger nearly gave us all a heart attack wandering into our camp in the middle of the night, but other than that, it hasn't been a very eventful trip."

"No. What were you doing swimming in the river?" MJ sounded almost amused.

"It's a long story, but I'll tell you all about it when I get home. Anyways, I better get going. We've got to play catch up to get to our RV point on time. I'll call you next time I get a chance."

"Okay, baby. Take care and come home soon," MJ said. She wanted to talk longer but knew Jensen would have a good reason not to stay on the phone for too long.

"Will do, speak soon. Love you."

"Love you, too," MJ responded.

Jensen ended the call before the chance to have second thoughts crept into his mind. He slipped the phone into the signal-blocking bag and folded the flap back over.

By some miracle, he'd pretty much managed to stay off the grid for now, but he was about to go to the center of Geneva. Remaining off the grid would be close to impossible for this next part.

He looked down at the phone in the signal-blocking bag and slipped it into his pocket, then took a deep inhale as he walked back to his hotel. It was time to prepare mentally for what was coming next.

He was about to walk into the lion's den.

Chapter 25

Walking past Lake Geneva as a part of their SDR, Jensen led the way as Marshall and Darius trailed a half step behind. Jensen made his way toward a huge park in the center of Geneva that was home to several useful means of spotting a tail. There was a large area of a black and white checked floor with giant chess pieces surrounded by two seater bistro style tables with chessboards for people to play if they weren't feeling like playing the giant version. Farther along one of the several paths that wove through the park, one led to a large water fountain with small restaurants and eateries orbiting it. A short stop for a quick coffee allowed them to take in their surroundings. They could take the time to see if anyone walked past more than once or looked out of place.

It didn't take long to spot the man on the bench reading a book but not turning the pages. The woman was sitting alone at the café with an empty drink, not showing any indication of intentions to move any time soon. Plus, the backpacker without Bergen on his third lap and one or two other potential operatives in the area. There appeared to be quite a team. The trio couldn't be sure if they were there for them or just operating in the area, but it was certainly yet another coincidence. After deciding they'd spent long enough sipping cappuccinos, it was time to move out and start shaking tails. They sauntered slowly into the park's depths at a steady rate that established a standard.

They picked up their pace gradually so it wouldn't be noticed. The transition from a slow stroll to a quick march was so subtle anybody following them wouldn't spot it. Turning into an area with a blind spot that Jensen was familiar with, the team followed his lead as he swiftly sat down on a bench while they were "in the gap." Shaded from the direct sun with a large hedge acting as a visual shield, the team simply waited for a moment. Within seconds, a man in plain clothing rounded the corner at a speed that would be considered way above the normal pace for somebody walking in the park. Then, he made the ultimate mistake. He looked directly at Jensen. Then he paused, glanced at Marshall, across to Darius, and realized his mistake.

"Oooooh. Feel the burn!" Marshall said with a huge grin on his face. Jensen simply watched Darius share Marshall's amusement before returning his attention to the man tailing them. He swallowed and ignored the comments, looked away, then continued at the same pace, rapidly leaving the area.

Under normal circumstances, you would never antagonize a surveillance team in this way. It would be handled with a lot more finesse. You would perform a pre-planned SDR, gracefully losing anyone following you. Leaving them questioning how and where exactly they lost you. Today, however, Jensen attempted to let Marshall and Darius have a little fun. After all, they were in Geneva, the chances of becoming completely surveillance free were low, and they were running out of time. So they decided a go-for-broke approach was the way forward. What did they have to lose?

The man who appeared to be following them faded out of sight.

"One burned, but he's undoubtedly working with a team. Who do you think's on our case?" Marshall asked, looking to Jensen for enlightenment.

"Not a clue at this point, but it's not the *who* that concerns me anywhere near as much as the why. We'll just have to press on and see if we can ditch the extra baggage en route." Jensen took a moment to make a couple of calculations, then continued. "Okay, let's split up for a short time, and each does an individual SDR, if they can keep teams on all three of us, then it's a large organization. If not, then it could just be a small private firm. Either way, it will give us more info on narrowing down the size of the opposition and a chance of a more educated guess as to who's locking heels with us."

Tradecraft: *"Locking heels" is a term usually used to describe tails being so close behind you that they're almost "locking heels" with you. On training ops, it's used by the instructor to state that you're too close to the "Rabbit." The Rabbit is the person you're following, and you are the "Eye." The "Eye" is the team member with visual contact with the Rabbit. As the Rabbit changes direction, the person whose role is the Eye will change. There are usually around four other team members in a box formation orbiting the Rabbit and the Eye as they move. If the Rabbit changes direction, then the Eye doesn't turn down the same street, they simply continue in the same direction, and one of the outer team members will pick up the Rabbit and now become the Eye. The previous person whose role was to be the Eye will move into formation with the other remaining team members to regroup as a box around the new Eye.*

This pattern continues until the Rabbit reaches their destination.

When in a vehicle, the term "Locking fenders" or "Locking bumpers" for the Brits is used as opposed to "Heels" to indicate the same proximity violation and state you're too close to the target.

Jensen gave them the RV point and an ERV as a backup in case of trouble. The team set about their separate SDR runs in different directions around central Geneva. Wandering around the city, it wasn't long before Jensen came across a large bed-type bench covered in AstroTurf. He remembered it well from his last trip here and how the first time he saw it, he thought it was real grass. He had laid there with his arm around MJ, and they'd chatted for hours. The busy city bustled around them, but for them, they may as well have been alone. So wrapped up in each other, time seemed to stand still as they conversed. It was only the setting sun that eventually brought them back to reality and made them aware of exactly how long they'd been lying there talking.

A smile formed on Jensen's face as he reminisced, thinking back to how they walked from there back down to the lake and bought the cuckoo clock for their future home from one of the gift shops dotted around the lake. They'd first spotted it when they were booking a boat trip and, at the time, thought it a daft idea to buy anything for a home they didn't even have. Still, during the day, they'd concluded it was only a matter of time before they were living together permanently, so they returned to buy one. That was the big turning point for Jensen, the moment when he realized this was forever. Never for a moment did he think he'd be in this situation where he'd be back here trying to cement the future safety of his family and passing through Geneva under these circumstances.

As he finished the last leg of his cleaning run, Jensen alighted the tram at the center of Geneva in an area he knew well. Diagonally opposite a Burger King, a bar on the corner sat adjacent to the market and large skate park. It was way too busy to risk trying to look around and have a last check to see if there was anybody he'd previously seen. Instead, he just had to have faith in his abilities and, after pretty much going full circle, walked toward the bar that was acting as the team RV point. The glorious sunny weather reinforced his desire to relax after his busy travels and enjoy a well-deserved cold and refreshing drink. He could feel himself unwinding at the very thought of the first sip.

Nearing the bar, a familiar sound caused an uneasy feeling to nest inside him. As he drew closer, his concerns grew with the confirmation of his suspicions. Marshall had completed his cleaning run a lot quicker than Jensen and decided to celebrate with a few glasses of Stella Act-A-Twat as Jensen had dubbed it. His slurred speech as he gobbed off to the locals seemed amplified as Jensen stepped into the segregated, outdoor seating area that ran along the immediate frontage of the bar.

Marshall was slumped in a seat, drinking and banging about the locals watching him and not understanding.

"Yeah, you just carry on about your lives, hic. I know what you're thinking, the crazy drunk waffling on about the love he lost. Well, it's not just a shob story."

At first, Jensen thought that maybe Marshall just seemed louder because he recognized his voice, but as he sat next to him, he realized that wasn't the case, and Marshall was, in fact, being far louder than acceptable.

"Hey buddy, you beat me back," Jensen said in an attempt to calm the situation.

"Yeah, I had a couple of drinksh while waiting. Hic." Marshall raised his glass, giving it a little shake like he was giving Jensen visual confirmation of what he'd said, seemingly oblivious to the fact that he would be more than aware of Marshall's level of inebriation. "The whiskeys are expenshive here! I had a couple to wash down my lunch." Marshall took another swig from his bottle.

"What did you have for lunch?"

"Beer!" Marshall replied with a burp. "But they won't serve me anymore. We should go shomwhere else."

Everyone was watching them. He was now being tarred with the same brush and didn't like it. One guy who'd been tutting and rolling his eyes since Jensen had got there had clearly had enough and pulled out his cell phone from his pocket. Jensen wasn't close enough to see if it was 144 for the emergency services or 177 to go directly through to the police but could tell it was definitely no more than three digits.

It was time to go.

"I think you're right. I know a great place we can go. Come on, Marshall, let's get a move on." He flung Marshall's arm around his neck and began the process of propping Marshall up as they walked out of the bar, trying their best not to bash into as many tables as they could. Jensen was concentrating so much on getting Marshall out of there quietly that he missed Darius approaching the bar, who was so focused on a Swedish girl walking by that he missed Jensen and Marshall leaving the area.

After about thirty painstaking minutes of dragging Marshall through town, Jensen slumped him onto a bench where Marshall didn't waste much time to drop straight to sleep with a snoring pattern only sporadically interrupted by the occasional grunt or two. This bench was their ERV. A carefully selected location not far from the US Geneva mission. A 1970s block of concrete and glass, given a touch of modernization with newly fitted solar panels on the roof. Access through a wrought iron gate and protected by a large wall and hedge, this was home to one of the NSA's sections of their Special Collections Service, where just about all mediums of communications in the area were monitored.

It wasn't too long before Darius trundled up after realizing the bar had been compromised, although he was completely unaware that it was Marshall who had initiated it.

Jensen sat silently as Darius joined them, his mind swirling. Could Marshall see this through? Is he okay? The whole Sandy thing seemed to have really knocked him about. Sure he'd seen death before, plenty of times, but was this because it was a girl he loved or the fact that she was an innocent party in the whole thing? How is it Darius had eased into tradecraft so effortlessly? Maybe Marshall had spent spare time training and practicing with him.

Who was the guy on the train? Who the hell was following them and why? This was a private situation. There was no need for any outsiders to be involved. How could anybody else even know what they were up to, never mind be on their tail?

Jensen's mental state was not functioning fully. Maybe it was tiredness, maybe it was the emotional rollercoaster of the last few days, maybe more. His thoughts were cut short as Marshall made a louder than usual snort with a jump as he woke himself up.

"Hey, I know that place," Marshall said, rubbing his eyes to focus and letting out a bit of a groan. "That's where you got me my first derog."

"What's a 'derog'?" Darius asked.

"Derogatory report," Jensen replied, his tone firm.

Marshall looked at Jensen, sensing the mood. Jensen didn't make eye contact, he just carried on looking over at the US mission as if he was trying to chase a thought slipping away from him. Voicing his opinion right now wouldn't help. Lecturing a person in grief who's already suffering is not going to have any form of positive outcome. At the same time, Jensen was also aware that piling on huge servings of guilt wouldn't help either. All he could do was to hope to get the mixture of words and feelings to the right ratio and hope Marshall would absorb enough of it to find the strength to stay on the straight and narrow until the job was done. After that, he could help him if he needed it but right now, finishing this job was more important than starting the next one.

"I didn't mean to have as many as I did. I just got carried away. I'm sorry, bud." Marshall looked down at the floor in shame.

"I know you're having a shit time of it, mate, but please, for the next few days, can you try your best to hold it together? We'll get revenge for Sandy and make them all pay for what they've done, to you as well as to me." Jensen attempted to give Marshall an area of focus instead of his attention straying back to bereavement and grief.

"I promise. I'll be okay, let's get this done. What's next?" Marshall tried his best to sound upbeat and move past previous events.

"We head for the Geneva train station and get our asses moving to Italy. We've got a meeting to make and road trip to be getting on with."

***

The tail followed them all the way to the train station. The Eye had switched several times, but the trio had detected a repeat of the same faces and footwear on multiple occasions.

Jensen sat outside the station's rear entrance at a popular sandwich chain with Darius. Marshall went inside with his shadow, almost locking heels. One of the members of the surveillance team following them sat diagonally opposite at a bistro table outside one of several eateries. Darius didn't leave it too long before hooking the tablet up to the WiFi.

Inside the station, Marshall's shadow was two back in the line as he waited to buy his tickets. One of the positions came free, and Marshall stepped forward to be served.

"Do you speak English?" Marshall asked.

"A little," the man replied with a smile.

"Ah, good." Marshall unwrapped a map with a bunch of paperwork and spread it over the counter. Using the map to disguise his actions, he handed the clerk a folded letter with large writing on it. "I want to get the train to Brussels. How long is the journey?"

"Brussels? Well, it's about five hours, with a couple of changes." The clerk picked up the letter and read it discreetly before folding it and placing it back within Marshall's papers. "I see, I'm sure I can help you out."

"Great, then I'd like to get three tickets to Brussels on the next available train, please." Marshall folded his map away as his tail was about to be served two spots down. The tail tried to discreetly order a single ticket to Brussels, but Marshall heard him. His face couldn't help but betray him with a slight hint of a smirk. The clerk printed the tickets and placed them in a folding glossy envelope as he handed them to Marshall.

"Is there anything else I can help you with, sir?" the clerk asked.

"No, that's everything. Thank you." Marshall turned and walked away.

Outside, Jensen finished his tea and cookies as Darius packed the tablet away. They walked up through the station's rear entrance, which was more like a shopping mall on the inside. Impeccably clean marble floors and gift shops surrounded the route up the stairs to the platforms. Polished chrome handrails complemented the immaculate corridors, the evident standards remaining just as high on the outdoor platforms and waiting areas.

They waited patiently for the train, their tail still on them, poised at the other end of the platform. This was when things were about to get tricky. They desperately needed to get rid of whoever had them under surveillance, but the stunt they were about to pull off had to be timed perfectly.

Chapter 26

The team was now down to one man on their tail. They avoided acknowledging him, luring him into a false sense of security as they waited for the train's departure time to draw closer. Giving the impression they were completely oblivious to the fact they were being followed, they stepped closer to the train's doors moments before departure time. The train to Brussels was seconds from pulling away, and Jensen was extremely grateful for the reliable Swiss precision. Just like their watches, the trains seemed to run equally as efficiently.

The digital clocked ticked from fifty-nine seconds to double zero, and the train pulled away on time. There was only a fractional window for the man following them to look out of the Brussels-bound train and see the trio smiling and waving from the platform. Moments later, they boarded the train to Domodossola, where they'd get the connecting train to Milan.

***

The trio sat at a wooden picnic bench outside the roadside service station where they had arranged to meet Gianluca's contact. The air seemed less harsh, and the summer warmth didn't seem anywhere near as dry as it did in England. To any observer, they were three tourist hikers relaxing in the sun as they drank their take-out coffee with premade snacks from the fuel station kiosk. The noise from the traffic droned in the background as they sat and carefully watched all the possible points of entry and exit. Although no one had vocalized it since their arrival in Europe, Bishop's execution had heightened their alertness. Yet, another ERV point had already been put into place should this scenario turn into trouble.

The morning was rapidly approaching double figures, and all three of them wanted to get on the road. They were becoming fidgety and irritable. Jensen decided it was time for another briefing before the inevitable "Where is he?" questions began.

"It's about a fourteen-hour drive from Milan through Slovenia, Croatia, and Bosnia before we reach Serbia. We'll stop there, get some downtime before we hit the road again, and start the drive from Bulgaria to Turkey. Once we make Istanbul, I'll get in touch with a friend of mine, Oruc, who'll hook us up with somewhere to stay and some food. Then it's the last leg of the journey to the Syrian border. If either of you wants to back out, now's the time." Jensen knew it was too late for either of them to change their mind, but the illusion of choice sometimes made people feel better. A shady-looking guy in a black leather jacket sauntered casually over to the table.

"Jensen?" he asked cautiously, peering over a pair of fake Ray-Bans.

"Have you got what we want?" Jensen didn't want to give too much away until he knew for sure who this guy was.

"Our mutual friend said you would be able to give me a keyword?" Slick Shady was taking no chances.

"Kent." Jensen volunteered nothing else until the man responded.

"Ah, and I'm supposed to say *gravesend*. The car is over there." He gestured at a Fiat station wagon parked near one of the exit ramps. "It's gassed up, and your stuff is in the back. Here are the keys." He tossed a bunch of keys over to Jensen.

"A Fiat? Of all the possible cars manufactured in Italy, Lamborghini, Ferrari, Maserati, and we get lumbered with a Fiat? An Alfa Romeo would have done." Jensen's disappointment was clear, but it was better than nothing.

"It was best I could do at short notice, and besides, Gianluca said you didn't want anything that stood out or could be traced back. This was all I could get on such short notice."

"I'll call a couple of weeks before I come next time." Jensen reached into his Bergen and pulled out a pouch with a bundle of euros from Bishop's safe. He wandered over and opened the Fiat's tailgate door. Once he determined no one was watching them and no CCTV were overlooking them, he peered under a rather grubby blanket. "Fuck me!" Jensen's grumpiness evaporated, and a big smile creased his face.

"You made up for it!" Jensen happily tossed the pouch of cash to Gianluca's man and summoned his comrades. "Come on, fellas, it's time to go."

He took a small canvas bag from the back of the car and jumped into the driver's seat.

Marshall noted that the spring had returned to Jensen's step. He was more like his usual self.

"Should I ask?" Marshall surmised that the sudden change had to be related to the contents of the back of their new car.

"I'll let it be a surprise." Jensen's smile grew wider. "But here, this will cheer you up for now." Jensen took one of three Berettas from the small canvas bag and handed it to Marshall, who passed it over the seat to Darius before taking his own. Jensen dropped the remaining weapon in his lap. The smiles of appreciation showed all around, and the mood had significantly improved.

"We really need to do this more often," Darius said.

Marshall and Darius happily sat in their new ride, making the checks to their weapons as Jensen started the Fiat's engine and negotiated his way out of the car park.

***

Since leaving the service station in Italy at about ten that morning, the trio had been on the road for about twelve hours with only three quick stops for toilet breaks and food. It was darker than usual for the time of year, but they were happy it was dry, at least. Cruising along the E70 at a steady pace, they decided it was time to start looking for a place to get their heads down for the night. Marshall took the exit for Niš. Being Serbia's third largest city with its own airport, they figured finding a cheap hotel that would take cash without ID wouldn't be much of a problem. Following the E-771, Marshall headed for the city's outskirts to find a place fitting their requirements. Even though Darius had the back seat to himself, he'd not managed to get completely comfortable or get into a deep sleep at any point. They were all tired and cranky, with the heat from the long drive during the day not helping any. The temperature had dropped, but they still couldn't wait to get their heads down for the night.

"Hey Darius, did I ever tell you about the surveillance job we did in California?" Marshall asked.

"I don't think so."

"Well, Jensen and I were working with a couple of guys. A huge fellow called Token …"

"Token?" Darius interrupted.

"He was the only black guy on the team. A big guy with a bigger ego," Marshall continued. "And another guy called Dwayn, who definitely had a face for radio." Darius smirked at Marshall's quip. "Anyway, we'd finished our assignment, and we all went back to the hotel for a few drinks in the hotel bar. Token was busy inflating his ego and blowing himself kisses in the mirror, and the rest of us were in the middle of pickling our kidneys. We had a good start to the night when this gorgeous, *and I mean gorgeous*, girl comes in and sits by the bar. Tongues hit the floor, and you had to wade to the bar for another drink.

"So she's sitting there with some exotic cocktail looking bored stiff, and during the course of the night, just about every guy in the bar had made a move on her or given her the eye. Well, she'd blown them all out, including Token, who was extremely disappointed at being rejected. He's cursing how a perfect guy like him had been kicked to the curb and was far from happy. So Token's knocking back the liquor after his pride had been seriously banjo'd, and Jensen saw an opportunity and decided to add insult to injury."

Darius eagerly listened to every word that Marshall spoke as Marshall glanced at Jensen to see a smile on his face.

"So Jensen got the devil in him and called Dwayn over to sit next to him. Now, like I said,

Dwayn had a face that only a mother could love. He sat on the sand once, and a cat tried to bury him."

Darius giggled, hanging on Marshall's every word.

Jensen just listened from the passenger seat as Marshall drove, knowing exactly what was coming.

"Well, Jensen being in his mischievous mood, decided to push Token right over the edge and gave Dwayn exact instructions on what to do and say. So Dwayn stands up, struts over to the stunning girl sitting at the bar, and whispers something into her ear. Her eyes lit up, she jumped off the bar stool, and Dwayn took her by the hand and led her off to his hotel room. Meantime, Token's standing there with his mouth wide open, just like every other guy in the bar." Darius was captivated as Marshall told his story. He'd gone from laying across the back seat in a slump to sitting forward and keenly listening to everything Marshall was saying.

The miles were clocking up as the drive into the night progressed. The city buildings were thinning out now, and they were approaching less densely populated areas.

"What happened next?" Darius asked eagerly.

"Token was spitting feathers. Here he was, this huge, muscular guy at the peak of physical fitness, and he got dismissed like a rodent! And there was Dwayn, who was so ugly that when he jerked off, even he had to pretend he was someone else!"

Darius chuckled away as Marshall continued the story that Jensen had heard so many times. "Jensen, in the meantime, is lapping all this up and chuckling his ass off at his cruel windup, watching Token boiling over. It was only the fact that Token was so vain and full of himself that Jensen even did it in the first place. In the end, Token downs his whiskey and demands to know what Jensen told Dwayn to say."

Darius was so enthralled at this point he was almost sitting in the front. Marshall carried on while Jensen sat silently in the passenger seat with a smirk on his face, recalling the memories of the night.

"So what did he say?" Darius asked, desperately wanting the answer.

"Jensen sat there with this smug grin and said I simply told him to tell her," Marshall's tone changed unexpectedly, "this is going to ruin the fucking night."

"What?" Darius was confused, and Jensen frowned, knowing that's not how the story went.

Marshall had gotten serious. All the hairs on the back of his neck stood at attention.

"Don't look back, but there's a cop car behind us." Marshall spoke in a lower tone. The color had gone from his face, and the concern had grown in his eyes. A feeling of dread filled all three of them as Marshall gave all his attention to the road. He concentrated on not making any mistakes and giving the police car a reason to pull them over.

"Don't worry, it's not trouble yet. Let's just hope he turns off somewhere." Jensen attempted to ease the tension, but the feeling in the pit of his stomach was overruling his rational thoughts at that moment.

"We're three foreign guys in an Italian car filled with illegal guns and explosives, driving through Serbia with no passports in the middle of the night," Marshall stated with an undercurrent of sarcasm in his voice.

"We've been in worse situations," Jensen said, trying to comfort Marshall. "Remember that time in Moldova?"

"Yeah, I really don't want to go through that again. I hated it the last time we went to prison. It took us weeks to get out, and the food was shit." Marshall scrunched up his nose thinking about it. "And as for Darius, he's a pretty boy, he'll never get near the soap!"

Darius had sunk into the back seat, not looking forward to the possible forthcoming events.

"Right, it's decision time. What's the plan if the disco starts?" Marshall asked.

"Can you outrun them?"

"It wouldn't be easy," Marshall replied. He'd spent years as one of the most experienced drivers in his field. Countless defensive driver's courses and vehicular evasive maneuvers training. He was what's known in the trade as a *wheel artist*. "We're in a Fiat, and they're in a BMW F10, even if we did manage to give them the slip, they'd be on the radio in no time with a mass of squad cars swarming all over looking for us. They'd have roadblocks set up in no time."

"Well, I'm not shooting a police officer just for doing his job," Jensen stated. "If we get pulled over, we'll just have to try and talk our way out of it first. Keep the guns hidden, and let's hope we don't need them."

Darius shuffled around on the back seat, trying to cover up anything that looked in the slightest way suspicious.

Jensen pulled the pistol from the back of his jeans and pulled the top slide back just enough to check there was a round in the chamber. Even though he was pretty certain there was, it always made him feel better to check. "And there's three of us, so just remember, we've got the advantage, we outgun them," Jensen added.

The tension among them grew as they all sat silently driving along the dark highway. Marshall signaled in plenty of time before approaching the turn onto a secondary road, hoping the police car would continue. He checked his rearview mirror just before turning, and the police car signaled, too.

"Shit," he whispered under his breath.

"Is he still behind us?" Darius asked.

"Yeah, he's followed us down here," Marshall said quietly as if it would make some kind of a difference.

They continued down the road at a reasonable pace staying within the speed limits and paying extra close attention to the road.

Marshall's mouth was drying, Jensen was feeling uneasy, and Darius did not like the situation one bit. Darius kept still in the back of the car, trying to control his nerves and not let the situation get the better of him.

Jensen's stomach churned as the cruiser's flashing lights illuminated the street.

"Fuck!" Marshall controlled his rage, slowing the car and fearing the worst. Darius took a deep breath as his eyes widened momentarily.

"Don't panic yet, it might just be a routine check. We could still be okay." Jensen wanted to keep the other two calm as Marshall pulled over.

Slowing to a stop, they waited as the police car pulled in behind them.

Marshall stared at his mirrors. “Let’s just try and see if we can get out of this without the situation getting noisy.” He watched as the two front doors of the police car opened, and the officers stepped out. He glanced at Jensen. “Here they come. You ready?”

Chapter 27

"We'll be okay, we've got through worse, remember." Jensen tried to sound positive, but his words betrayed his thoughts as he, too, was filled with dread from the possible outcomes of the situation.

The two officers moved toward the Fiat, splitting off and walking up on either side until they reached the front of the car, where Marshall had already lowered the driver's window in anticipation.

Tradecraft: *When operating in a foreign country, attempting to bribe a police officer can make things go from bad to worse. There's a way it can be done that can help you to offer a bribe without it looking like you're actually trying to bribe the police officer and afford you a degree of deniability. The first and most important thing is to be as humble as you possibly can and apologize for any wrongdoing. Even if you don't think you did anything. If it doesn't seem to be getting you anywhere, you continue to be apologetic and ask if there's any kind of a fine you can pay. You indicate that you're happy to pay an on the spot fine in cash and promise you will continue about your day within the confines of the law. It is a must to always carry cash and be prepared to give it all if need be (separating your cash into different areas between you and your luggage can help). Take out the cash if you think the officer is considering your offer, and repeat that you're happy to pay a fine for whatever you did.*

The officer on the passenger side unclipped the strap that held his pistol in its holster and rested his hand on top of it. The other officer bent down to the level of the open driver's window and barked something at them that none of them understood. Marshall looked at Jensen as if he would know what was said, but Jensen was blank-faced.

The officer snapped, repeating whatever he said the first time with less patience.

"Do you speak English?" Marshall asked.

Yet again, the officer reeled off something in his native language that none of them understood.

"English?" Marshall asked again, a fraction louder.

The officer stood upright and jabbered over the car's roof to the second officer on the passenger side. There was a harsh exchange of words between them before the police officer finally bent down and looked through the driver's window again.

"Iddy," he snapped and waited for a response. Nobody moved, and none of them knew what to do.

Marshall looked over to Jensen yet again. Darius had his finger on the trigger of his pistol hidden under his jacket in the back.

"What do we do?" Marshall asked.

"I'm not sure. Just stay calm for the moment." Beads of sweat had formed above Jensen's temple.

The officer waved his hand "Iddy, iddy!" he shouted again.

Darius was getting twitchy, and Jensen's concern was growing. The longer they were here, the more chance there was of the situation worsening.

"Just go," Jensen said softly.

"What if it doesn't mean go?" Marshall asked.

"Just go. Go!" Jensen repeated firmly, reasoning that iddy sounded the same as the |Russian word for go. The officer stepped back, and Marshall pulled away, hoping for the best. Taking a deep breath and moving forward steadily, he looked into the rearview mirrors to check the policemen weren't about to pull their pistols out. Watching them turn to walk back toward their patrol car, he picked up the pace and moved out of the area, taking the first turn he came across to get out of sight. They all sighed and relaxed as Marshall put some distance between them and the cop car.

"That was close," Jensen said, blowing out a huge puff of air.

"You're telling me!" Marshall agreed, a slight sheen of sweat covering his face.

Darius relaxed his shoulders and released his grip on the pistol. He pushed it aside, still wrapped in his coat, and rubbed his face with his hands.

"Let's call it a day, yeah?" Jensen glanced at Marshall. "Find the first place we can to stop and get a room each for the night."

Both Marshall and Darius nodded.

Marshall pulled in a couple of kilometers down the road, having lost total track of where he was or even which direction he was heading. He parked outside a cheap, half-star motel with more concrete than windows, shut off the engine and relaxed. The neon light had only three of the seven letters lit, and one of those twitched. Bars covered the ground floor windows, and graffiti covered the bars and wall.

Marshall yanked at the pull handle on the main entrance, but it didn't budge, so he pressed the buzzer. After a couple of more presses, the door finally clicked open with a buzzing noise that followed to keep the lock from shutting them out. They funneled in and walked up to the reception desk.

A short fat guy who looked like Mario and Luigi's missing brother stood behind the pine counter smoking a cigarette. The smell of cheap bleach and cleaning fluids filled the room, and the décor consisted mainly of varnished pine panels. From behind the smoke, the hotel owner stood in his once-white sleeveless vest and grunted something at the three of them.

"English?" Jensen asked.

The hotel owner rolled his eyes with a look of realization on his face and a dash of disgust thrown in for good measure. "Passports." He grunted at them with a harsh tone. His bloodshot eyes indicated he just wanted to get back to sleep.

"We got mugged," Marshall interjected.

The hotel owner just stood there with a look of sarcasm on his face as he stared at the three big guys in his reception who looked like they could take down a herd of rhinos between them, claiming to have been mugged for their passports. He weighed up the situation and decided to push his luck.

"Three hundred dinar," he barked.

"We don't have any dinar, but we have US dollars," Jensen said, showing him a couple of twenty-dollar bills.

"Five hundred US dollars." The hotel owner was getting fed up and just wanted to get back to bed now.

"Okay." Jensen went to pull his cash out.

"Each!" the hotel owner added.

"Each?" Marshall was fuming. "That's robbery. I'm gonna …"

"Don't worry." Jensen held Marshall back from doing anything stupid and tried to calm him down. “We don’t need any attention right now. Let’s just pay for it and get a good night’s sleep. It’s not as if it’s our money anyway.”

Marshall calmed, giving Jensen a sideways nod.

Jensen handed over the money, and the hotel owner dropped three sets of keys onto the counter.

“Out by eight o'clock.” The owner turned and walked through the door behind him.

They grabbed a set of keys each and made their way to their rooms. Within no time, Jensen was in bed, physically and mentally exhausted. He lay there justifying to himself that it was too late at night to call MJ and would call her in the morning. He was so worn out he drifted off within his thoughts.

In the next room, Marshall was drained from one of the longest drives he’d done in a long time, topped off with the night’s events. He was grateful to be settling into a hotel bed for the night and not banged up in a cell. He was so exhausted he pretty much passed out as soon as his head hit the pillow.

Darius lay on his back, looking up at the ceiling, wide awake and unable to drift off. He was finding it impossible to sleep without knowing what Dwayn said to the hottie in the hotel bar.

Chapter 28

The trio finally crossed the border into Turkey, but the road trip was really taking its toll on the three men, who by now were suffering numb butts and cramps like never before. Even the overnight stop in Serbia hadn't seemed to help, and all of them wished that they'd been provided with anything other than a Fiat. Sitting at a constant speed on the main highway, Jensen was glad of low traffic volumes allowing a steady cruise.

Tradecraft: *When MI5 (The British Security Services) do their advanced driver training, the final part of the exam is to drive from London to Glasgow in the safest yet quickest possible way, frequently topping speeds of 150mph. It's not uncommon for highly trained operatives to exceed 100mph, especially in Europe. Most people have heard about German Autobahns, and the deeper into Europe you go, the less the actual rules seem to apply. Mostly, it's down to what drivers can get away with and using your discretion. Not to mention being prepared to use a little bribery if required.*

"So, who is this Oruc?" Marshall thought he'd ask while Darius was sleeping in the back seat, just in case Jensen didn't feel secure revealing the link in front of the Lithuanian.

"He's an asset I flipped a few years ago for the agency. After they'd milked him for all they could get from him, they relocated him to Istanbul. He's useful, he knows a lot of people and can really help with some insider knowledge. He will be able to get us to places we might not ordinarily be able to get."

"Will he be okay with us dropping in on him unannounced?" Marshall seemed dubious.

"Yeah, sure. I made certain he had a good payday when we finally relocated him. He'll be happy to see me again." Jensen sounded confident, but he could tell by the way Marshall looked through the corner of his eyes, with a sort of sideways, head-tilted glance, that Marshall wasn't buying it that easy.

It took about twenty minutes for Jensen to familiarize himself with the area and confirm that he'd definitely got the right place. They parked in the immediate vicinity of the two-story apartment block for a short period of surveillance. An open archway in the center of the building allowed them to walk into the main foyer and up an exposed stairway to the first-floor landing. Plants in ceramic pots dotted about the place seemed to add a personal touch to the open-plan communal area.

Marshall and Darius stood behind as Jensen knocked on a door. The woman who answered didn't speak any English and didn't seem thrilled that three foreigners were asking questions and pestering her. It took a while to find someone who not only spoke English but was also willing to help translate for them. A girl of about college age finally agreed and knocked again on the door that Jensen was convinced belonged to Oruc. The girl spent a few moments in conversation with the older woman before returning to Jensen.

"She told me that Oruc's family moved to Antalya after he was found shot dead in his apartment. I live here now and want nothing to do with you Americans. I'm not sure the next words have an exact translation." The girl looked a little embarrassed.

"We get the idea." Marshall looked over at Jensen. "What now? Man with the plan."

"Back to the car. I need to use the sat phone."

"Holy cow, sat-man; that might just save us." Marshall's parody was said in jest, but the long drive and the oppressive Turkish heat had made him cranky, not to mention that too many people linked to Jensen were dead.

"Don't worry, I have a contingency plan," Jensen reassured them.

"I hope it's better than the primary one," Marshall countered. He was concerned that Jensen's plans appeared to unravel faster than a fat kid's candy wrapper. His survival instinct prompted his mind to wonder about making a contingency plan of his own, so he could get home if the shit hit the fan.

"I'm going over there to get some chilled drinks. I'll meet you back at the car." Darius moved toward a group of shops over the road while the other two plodded back to the car.

Jensen sparked up the sat phone but stopped mid-process.

"What are you waiting for?" Marshall's tone was surly.

"I haven't dialed the number for a few years." Jensen was frowning intently.

"Well, this is no time to get butterflies, loverboy, get on with it!" Marshall was becoming increasingly tense.

"No, it's not that, I'm working back through my long-term memory to recall the number."

Marshall was slightly taken aback by Jensen's response, and he appreciated how, with machine-like precision, the man could backtrack through his mind to retrieve data from years ago. This amazing capability was not easily accomplished, given the distractions of the last few days, and Marshall's admiration for Jensen was revived—this man was truly remarkable.

Marshall could tell from Jensen's expression the exact moment the number registered in his mind, and he dialed as if he'd just rehearsed it. It seemed to take ages before there was a connection and even longer until a voice answered on the other end.

"Who?" The thick American accent was making sounds but not much sense.

"Max, it's Jensen. I'm in Istanbul and need some help. Can you guide me to a CIA castle or safe house?"

Tradecraft: *A Castle is a name given to a secure base of operations or an outpost. Even though the CIA occupies the entire top floor of the American embassy in Turkey, they also have several other buildings they utilize around that area.*

"What time is it?" Max was still coming around, and the information was a little slow to register. "Jensen? You're in Istanbul? Hold on, let me get some pants on."

After a few more minutes on the phone, they were up to speed. Jensen had got an address, and Max was up to date on the situation. Although Jensen couldn't be sure, his instincts told him something seemed off. It might have just been the surprise call from a long-lost friend in the middle of the night, with California being ten hours behind Turkey, that had thrown Max off guard, but because he wasn't there to see his face, it was hard to tell.

Tradecraft: *Reading someone's body language, Jensen was good at. After all, as his trainer told him, most people only tend to listen and ignore what the rest of the body is openly saying. Once his training kicked in, he seemed to use it all the time. It was difficult when he first started. He was either listening to what someone said and missed the tells or got the tells and missed what someone said. Combining the two, the CIA refers to as going into "L squared" mode. You literally have to use internal dialog to tell your brain for the next few minutes, I want you to look and listen! It can actually be quite taxing on the mind at first, but in time it becomes second nature. As with anything, the more you use it, the easier it becomes, and if you don't use it frequently, then, like anything else, it becomes subject to "skill fade."*

But now, he was relying solely on his instinct. Max's instructions had been quite clear. "Go to the address I gave you and ask for Mason. He's the C.O.S., he'll look after you. I'll let him know you're on the way." But when Jensen shut off the sat phone, he still had a vague impression that something was off.

Everyone was more than a little irritable now, and the heat certainly wasn't helping, so the ice-cold fruit juice drink Darius returned with was greatly appreciated. As they glugged away at the orangey-red drink, it seemed to cool the tension as well as the body. They all took a breath and, after feeling a bit more relaxed, were almost ready to move on.

After a few snacks that Darius also took the liberty of collecting, all three of them managed to compose themselves and get back into the car. The safe house was about twenty minutes away, on the other side of Taksim Square, just off the E80 toward Maslak. They were all more than ready to get some down time. Jensen was desperate to check in with MJ and hear his daughter's voice on the phone.

***

The apartment above a local store adequately met the criteria for a quiet rendezvous point. Multiple exits, a parking garage at the rear going straight into the property, iron gates protecting the doors, and windows that could be opened from the inside in the event of an urgent need to escape. Above all, it was in such a busy part of town that nobody would ever notice whether or not it was being used. The most important thing was that it looked nothing like a safe house, and access was achieved by saying the right words to the man in the store who would show you to a door at the back of the store room.

This was perfect for use as a FOB (Forward Operating Base). They could set up equipment, lay plans out, and create an intel wall, all without the worry of housekeeping coming in to change the sheets and discovering a control room set up.

Leaving the others in the Fiat while he checked out the situation, Jensen went into the store. He'd been told to look for a man with one eye, a scar down the side of his face, two missing fingers on his right hand, and a walking stick. When Max had told him the man's name was Lucky, he was sure he was taking the piss.

There was no sign of him in the store, but a young guy in shades stood behind the counter, bopping away to music that must have only been going on inside his head.

"You're not Lucky." Jensen looked over to him, and the head dancing stopped. The guy's face lightened up, and he wandered around the counter.

"No," the man said. "Fortunato is my brother, and he got shot again. The bastard can't keep it in his pants. My brother is lucky in some ways, but in others, not so much. Here, come this way." Jensen followed the young man through the shop to a store room at the back, where he pressed a button to the right of the door.

"Please." He gestured with his hand to instruct Jensen to wait there and walked back into the shop. The door opened outward with a buzz and a click, and Jensen walked inside.

Nothing but concrete steps to the next floor were on offer on the other side of the door, with not even enough room to close it without climbing a few. The top of the stairs led straight into an open plan apartment, with old furnishings, rugs covering the floor, and a distinct lack of ornaments to display the personal touch. Jensen was no more than three or four steps into the room when US Marines, in digital camo and sporting M4s, burst out of nowhere.

"Hands above your head! Get down on the floor!" Jensen's heart jumped into his mouth as he dropped to the floor. There was no other option at the moment but to comply.

"Where are the other two?" one of the Marines yelled at him.

Jensen didn't answer. Two Marines pulled him up so fast that he nearly left his lunch behind. Relieving him of his Beretta, they slammed him into a chair and restrained him. A broad-figured man entered the room and paced toward Jensen.

"Get the other two up here now!" he snarled. His face contorted with anger at Jensen.

Chapter 29

Jensen's captor stood with his back straight. The tall posture and stance revealed he was former military. More than likely a Marine, too. He'd obviously managed to climb to the top of the chain and land a job somewhere in one of the intelligence agencies. His white hair made him appear older than he probably was, but it certainly seemed to define the "no fucking around" glint in his eye.

"I need my phone." Jensen had weighed up the options as quickly as he could. They didn't want them dead, or he wouldn't be sitting in the chair, he'd be floating in the river, and whoever Silver Top was with already knew there were two others in the mix, so the best option at this point was to lay the arms down and listen.

Silver Top nodded to one of the Marines holding Jensen, and he released his hand. Jensen grabbed his phone out of his pocket and called Marshall.

"Come on up. Leave your weapons behind and keep your hands in view." Jensen shut off the phone. He deliberately told him about leaving his weapons behind, because these guys might know about the Fiat, and it also gave a signal to Marshall. Now he knew what to expect when he came up the stairs.

***

Jensen, Marshall, and Darius sat in restraints in three lined-up chairs, Marines dotted around the room, with Silver Top pacing the soon-to-be-worn-out silk rug covering the floorboards. They took in as much of their surroundings as possible and mentally calculated what the worst and the best outcome could be.

Then Silver Top launched into a tirade. "You bunch of shit dribbling fuck ups have fucked up so bad that a normal fuck up would be jealous." Like a drill sergeant, he erupted and fired abuse at all three of them. "I got a top CIA deep cover operative playing step mommy to a couple of spoiled shits because you thought it would be a good idea to take their daddy for a ride in the trunk of his own Bentley. I got a whole lot of shit trying to crawl back up my ass because it's too scary to come out and land in the worse shit you guys made. One of the biggest drug and arms dealers in the Middle East is off the grid because he came after you for slitting his little brother's throat, and the vulture PMCs are tearing themselves a new one trying to secure the contract for the supply route. And that's only the bits you're allowed to know about." Silver Top's rant didn't seem to calm him down any. He glared over at Jensen.

"We didn't know anyone was watching him." Jensen's defense didn't seem too solid.

"Well, you're about as much use as a cock-flavored lollypop then, aren't you? Of course, we were watching him. We watch everybody, especially if they're running around with millions of pounds of military equipment and shipments of heroin!" While Silver Top fired off blistering verbal responses, his body language showed signs that he was calming.

"So what happens next?" Jensen asked.

"I'll tell you, shall I?" The black leather reclining office chair creaked as Silver Top sat back into it. He steepled his hands, closing all but his index fingers, and moved them under his chin. "You three might have the brain power of a spunk stain in a retard's diaper, but you got further than we expected. So," a dramatic pause emphasized his point, "you're going to finish the job. Only you're not gonna kill your target. You're gonna bring him in for tactical questioning as a ghost detainee."

Tradecraft: *Tactical questioning was the polite way of saying we're going to water board and torture the shit out of him. As a ghost detainee, he would be kept anonymously in a detention center.*

"And if we refuse?" Jensen thought he might as well check the alternatives.

"Then you and Marshall will be dropped straight back in the UK for a long life in prison. Kidnapping, extortion, robbery, breaking and entering, perverting the cause of justice, theft, withholding information, trespassing on restricted harbor property, murder, possession of illegal firearms, grand theft auto. Not to mention a DGSE officer who's never going to wake up from his nap on the train! Need I go on?"

Marshall leaned closer to Jensen. "Just agree to do it. Let's get the hell out of here."

"Oh, gas comes out the other end, too? Well, princess, welcome to the party. You're a lot deeper in the shit than you think, and I'm about to piss in your snorkel. Unless you got something I wanna hear, keep your hole shut!" Silver Top looked back at Jensen while Darius just did the sensible thing and kept quiet. "I'm gonna let you go with a bunch of instructions on what you're gonna do when you get Aram. You'll be naked, with no diplomatic cover at all. Call this number when you have him, and I want him delivered to me, *alive*. Do you understand?" Silver Top tucked a piece of paper in the holster and tossed the Beretta back over to Jensen as the Marines cut them loose.

"Yeah, okay. And what's your name, sir?" Jensen sounded despondent.

"Why the hell would you want my name?" Silver Top couldn't hide the curious look on his face.

"For the invoice, sir!" Jensen couldn't help but display a smirk as he said it.

"Get the fuck out of here! And don't come back until you got what I want." Silver Top's rage had fired up afresh. Jensen hadn't known the man long, but he already knew exactly which buttons to press.

"Great move! Your friends are a hoot. I bet your barbecue parties are so much fun." Marshall's sarcasm was causing Darius to stifle his laugh as he walked a couple of paces behind the other two.

They walked back to the car, and as much as they were unhappy about the situation, they were grateful, too. That meeting could have ended a lot worse.

"Why do you think they let us carry on?" Darius wasn't sure about the whole situation.

"Simple, we get this done, and CIA takes all the credit, while we're lucky even to get a lift home. If it goes to rat shit, then they have complete deniability and can blame it on the three vigilantes gunning for revenge. You know, the guys KIA." *It's common practice in this industry. The contractor usually gets the shit end of the stick, but the rewards can occasionally be worth it.*

Jensen didn't know why the CIA wanted Aram and didn't really care. Now he was out of the way of Silver Top and his marines, his mind couldn't help but ask when it comes down to it, could he really hand over Aram, or would the urge to end him get the better of him? He decided not to ponder it any further. There were bigger issues that needed resolving right now. He could worry about how he was going to deal with that later.

The deeper into Turkey they went and the closer to the Syrian border they got, the more the Fiat became coated in road dust and sand, so much so that it became difficult to tell what color it was underneath. The trio rallied against the blistering heat, hoping to find somewhere to lay-up for a while, and get a drink. The tires slapped the sand-coated tarmac, and the engine's heat caused a mirage-like effect behind the car. A clunking sound, a stifled cough, and a splutter from the Fiat's engine announced the car was about to give up the ghost. The power drained, and the final clonks and ticking of the engine as the car died on the side of the road was the icing on the cake of what had turned out to be a shit day.

Marshall lifted the hood, and the three men stood for a moment gaping at the dust and sand that caked the engine. All of them had experience in desert driving and should have known to strap a rag over the air filter, at least. But they had been anxious to put as much distance as possible between themselves and the CIA that they had simply forgotten.

"Well, we knew it was going to happen sooner or later. Doesn't Fiat stand for Fix It Again

Tomorrow?" Marshall, as usual, tried to lighten the mood, but his banter didn't quite have its usual effect.

"We'll have to TAB the rest of the way. Find a good spot and set up an OP." Jensen was saying the words but not looking forward to the action one little bit. It was at least another thirty kilometers to their destination.

Tradecraft: *This is where military fitness plays a huge role. Army workouts are structured in a different way to most civilians just joining the gym in January. A lot of the time, newbies seem to want to work on numbers ten, fifteen, and twenty and, using that pattern, go from there. Thus setting the typically vast fail rate. The difference is, doing an army workout, you start from the target number and work down. So instead of trying to get to twenty bench presses, for example, and only making it to seventeen before you quit. You would start the count at twenty and work toward the end/ You would say, "three left, two more to go, last one!" giving you a psychological advantage and higher success rate. This, combined with several other factors, contributes to the mental attitude of soldiers worldwide and yields great results in keeping the military at the peak of its physical fitness. A thirty-kilometer TAB would work pretty much the same way. Instead of thinking about a thirty -kilometer run, you simply count backward, giving you a higher sense of achievement the lower the number gets. It keeps mental morale up and changes the soldier's attitude. Instead of the frame of mind being, "I just ran twenty-seven kilometers," they think, "Only three kilometers to go." And let's face it, nobody wants to quit just before the finish line. Again ensuring a higher success rate. This method works really well for the majority of soldiers around the globe. That's another reason the British SAS use a mentally cruel and exhausting training tactic during recruitment known as false endings. Just as you think you've got to the end, they tell you you're nowhere near and have twice as much to go. It demoralizes the recruit and is mental cruelty to a degree, but it filters out a good amount of the weaker candidates pretty rapidly.*

The hissing of steam from the Fiat's radiator continued as the trio weighed up their options.

"What about we requisition a vehicle?" Marshall volunteered.

Tradecraft: *Requisition of a vehicle is the military terminology for "stealing" a car. It might not be the best long-term move, but it beats the prospect of a thirty-kilometer TAB to the Syrian border.*

Jensen grabbed a few items from the back of the car and stuffed them into his Bergen. He distributed three, easily concealable, Heckler & Koch 30mm MP7s and watched with amusement as Darius and Marshall's eyes lit up as they took possession of them. "It gets better he said." Watching Marshall's face evidently recognize the H83 container.

"Oh yeah," Marshall said as Jensen popped it open and dished out the contents between all three of them.

"It holds eight, so you can both flip a coin to find out who gets the extra one," Jensen said.

Marshall wasted no time as he pulled a coin from his pocket.

"Tails," Darius said with enthusiasm.

"Yes!" Marshall exclaimed as he showed Darius the head side up of the coin.

It was time to get back to business. All three donned their Bergens and set off to find the optimum place to acquire a car.

Chapter 30

The sun was setting, and the sky was turning a beautiful orangey red. The heat, however, was still oppressive. A couple of miles of walking brought the threesome to a dimly lit urban area on the edge of a small roadside village. There didn't appear to be any shops nearby that they could make out, but a parking lot was getting a fair bit of short-term use. This looked like the ideal place to get what they wanted.

"What about that one?" Darius asked, pointing at a sporty-looking convertible

"No, the Taliwagon." Jensen pointed out the Toyota Hilux Double Cab. "See it, there?"

Marshall grabbed a chunk of steel bar left at the edge of the breeze block wall and bent it out of shape. He took a length of paracord from his Bergen and tied it around the middle of the bar.

"Darius, get into place. Drive it around the corner and pick us up after you've procured it."

Darius dropped his Bergen next to Jensen, and Marshall ran to the back of the truck. Procuring was yet another posh military way of saying stealing. He crawled down at the back of the Toyota and tied the other end of the paracord to the underneath of the car. Tucking the bar well under and out of sight. He leaped up and ran farther down the parking lot behind one of the other cars.

Marshall waited with Jensen around the corner, where they sat poised with all three Bergens. It wasn't long before the Hilux owner showed up and jumped into the driver's seat. The engine burst into life, and the car moved forward. Just as anticipated, after a few yards, the truck came to a halt. The driver opened the door and, leaving the engine running, moved to the back of the truck to see what was causing the clanging sound.

Darius swiftly shot in through the open door and drove off before the Hilux owner even knew what was going on. The door swung shut as Darius pulled away, the bar clanging away as it dragged behind. He pulled over for a moment where Jensen and Marshall were waiting. They chucked the Bergens and weapons into the cab, then jumped inside.

Darius shot off as quickly as their new Toyota would let them. One extremely angry local chasing behind and running as fast as his sandals would let him.

They managed to catch their breaths, and their heart rate slowed the farther they drove down the road. Jensen unscrewed the cap of his canteen that was stashed in the side pocket of his Bergen. He took a swig and passed it around. Old habits die hard.

Tradecraft: *When first joining the army, most recruits don't understand why they're always instructed to fill their canteens right to the top. It makes sense before long, and you can tell the recruits that hadn't. Mainly because when you're all out learning field craft, most of you would be sneaking around while the odd recruit that didn't listen would be making a bunch of sloshing noises. When it comes to having a drink, one person opens their canteen and passes it around for everyone to have a mouthful. That way, you aren't in the compromising position of taking a swig, and then you're one of the recruits sloshing about, too. Your canteen would be either full to the brim or completely empty. It's what's known as noise discipline. Soldiers that rattle, clang, and slosh aren't very effective when trying to use the element of surprise. It's the knowledge of these simple things that can save your life.*

"Give it a good mile or so and pull over," Marshall said. "That bar dangling at the back is driving me crazy."

Darius was happy to continue as driver while the other two made themselves comfortable in the back as they sped toward the border, all of them relieved at avoiding the long trek on foot. The last few rays of sunlight defiantly continued to shine in the distance, but nighttime was closing in fast. The stress of the day was beginning to tell on the three, and a few hours with their heads down was the sensible choice. Tomorrow was only the beginning. They would have to set up a hide and figure out how they were going to achieve their recently changed objective. What had commenced as a simple "neutralize the target" mission had now turned into a "target acquisition assignment."

It's amazing how quickly agendas can shift in this industry, Jensen mused, far from thrilled with the circumstances in which they now found themselves.

After passing through the town of Silopi in Turkey, they drove across the Khabur river, making their way to the arched Frontier Gate at Ibrahim Khalil. It had been a long drive. The tension rose as they approached the Kurdish guards manning the border.

"What are we going to do?" Marshall asked Jensen.

"Roll up and see if we can talk our way through," Jensen replied. Kurdistan was a nation within a nation. A place the CIA had never really left since 1991.

The slowed as they reached the border control. Before they even had the chance to wind down their window, a man in the indigenous CIA desert tiger strip uniform came out of nowhere and took over. He raised a hand and indicated for them to stop. Marshall wound down the window.

"Jensen?" the American asked

"He is." Marshall pointed at him sitting in the passenger seat. The American looked over at him.

"Have a good day." the American said with a smile as he waved him through, letting all three of them continue unimpeded.

Marshall didn't wait or second guess. He got moving and drove out of there quickly.

"I'll get us a few miles in and find somewhere out of the way to pull over," Marshall said, happy at how that border crossing went. They'd opted to enter Iraq from the Turkish border and then slip into Syria through the back door rather than risk exposing themselves to the locals and giving a heads up and announcing their presence that they were in town.

***

Jensen's neck was stiff from sleeping against the door in the passenger seat. Darius's feet had crept over from where he had slept on the driver's side, Marshall having the best deal laying across the back seat, snoring like a beast. The sun was low in the sky, and Jensen was squinting to see as he came to terms with the idea of waking up. His spine argued that moving was a bad idea, and his head was thumping. The need to stretch his legs won the battle, with his spine trying to stop him from doing anything.

The car door opened with a creak, Jensen being uncertain if it was a noisy hinge or his back bone. He stepped out of the truck and stood a couple of paces in front of it. Stretching out and yawning, he raised his arms above him, needing to clear his head. There had to be a way to sort this mess out with a happy ending all round, without the risk of it all going FUBAR. He knew that Silver Top's threat of life in prison was a fallacy; it simply wasn't going to happen. Earlier in his career, he'd had the sense to put in place what is known as a 'security blanket' to avoid just that kind of situation.

Tradecraft: *A security blanket is a collection of incriminating documents or secrets that could cause huge devastation if leaked. Over the years, he'd compiled valuable intel to insure he could gray mail his way out of most serious situations if it actually came to that. He'd even had the sense to back it up with a dead man's pedal. This was a little extra insurance against his simple unexplained disappearance. If he was locked up and denied access to the outside world after the elapse of a predetermined amount of time, a trigger was in place that would result in all the incriminating intel being sent to the relevant places.*

On top of all that, Jensen was supremely confident that if all failed, he was skilled enough to get himself out of incarceration anyway. Escape would just be a matter of time; when not if.

From there, it would just be a case of implementing his relocation plan and getting to the Philippines. A location specifically chosen in the event of everything going south and wanting to drop off the grid completely, remaining unfound.

If he spent just one day on each of the islands in the Philippines, it would take almost twenty-one years to visit them all, making it the perfect location to drop off the grid and hide from the world in the event of needing to disappear.

The ground crunched under Jensen's feet as he shuffled farther away from the truck. He was about to go up against a titan. A man who was the head of organized crime in an almost lawless area. *How do you bring down the biggest drug baron in the Middle East?* Jensen asked himself. *Well, the theory for that is simple. You go to the second biggest drug baron of the Middle East.* Jensen fired up the sat phone. This time he was going to try a friend from his own side of the pond. He dialed the number and waited for a connection.

"Switchboard." A neutral female voice spoke at the end of the line.

MI6 operators are trained extremely well in not giving any information out over the phone. There was a process of getting through to the extension you wanted, and if you didn't know what it was, your call would be a total waste of time.

The line rang a couple of times before the click on the other end informed Jensen the call had been answered.

"Ashley? How's life in the Ziggurat?" Jensen's tone was upbeat. Ziggurat was the nickname used by staffers for the new MI6 Headquarters in Vauxhall Cross. Sometimes called LEGO Land. Since they'd moved from Century House in Curzon Street, a lot had changed. The two men had known each other since Ashley's service in Special Reconnaissance. With a downturn in the availability of decent work on the close protection circuit, he had a tap on the shoulder to work for the SIS. Jensen had stayed in touch with Ashley all through his training and while he was at the secret MI6 training facility called Fort Monckton, usually just referred to as the Fort, in Portsmouth. He had stayed in close proximity to help him out if he needed it. Due to the nature of his new career, however, Ashley had been forced to make certain social sacrifices and had distanced himself from Jensen recently.

"You shouldn't be calling me." Ashley spoke quietly into his phone as if it would make a difference. Jensen ignored the tone of reluctance in his voice.

"I need your help, mate," he stated evenly.

"No, no way. I'm not getting involved. You're in way over your head, Jensen. The Americans are all over this like spaghetti on a toddler. It's messy and will leave stains." Ashley seemed extremely unnerved, but Jensen wasn't fazed and just pressed on.

"I need to have a meeting with Prince Nadir." Jensen's tone was still in catch-up mode.

"No, absolutely no way. It's impossible." The tension in the man's voice was palpable over the satellite connection.

"Come on, Ashley, I know you have assets in place there, and it's really urgent I get to see him within the next twenty-four hours." Jensen's tone was more insistent.

"I already told you, there's no way it's going to happen." Ashley's attitude had shifted from tense to irritable, but Jensen, too, was about to up his game.

"Oh, it's going to happen, mate, it's just a question of how much help you're going to be. Because very soon, I'll be dropping names left, center, and right to get in there, and by dropping names, I mean letting Prince Nadir know which members of *his* staff are actually members of *your* staff. Now make it happen, or you'll be deaf, dumb, and blind without a single agent in place by midnight." Jensen had no choice but to put pressure on Ashley. He wasn't particularly keen on it, but it was the only way he could make the situation play out the way he wanted.

"You would blackmail me?" Ashley's tone was anger now.

"Actually, in our trade, the official term is gray mail when somebody threatens to expose an operation of this scale. Don't they teach you anything in training anymore? Either way, *today, the prince, make it happen*!" Jensen shut down the phone.

"Did I hear you say, prince?" Marshall asked. "So that's the plan? We're gonna do a live performance of *Purple Rain*. Send tickets to Aram and bag him when he gets here?" Marshall had emerged from the back seat of the Hilux.

"Don't be stupid, it's not Prince anymore, he's a symbol." Jensen returned the sarcasm, and the pair of them smiled, enjoying the banter again.

But the smile on Marshall's face faded. "Seriously, though, Jensen, I'm gonna need a season ticket to shit creek soon. What's the plan this time, mate?"

Darius, too, had emerged from the Toyota, his mouth working in an attempt to get some saliva flowing. His tongue was so dry it could have featured in a Sure antiperspirant advert. He ambled over to complete the team, just as curious about what would happen next.

Jensen had their full attention. “Darius, I need you to go into town and get me a decent suit, some food and water for all of us, and five animal porn DVDs. Marshall, go with Darius and get us into a hotel for the night, as posh as you can get while paying cash. Drop me off at some kind of bar or restaurant on the way where I can make some calls and get a cuppa.” Jensen’s instructions set the others off on their appointed missions and bought him enough time to iron out some of the wrinkles in his half-thought-out, long shot of a plan. The journey so far had been tough but what lay ahead was beyond treacherous.

Chapter 31

With their tasks complete, Marshall and Darius took their positions as close to the palace as they could get without raising suspicion. Tapping at the steering wheel impatiently, Marshall fidgeted in the uncomfortable heat of the blazing sun. The pair of them were playing the waiting game. All they could do was sit it out until Jensen came back. Sitting with his feet up across the back seat, Darius fished the tablet out of his Bergen and unlocked the screen.

"What is Max's full name?" he asked.

"Why? You gonna add him on Facebook?" Marshall quipped.

Darius said nothing and waited for Marshall's reply, so Marshall told him, and Darius tapped away at the tablet's screen, ignoring Marshall's glare. The usual arrangements of pre-agreed emergency RV points were put into place in case things all went to hell.

The moment of truth was looming. With a few strategic, well-placed phone calls, Jensen managed to accomplish the seemingly impossible, and the meeting with Prince Nadir had been arranged.

Jensen took stock of his impressive surroundings. The large Audience Room in which he had been instructed to wait was indeed palatial. With white marble pillars and opulent gold embossed furnishings, the spacious salon opened on one side to a magnificent oasis garden where a couple of tame hunting leopards wandered freely. The garden was surprisingly cool, and Jensen suspected that some kind of concealed air conditioning was working its magic. The whole scene was like a setting from *Arabian Nights*.

Although, over and over again in his mind, he had rehearsed the specifics of his one-shot proposition, Jensen was willing to freely acknowledge that it had more holes than Harrison's Jag. His pulse raced and his palms were sweating as the time of the meeting drew closer. There were a lot of barriers to break down within a short time, and he was beginning to experience an element of self-doubt about his ability to pull it off.

The imposing surroundings amplified the situation, and imposter syndrome was setting in. He was feeling out of his depth. It was time to employ his secret mind weapon: His bad ass list.

Early on in his training Jensen was taught how to combat self-doubt. His mentor had told him to make something called a bad ass list. He instructed him to compile a list of twenty or more times in his life when he had felt extremely confident through something he'd done. Some of his greatest achievements or moments in life where he just pulled off something incredible. It could be anything from acing a test to asking the love of his life on a date and getting a yes. The time you get a strike or win the game of pool when it's all down to the last ball. Whenever he needed to boost his confidence, he remembered each moment on his list. Replayed them in his mind, relived them in as much detail as possible. The sights, sounds, smells, temperature, and feelings, all the senses included to take him back to the moment. One by one, Jensen could go down the list and re-create every single moment in his mind until his confidence was back to full power. Like an impenetrable force field that had just been recharged.

He said a silent prayer that Marshall and Darius had managed to pull off their part of the plan amongst some of the staff they'd managed to bump.

Bump is the term used for a planned meeting with a specific person that appears to be a chance encounter by the recipient. Usually, POL (patterns of life) have been established by the operative performing surveillance on the target or potential asset.

His high levels of faith in his friends were equally as important as his faith in himself at this point. They'd been tasked to start rumors of Jensen, the English super spy, capable of the impossible and the fact that he was in town on business and how much of a unique opportunity it was. Normally he would have liked to have made this happen over time, but that was a luxury they couldn't afford at the moment. The deliberate rumors were set up to be overheard by the prince throughout the day by select people whom the prince trusted. The subtle foundation of planting these seeds was as important to his task as distance calculations are to a sniper. When you have one shot, everything has to be worked out in advance perfectly.

Jensen turned to face a twenty-foot mirror on the wall behind him and looked at his reflection. Satisfied with the outfit that Darius had chosen for him, he stared into his own eyes and voiced his thoughts. "*I'm trained for this*," he told himself quietly.

Chapter 32

With his self-assurance restored, like an actor going on stage to face his audience, Jensen turned just as the massive doors opened and the first of the prince's entourage swept into the lavish chamber. The group parted, and the room fell silent as Prince Nadir made his grand entrance, flanked on four sides by armed bodyguards. The prince greeted Jensen with the traditional hand-on-shoulder-double-cheek kiss and gestured to a place at a small table where serving girls promptly arranged food and drink. The audience was now in session.

It was time for Jensen to go in all guns blazing and perform the whole seven-step process. Jensen cleared his throat to deliver the big promise, steepled his hands in front of him, and in a clear and controlled voice, spoke confidently.

"I'm going to do you a favor the likes of which nobody has ever done for you before." Jensen took a breath as he watched Nadir's reaction. "I'm going to remove your competition. I'm going to make you more than double the money you already make, and I'm going to make Prince Nadir the biggest and only name in the land." Jensen stepped forward to continue his delivery, never once breaking eye contact with Nadir.

Prince Nadir's ego was already inflated, but he watched closely, mildly skeptical with deep intrigue, as Jensen continued his speech. Servants flanked him, waiting for instructions as Nadir picked at the spread of sweet fruits around them. Jensen moved onto selling the dream with an emotional link.

"I'm going to fill that missing void you might not even know that you have. That yearning to complete your life. To finally reach empowerment. Your life is fulfilled with the desires you have yet to achieve."

Nadir stopped picking at the fruit and looked up at Jensen. Jensen moved in and sat next to the prince. Putting his arm around the prince's shoulder, he broke the patterns and norms, showing there was something different about him. His forward and friendly demeanor removed the usual boundaries that would prevent this type of behavior. Jensen waved his other hand out in front of Nadir as if painting an imaginary picture in the air.

Now he had to ensure the prince visualized it. "Imagine, Prince Nadir, the envy of every person in the world. Every house knows your name and speaks of the all-powerful Prince Nadir. The man every boy dreams of growing up to become. Every man models themselves and idolizes, and every woman dreams of being married to. The money, the power, everything you could ever want, all delivered to your feet." Nadir was lapping it up as Jensen deliberately filled his voice with excitement. Now it was time to sprinkle some razzle dazzle on it.

"Prince Nadir, *Time's* magazine man of the century, Prince Nadir the first prince to marry three western princesses. Prince Nadir is the most powerful prince in all of the history books around the world." Jensen increased the volume of his voice slightly with each sentence, getting more excited with every statement.

Nadir shifted in his seat, listening intently to Jensen.

Jensen smoothly transitioned to step five; back it up with proof. "This isn't the first time I've done this for people. I've made ordinary men become men of power. You've heard of Sheik Al Saud Nahyan, haven't you?"

Nadir nodded, pretty certain he knew who Jensen was talking about.

Before he could ask any questions, though, Jensen continued. "Well, I put him where he is now. Call him and ask. Ask him about the English man named Jensen and what I did for him." Jensen did something he doesn't normally do—he bluffed. He was pretty certain that Nadir wouldn't have Al Saud's number, and even if he did, he probably wouldn't call him. He just swept over it and carried on before the prince had a moment to give it another thought. "But why would a prince as smart and as powerful as you waste your time checking such trivial things. You are a clever man, and somebody as intelligent as yourself can see that I can do what I promise." Jensen stood, ready to move to the next stage. The prince was now filled with excitement and hanging on Jensen's every word.

"I am your chance to make this dream a reality." Jensen stood in front of Nadir, matching his posture as best he could. He looked him directly in the eye. It was time to deliver the final stage. Take it all away if he doesn't agree to a deal right now. Hold a pin to his bubble. This was the clincher. After the sale came the close. This was where it happened.

"But …" Jensen paused for effect. "If I leave, then my offer leaves with me. Never to be offered again. I can only do this while I'm here. Once I leave the country, it cannot be something I could make happen again. And I leave today unless you want me to deliver everything I promised."

"I do, I do." The prince edged forward on his seat. "What do you want from me to make this happen?"

"For a man of your stature, it will be almost nothing to provide me with what I need. I have a very short list of requirements, all of which will be nothing compared to what you will receive."

Jensen used the whole seven-step process. All that, with a load of NLP and ego feeding, and Jensen was good to go.

If you know nothing about the world of espionage and spies, then that little gift was probably the most important bit of tradecraft you could ever ignore. That seven-step process is gold. Do not underestimate its value. People have paid big money to find out what you have just read.

Jensen had given it a whole load of silver tonguery, and the prince was under his spell. The hapless trio had gone from being at the bottom of the food chain to being off the menu in one afternoon. With a huge royal backing, whatever they wanted was just a phone call away. The prince introduced Damien, a friend from the west whom he trusted to "take care of his desires."

"From now on, you just ask Damien, and he will give you whatever you need, you have my word." Nadir's conviction was solid, and Jensen knew he'd pulled it off. Nadir had found a new best friend, and while Jensen was flavor of the month, nobody was getting him off the stage. Jensen finished his performance feeling like a little tap dance in there wouldn't have gone amiss. As for Nadir, he was happier than a fat slag in the army barracks. The final result was a win, but now, it was time for Jensen to get back to Marshall and Darius and give them the next piece of the puzzle.

Jensen walked out of the building with Damien in tow. Damien's manner gave the impression of a stereotype of the old British Diplomatic Corps. Eton educated that he had probably ended up in Sandhurst to prove a point to Daddy and had, more than likely, wound up in this situation through a few too many glasses of Pimms in the Conservative Club. Jensen was skeptical and put his suspicions to the test.

Many secret societies such as the Freemasons, have specific secret coded questions by which members can identify one another without raising any eyebrows. For example, Freemasons will casually slip a question into a conversation. "Are you a traveling man?" Fellow Masons will know how to correctly respond, while ordinary public members would be none the wiser. MI6 uses a similar system. Whether or not it's official or just something MI6 staff have invented is unclear, but it works, and "If it ain't broke, don't fix it."

Damien's fine ginger hair stood on end when Jensen asked the question, the color draining from his face, leaving only the freckles behind. His posture immediately changed, and his body language screamed panic.

"Did I do something wrong? Have I been blown off?" Damien's voice trembled as he spoke.

Jensen kept the pace with Damien tagging along behind him. "It's just blown and no, I just need your help with something. Your cover's still fine, and you'll be back to work in no time. I promise."

Jensen's words put Damien at ease. Away from the palace, Jensen opened the back door of the Hilux and gestured for Damien to get in. He shuffled over as Jensen climbed in behind him.

Darius stuffed the tablet back into the Bergen and pulled out a carrier bag as he looked over at Jensen.

"It all went to plan, fellas," Jensen said with a proud grin. "This is D'Artagnan."

"Actually, it's Damien!" the newcomer corrected, failing to grasp what was so funny, as Marshall and Darius laughed at the private joke.

"Here." Darius handed the carrier bag to Jensen. "I understand why you needed the suit, but why these?" The animal porn DVDs were neatly wrapped, and Jensen let out a short burst of laughter as he peered inside the bag.

"I don't actually need these, I just wanted to see if you'd do it." He laughed.

"You prick, took me nearly two hours to get them." But Darius was also laughing.

"Well, it gave me time to put the finishing touches to my plan," Jensen replied.

"Which is what?" Marshall asked. "You've had Darius and me running around like personal shoppers. I think it's about time you let us in on what we're about to do." Marshall's face belied the serious tone in his voice.

"Okay," Jensen said. "Previously, all we set out to do was shoot a drug dealer, but that soon got complicated by the silver-tongued and silver-haired drill sergeant. Now there's a slightly different agenda." The three men hung on Jensen's every word, taking in each minor detail. "To start with, Prince Nadir isn't a real prince. In fact, I don't even think his name is Nadir. He's a super-rich drug lord who gave himself a title and lived like royalty. The self-crowned crime boss only has one issue. His shipments are having problems completing the journey to their destinations. They can't use the supply route, which up until now, was controlled by the recently deceased Bishop, and if they take the alternative route, they risk getting hit by local militia. I convinced the prince that with my help, he could control everything. The supply route, the product monopoly, and that I'd even take out the competition. But to get my help, he needed to help me." Jensen laid it all out, and soon it was coming together for the others.

Marshall frowned. "All we do is kidnap a drug baron for the CIA and hand his business and that of an already dead CEO of a security company to a deranged, psychotic crime lord who thinks he's a prince?" Marshall's sarcastic tone made Darius chuckle uncontrollably.

"Exactly!" Jensen smiled with his answer.

Marshall shook his head. "What could possibly go wrong?"

"It's what's going to happen anyway, so we may as well take the credit for it and make it happen our way," Jensen replied, ignoring the irony in Marshall's question.

"What do you mean by *our way*?" Marshall was concerned about where all this was going.

"Well, as it turns out, we are part of a lucky few. The guy we are after prefers to live as a recluse and has been seen fewer times than the credits at the end of a porn movie. Nobody around here even knows where he lives. Except us. We were guests at his exclusive residence three years ago."

"And that benefits us how exactly?" Marshall asked, still waiting for some good news.

"Sheikh Aram is head of a large drug and arms cartel. But where Prince Nadir operates out in the open with his large palace and his ostentatious lifestyle, Aram stays under the radar. He feels safer here in the desert, directing the family business, like a giant octopus, with tentacles reaching all over. Our well-tailored friend in London, with the Gucci suit and the bling, is one brother; he runs the operation in the UK. Aram has contacts with the Russian mafia and the Sicilian mob. Other family members in various locations around Europe and the Middle East use legit import/export businesses as cover for their contraband trade. One of the younger brothers was being trained for a key position, so they gave him an AK47 and a job in Aram's private militia, which is why he was in the wrong place at the wrong time and got his throat cut.

"But Aram doesn't trust anyone, especially when it comes to money. Even members of his own family have been known to disappear if they cross him. So the profits from all of his ventures are funneled back to his headquarters here to be reallocated as he sees fit. So the way I figure it, if we're going to put him out of business and we're not getting paid by our new employer, we may as well dip into petty cash and get ourselves some financial compensation from the job itself along the way."

Jensen saw the smile appear on Marshall's face and could almost hear the cogs ticking over in Darius's mind, followed by a satisfied grin and an approving nod. Completely bewildered, Damien just sat there with his jaw a few inches lower than normal.

"I don't know who you people are, but I take it that you do this kind of thing all the time. Highly trained professionals with masses of experience in this kind of thing, right?" Damien's questions were more for his own reassurance of how capable they were and how safe his future was.

"Nope, I'm a full-time Daddy, he's an old friend, and I only met this guy two days ago, but he seems to know what he's doing," Jensen said casually, pointing at Darius.

"Oh my Lord, I'm going to die!" Damien turned an even paler shade than before, and every hair on his body stood to attention.

"Does he always turn that color?" Marshall asked, taking in Damien's pale complexion.

"Will this crazy ass prince be as good as his word, do you think?" Darius asked.

"He might be one wave short of a shipwreck, but he's rich and powerful. He certainly didn't get there by chance. He knows what's good for business, and that's us. That's why he sent Damien with us. He said he'll do whatever we want him to." Jensen's words sounded cheerful as he patted Damien on the shoulder.

Damien gave a huge gulp and sat with his hands between his knees in the naughty school boy position. The color returned to his face, then did a rapid U-turn and drained again.

"I guess he does always turn that color," Marshall said to Darius and Jensen. "I had a toy that did that once. Whenever you picked it up, it changed patterns and colors."

"We should do this more often." Darius laughed, enjoying the banter.

Chapter 33

The coolness of the air-conditioned hotel suite was welcomed as all four of them shuffled in through the door. Marshall immediately poured a drink from the mini bar as Darius sat on a winged-back chair and pecked at Jensen's tablet, which he'd recently seemed to have adopted. Damien sat on the edge of the couch, leaning forward with his hands between his knees. He sat silently, feeling about as comfortable as a fart in Batman's rubber suit.

Marshall knocked back the glass of whiskey before pouring a second one.

Jensen eyed Marshall's actions hoping it wouldn't get out of hand, then quickly dismissed the thoughts of Marshall drinking too much to deal with the more pressing matter at hand. He walked to the center of the room.

"Right, I know Damien is an MI6 asset, but he'll have to be treated like a civilian under naval training." Jensen smiled with his words, looking over at Marshall, who was beginning to chuckle.

"Is that because you'll be talking about a load of top secret stuff?" Damien asked.

"No, mate. It's because you're ginger." Marshall laughed.

"What's a civilian under naval training?" Damien was none the wiser.

"Ha ha, it's good to know in an era of political correctness, it's still safe to take the piss out of ginger people." Marshall chuckled.

"Okay, being serious now, it's time to figure out how we're going to pull this off."

Jensen invited the group to form what the British SAS referred to as a Chinese parliament. It's where all parties involved give their input and form a plan together as a team. The plan only being finalized when all parties are happy with all the details. Within half an hour, they'd ruled out a dozen or more possibilities. Jensen continued to press forward.

"How much sway does his royal anus have with the local law enforcement?" Marshall asked, looking over at Damien.

"Why, what do you need?" Damien's reply was sheepish, although he knew the locals in all areas and departments did pretty much whatever they were told.

"Well, to start with, there's that stolen truck we could do with getting back to its owner when all of this is finished, and how likely are they to turn a blind eye to an explosion or two?"

"Explosions? I'm not—wait, I've been driving around in a stolen truck?" Damien changed color again, and Jensen stood before the traffic light puns started.

"I think we need a break. I'll call room service and get us something to eat." Jensen sounded exhausted. He picked up the phone and dialed. It barely rang when a friendly voice answered, saying something he couldn't quite make out. His English accent seemed even more prominent as he spoke. "Good afternoon, I'd like to order some food, please." He rattled off a few options from the menu and looked around, receiving thumbs up, nods, and smiles from the team.

"Would you like anything else, sir?"

"Anything else?" Jensen asked, looking around the room.

"A couple of bottles of Guantanamo sauce," Marshall mouthed more than said.

"And two bottles of water, please." Jensen relayed down the phone. "Yes, that's everything, thank you." Jensen replaced the receiver and joined the others now sitting around the dining table.

Over half an hour later, the group had the makings of a plan. Active intelligence, through Damien's MI6 sources, had informed them that the property would have minimal amounts of personnel at about ten a.m. due to a planned regular road trip in the trucks, although details were slightly sketchy.

Tradecraft: *Active intelligence is directly developing information from sources in the field and can be used to make operational decisions on the ground in an AOI or Area Of Interest.*

This ruled out the ideal option of a predawn raid, which they all would have preferred. The other factor was that local law enforcement and other military bodies were allowing a window for what they called a pre-arranged staff break, where nobody would be available to answer calls for a short while. It would have been expensive to arrange, but they weren't footing the bill, so it didn't matter to them. Attacking the compound knowing there was a skeleton crew inside and nobody was going to be rushing to the scene was a bonus and, in some ways, probably outweighed the option of a predawn raid anyway.

"We have to make sure that when the trucks leave, they won't get a call and turn back around to join the fight," Marshall said.

They were interrupted when a knock at the door caused the trio to draw their weapons rapidly. Damien pulled his feet up onto the chair like a frightened child who'd just seen a spider. Marshall and Darius went out of sight into opposite sides of the room, and Jensen hid his pistol by his leg as he walked closer to the door, standing slightly to the side of it.

"Who is it?" Jensen asked through the doorway.

"Room service." A soft female voice answered.

Everybody exhaled, and Jensen opened the door a crack. After visually confirming it was indeed room service, he held the door open as the young girl wheeled the trolley into the room, completely unaware of the reaction she'd caused moments ago. Discreetly re-holstering their pistols, Marshall made his way over to the trolley and lifted the silver lid. Darius came over and sampled the food, too. Jensen took a wedge of cash from his pocket and handed over a fifty-dollar bill to tip the waitress.

"Thank you, sir. Will that be all?" she asked with a smile.

"Yes, thank you." Jensen closed the door behind her and looked around to see the others tucked into the food. It was at that point he realized how hungry he was. All of them munched away at the freshly prepared lunches making noises of appreciation.

"This ham's lovely," Damien said between mouthfuls. "Makes a change from the type of stuff we get at the palace."

"It's not ham," Jensen informed him, but Damien didn't seem to hear as he continued chomping away on his sandwich. A sudden look of realization formed in Damien's eyes.

"Oh, I get it. Civilian, C. Under, U. Naval—" Damien's sentence was cut short by the laughter of the other three.

"It took you long enough!" Jensen spluttered, laughing as he chewed his sandwich.

"We should do this more often." Darius chuckled.

***

The post-lunch finishing touches were put in place on the plan of attack, and they all agreed some down time was in order before they got to work. Jensen looked at the body armor in the kit that Damien had managed to have delivered. It was old Russian gear that looked like it belonged in an antique shop rather than being used in the field. He didn't expect it would stop too much, but anything was better than nothing.

Damien had been volunteered to go into the city with a shopping list, and Marshall watched as Jensen went out onto the balcony to call MJ on the sat phone. Darius sat back in his chair, tapping the tablet again, likely messaging Olivia. A sudden wave of loneliness washed over Marshall. When all of this was over, life was as normal for everyone else but him. Sandy was never going to be there again. The sadness swirled inside him, and his eyes welled up. It didn't take long before the pain turned to anger and his thoughts returned to Gucci and his part in all of this. Darius peeked up from behind his tablet momentarily and spotted the look on Marshall's face.

"I think I could do with vodka. How about you, Marshall?" Marshall snapped out of his almost trance-like state and was back in the room. Darius's distraction had worked.

Marshall grabbed a couple of bottles from the mini bar as Darius sat at the table. "A glass of Jack for me, I think." Marshall placed a couple of tumblers on the table and poured. Darius grabbed the Vodka and joined him in a toast.

"To friendship," Darius said, raising his glass. Marshall clinked his glass against Darius's.

"Good health," he said before swigging the first mouthful.

These few minutes of normality were greatly appreciated with what was looming for them later that night. What they were about to do was not only high risk, but the entire operation was a "single bullet." Mistakes could not be made, especially before they had the chance to take their one shot.

The countdown had begun, and they'd soon be in a critical position as they set everything up. The last thing they wanted was for the whole thing to come undone before it had even started. Marshall opened his mouth wide and knocked back the last drop of alcohol. It wasn't going to be long before he needed to be on top form and switch to work mode again. He placed the glass back on the shiny table top. His mind drifted to the new orders. Bring Aram back alive. The logical part of him wanted to do it, but there was a deep emotional side that was questioning his ability to follow those orders. He wanted blood. He wanted Aram to suffer, Gucci to suffer, and the entire family to suffer. The thoughts of how he would react when he came face to face with Aram swirled around in his head. Could he do it? Could he hand over the man behind the death of his girlfriend? He decided not to overthink it. In the next few hours, he'd find out and would have the answers to all of his questions.

Chapter 34

Jensen was already awake before the phone sounded with the hotel's early morning wake-up call. He answered and thanked the concierge as the other two stirred. They'd completed all their preparations the night before and got their head down early, ready for the 0300 hrs wake-up call. Darius was first in the shower as Marshall made his way into the main area of the hotel suite. Jensen walked in to grab a bottle of water to see the mini bar already open. Nearly all the liquor was gone, except for the bottle Marshall was taking a swig from.

"Seriously? Marshall, you just woke up," Jensen said, worry in his voice.

"It's rum," Marshall replied. "That makes me a pirate, not an alcoholic." He took another swig and replaced the bottle, wiping his mouth with the back of his hand. Jensen didn't press the issue. He knew Marshall was still grieving.

After all three of them had freshened up and were ready to go, they looked over at Damien, still sleeping on the couch sporting the hotel's complementary eyemask.

"Where did he get pajamas from?" Marshall asked, stifling a chuckle. The other two gave a little snigger as they left Damien sleeping in the hotel and made their way down to the truck. Jensen stayed in the lobby to grab a couple of phone books from an area near the reception. He chucked them in his Bergen and caught up with the other two. The parking lot was in darkness as Marshall made his way to the driver's door.

"Are you okay to drive, Captain?" Jensen asked.

"Captain? I never made captain." Marshall replied with a touch of confusion.

"You will the way you're going. Captain Jack Sparrow." Jensen smirked.

Darius giggled to himself as the three men clambered into the truck. Marshall turned the key, the engine shuddered as it burst into life, and the smell of diesel fumes permeated around them. The truck roared away, and they started the drive into the night.

When they arrived, they parked the truck up out of the way, about half a kilometer from Aram's house. They picked an ERV as back up in case the truck got compromised, then got ready to move into the target area. In the darkness before sunrise, all three checked each other's kits. Jumping up and down on the spot, in turn, they did their noise discipline checks. After making sure they weren't going to rattle or clink as they TAB'd the rest of the way, they set off.

It didn't seem to be too long before the pace of the march was slowing with Aram's home in sight. Heart rates increased slightly, and breathing heavily decreased their speed to a slow walk. They stopped short of Aram's compound to observe and orientate before the final approach. Memories came flooding back of their last visit to this place. Jensen remembered the eager look on James's face before they went in. The same keen look was displayed by Darius now.

"Darius, stay focused and try and remain between Marshall and me. Okay?"

"Sure. Are you okay?"

"Yeah, just don't want you in harm's way if it can be avoided, mate," Jensen said in a solemn tone. Darius shrugged. He wasn't sure why Jensen was so worried, but he took heed of what he'd said and carried on.

The house was in darkness, and all was quiet. The anticipation of what was to come next rose, and the tension seemed amplified by the silence of the night. The moonlight was more than enough to give them sufficient vision of their surroundings. No lights were on within the property, and the stillness of the local area made every sound seem ten times louder than it actually was.

Jensen gave the signal, and Marshall advanced. Jensen remained right behind him, and Darius watched the rear. They moved in and progressed slowly toward the five-foot outer cinderblock wall.

Darius was the first over the wall. Marshall followed, and when all three were over the wall, they slowly crept toward the two personnel carrier trucks parked in the yard.

Marshall crawled quietly under one and Jensen the other as Darius took the role of the lookout. They lay on their backs, securing remote IEDs in place with tie wraps.

Tradecraft: *Movies tend to show a magnet being used to secure explosives in place, but it's not the best way to operate. A magnet wouldn't hold an IED in place very well, and it could drop off the moment the truck went over a bump in the road. Using a high-powered magnet could fry the circuits in the phone attached as a remote trigger to detonate the device. So, tie wraps are usually the best method.*

That doesn't mean magnets aren't used–they're just not best practice.

A film of sweat covered Marshall's body as he worked away under the truck. Pulling one of the tie wraps tight caused a layer of gritty dirt to crumble from the truck's chassis, peppering Marshall's face. A tiny piece of grit landed in the corner of his eye, causing it to water. Crumbling and crunching sounds from the ground underneath him seemed to get louder as he wriggled to finish the job. A trickle of sweat ran down the small of his back to add to his irritation as the grit in his eye increasingly agitated him. His palms were covered in black dirt from the chassis as he pulled the last cable tie tight. Wiping his eye with the back of his hand, he lay back, ready to shuffle from under it. With the explosives in place, it was time to move out.

Darius moved in toward the truck Jensen was under. "Jensen?"

"What?" Jensen whispered.

"What did Dwayn say to the girl in the hotel bar?"

"What?" Jensen wondered about the timing of Darius's question.

"What did you tell him to say? You know, to the girl in the bar?" It had been bugging Darius, and the not knowing finally got the better of him. The thoughts of the team were cut short, though. An unexpected clang from somewhere within the compound startled them, and all three momentarily froze. Remaining motionless on the spot, Jensen lay on his back, listening to try and work out where the noise had come from. His heartrate increased, and with his senses heightened, he turned and scanned the area. Marshall kept painstakingly still as he fought the sensation to wipe his eye again. The grit was still there and driving him wild.

Movement caught Jensen's eye, and he spotted a black and white stray cat jump onto the roof of one of the outbuildings. Sighing relief, he mouthed, "It's just a cat."

They slid out from under the trucks. Marshall used his shirt in an attempt to finally wipe his eye clean. Adrenaline still coursing through them, they fought the urge to drop their guard and move out quickly. It was imperative not to get caught at this stage. This was the point of vulnerability, the last thing anyone wanted was to be compromised while they were still in the process of preparation. Letting the explosives off early would be a disaster.

There's nothing worse for a man than premature detonation.

With this stage completed, they needed to remain just as vigilant as ever. Backing out slowly, they made their way to their truck. Dawn would be approaching before long, and it was time to prep for the last stages of the plan.

Chapter 35

The hide they'd set up was just about big enough for the three of them to operate. Working on stag, they'd managed to get some downtime in turn as the one slept and the other two kept continuous surveillance on the house. The temperature was rising dramatically since sunrise, and they were getting through the water supplies from the truck pretty rapidly. Even in the shade of the hide covered in camo netting, they still seemed to be baking. They monitored Aram's home, which had a larger industrial-type building off to the left with scattered outbuildings surrounding it. Back and slightly to the right, the residential area was elevated to allow for three double parking garages underneath. The well-kept, mid-level patio housed a pool that seemed slightly out of character compared to the rest of the dwellings, which appeared run down externally. The whole compound was surrounded by an almost kidney-shaped cinderblock wall with a smaller gate at the back and two large gates on the side.

The flaking green paint on the double gates covered the steel frame underneath. Opening outward, they allowed the vehicles from the yard and garage area onto a track that eventually joined the road. A total of five armed guards were patrolling the house. All brandished AK47s with zero trigger discipline. Two of them sat in the shade most of the time, but the other three performed some sort of half-hearted patrol around the outside of the wall.

Jensen slept on a roll mat while Marshall watched closely through binoculars, relaying the details to Darius. Darius kept notes of the action within and around the compound as they watched the rebel warriors prepare for their excursion.

"The trucks are about to leave," Marshall grunted to Jensen, giving him a nudge to bring him around. Jensen stirred and rubbed his face with his hands, stretching as best he could in the confined space of the hide. His mouth was dry, and dust seemed to be sticking to every exposed bit of skin that was leaking sweat.

"Okay, let's start prepping." He came to terms with what was to follow. They topped up their water canteens and double-checked their kit. They gave it a full thirty minutes for the trucks to drive off into the mountains and be well out of the way of the action. Jensen had been briefed and brought up to date, and the trio tactically made their way toward the cinder walls bounding the compound. Darius at the northwest of the property, Marshall at the northeast, and Jensen sneaking up from the south. Jensen saw the guard he had to take out and controlled his breathing as he slowly approached from behind. The guard was standing, leaning against a post just outside the yard in an area shaded by the perimeter wall.

Jensen drew his knife with his right hand and, creeping as silently as humanly possible, neared the guard from behind. With his left hand, he pulled the guard's forehead back, simultaneously thrusting the knife into the side of his neck. The blade was facing forward with the tip sticking out to the left of the man's windpipe. Jensen pulled back hard on the guard's head while pushing on the knife, cutting through flesh, blood supply, and the windpipe all at once. The outward motion tore through the front of the guard's neck, killing him instantly.

Tradecraft: *Most people seem to think that you would wrap your hand around the neck and slice from one side to the other, but unless you're using a razor or extremely small blade, this isn't actually the case. The two separate motions of grabbing the forehead and wrapping your arm around the front of the assailant allow for reaction time. There are too many windows of opportunity for the assailant to defend themselves or pull the trigger of a weapon etc., and the time before the assailant finally dies is too long. It can take a while for him to bleed out while grabbing his throat and again possibly detonate an explosive or pull a trigger. By stabbing the knife into the side of the neck and pushing forward to cut the throat, it's quicker, more efficient, and gives less chance of the assailant reacting before death. Less of the gargling noises, too, which decreases the chance of being compromised.*

Jensen nearly toppled as the man's dead weight fell, pushing him backward. Bending his knees, he lowered the guard to the ground, resting him between the pole and the wall so he just looked like he was napping in the shade. He pulled the guard's shemagh around the front of his neck to cover the wound.

Four clicks sounded in his earpiece, which was Darius's radio silent signal to say he'd cleared his area. Jensen gave two clicks for his signal, and a moment or two later, three clicks came through to signal Marshall had completed his task, too. The three of them made their way to the side gate in the outer wall where they'd escaped the last time they were here. It was now time to detonate the explosives on the trucks. They needed to blow them both up while they were well out of the way. That way, any survivors would be stranded up in the mountains and unable to join the fight here.

Jensen did the deed, then glanced up. "Shit," he whispered.

Only one explosion had erupted in the mountains. He wasn't sure what had happened, but he could only see one cloud of black smoke. Maybe it just seemed like one explosion because they both went up so close together. Maybe the smoke had merged to look like one in the distance. Either way, there was nothing they could do about it now, so they pressed on.

The trio made their way through the gate, and advanced toward the side door of the property. A window entry would have been a favorite, but Damien's intelligence sources suggested there might be bars on the other side. Marshall and Darius stood on either side of a door, weapons at the ready and watching Jensen's back as he strategically placed a homemade charger on the door.

They backed up from the door and moved alongside the house wall farther than normal practice would dictate, mentally preparing themselves for the blast. The normal procedure would mean they would be closer to the door, but the exact actions that the improvised explosives Jensen had made were unpredictable. All was quiet as they steadied their breathing and got into the mental state of mind that would allow them to do their job with speed and accuracy.

Chapter 36

The explosion made everybody jump, even though they'd been anticipating it. The dust from the crumbling wall continued to fall and, combined with the cordite smell from the blast, filled the air with an acrid mixture of explosives and old masonry that stimulated the adrenaline rush Jensen got every time he found himself in a situation like this. His senses heightened, his heart raced, and his raw emotions seemed to guide his every move. The door was gone, not blown somewhere out of the way or blown to the back of the room, it was gone, and most of the wall with it. Jensen was through the gap in an instant, moving to cover as fast as he could. Marshall and Darius were a split second behind him. Most of the tenants who could pose a potential threat were located in the room to the right of them.

After opening the door a fraction, Jensen rolled a HE L109 series hand grenade through the gap and waited for the guys in there to get the news.

The three-man force burst through the door and continued to clear the rooms with their MP7s, recently purchased from an Italian friend of Gianluca. It was obvious that the prince's influence had stretched far, with the local law enforcement taking an extended coffee break. Either way, they were safe for the moment.

A couple of servant girls ran out screaming, and the men just let them go. They were no danger, and killing them would have served no purpose. The door on the other side of the room led to a short corridor that formed an upside-down L shape at the end.

Tradecraft: *People inexperienced in room clearing and close-quarter combat would more than likely believe the correct procedure would be to stay close to the wall and quickly pop your head around the corner to take a peek before giving it a second go with your weapon raised. The opposite is actually true. You walk with your back to the wall on the opposite side of the corner. You wish to look around and slowly clear a small section of the corridor at a time until you can see all of it. The terminology used is to pie the corner, clearing each slice of the pie as you go. It's a slower method, and you clear each segment a bit at a time until your way forward is clear. Then, and only then, can you move out.*

Darius cleared the corner with Jensen by his side while Marshall secured the rear. When Darius gave the signal, all three moved toward the heavy steel door of what appeared to be a storage room at the end. There was no handle on the outside, and the door was hinged to open outward, obviously intended to make it more difficult for anyone trying to kick it in.

Marshall stepped forward. "Let me!" He reached into his pocket for some Kevlar cordage which he pushed into the slight gap between the door and the frame. He fed it at the top of the lock area and pushed it out under where the latch slotted into the housing on the frame. Looping each end around each of his hands, he gave one big tug, and the door clicked open. The trio got into position and, using the door as a shield, slowly edged it toward them, opening it a quarter of its width. The response was immediate as two AK47s with untrained and ineffective Syrians behind them started spraying the room with 7.62s at waist height.

The trio simply dropped to the floor for a period of seconds as both mags were emptied, and the two guards, with a room temperature IQ figure, stopped to look stupidly at their now empty weapons. Marshall was the first up. Crouching low, he ran into the room firing two short bursts, a total of six rounds; three rounds, neatly grouped on each target. In the background, he'd managed to catch a glimpse of a figure in traditional Arab dress, which he assumed to be their quarry, disappear through a door behind some pallets which were stacked to about waist height and shrink-wrapped.

"Aram, there's nowhere left to go. Come on out!" Marshall shouted through the heavy steel door of what was obviously a safe room.

"There's no way you will get through this door before the rest of my men get here. Your efforts have been for nothing, and now I will have all three of you killed like animals," came the muffled reply from within.

Jensen dropped to the gap at the bottom of the door, putting his face as close as he could.

"Aram, if you come out now, we won't kill you, but this is your last chance before we come in and get you."

"Ha, you'll never get in here. This panic room is built for just such a situation. Your time runs short, infidel, my men will return soon, and we will make sport with your deaths."

Jensen looked around. Marshall and Darius were fiddling with the shrink wrap on one of the pallets. He wandered over to examine the contents of some metal shelving lining the storage room's walls. In less than a minute, he had a plan. Jensen called his team together.

"Darius, there's a swimming pool out back, get up there and get me some chlorine tablets or powder, whatever they're using. Marshall, you go to the garage and get me some brake fluid. If you can't find any, try the cars." Within a short time, Darius was back with a bucket filled with chlorine tablets, shortly followed by Marshall, who came in with a plastic bowl filled with brake fluid.

"I couldn't find any bottled brake fluid, so I had to rip the reservoir off a couple of the cars and drain it into this." Marshall looked proud of his little accomplishment as he handed over the bowl. Jensen slowly tipped the brake fluid through the crack at the bottom of the door and watched a puddle form on either side as it all trickled out.

"You see this, Aram? This is brake fluid. In a moment, I'm going to add chlorine to it. It won't take long before it creates a chemical fire, but in the meantime, the deadly toxic fumes will certainly kill you. This is your final chance to come out." Jensen chucked an Israeli respirator, a gas mask as they're more commonly known, to Darius and Marshall. He'd found them among the supplies on the shelving, and it was this discovery that had triggered the idea. They each ripped open the foil seals with the filters inside and screwed them to the masks, and once they'd got them on, Jensen dropped a line of chlorine tablets by the strong room door in the puddle of fluid.

Within seconds there was a chemical reaction, the hissing and fizzing began, and smoke rose from Jensen's concoction. The ventilation in the safe room caused a pressure difference, and the smoke was drawn under the door. Aram's coughs and splutters began, and seconds later, he burst from the safe room, choking and retching. Marshall and Darius grabbed an arm each and dragged him out. Jensen scooped up the tablets in a piece of waxed canvas and ran them outside, dropping them over the wall. The timing was so close as the chemical mix burst into flames the moment he dropped it. No sooner than they were outside, they all whipped their respirators off, gasping for breath. Marshall had wasted no time restraining the still gasping Arab, and Darius was ready with the sat phone.

"Okay, call Ginge and get the trucks up," Jensen instructed. Darius dialed, and Marshall gave Jensen a nod.

"It was all in the pallets. Every pallet in there, all shrink-wrapped and ready to go."

"Is it in US dollars?" Jensen already knew the answer before Marshall replied.

"Every single one." Marshall had a bigger grin than normal.

"Brilliant. Better in our pocket than in a black vault somewhere. You go with the money, Darius, and I will go in the taliwagon with this piece of shit." Jensen looked down at the captive, and a burst of rage welled up inside him. The man who had caused so much of his recent grief sat in the sand in front of him. Could he really hand him over? The man that had caused so much pain and anguish. All he had to do was pull his pistol out, and the whole thing would be over. Jensen could explain it by simply saying he got killed in a crossfire. It wasn't an unrealistic possibility. He'd probably never get hired by the CIA again, disobeying a direct order, and his life as a contractor would probably be finished. Then what would he do? Live as a retired spy, writing books of his misadventures as fiction? Maybe one day, when he was a bit older. He wasn't ready for that yet.

The logic battled his emotions, and his mind was in turmoil. The temptation to just pull the trigger and finish him increased. His hand moved to his sidearm. His muscles tensed, like his body and mind were fighting each other. The battle of what to do exploded within him. Putting all his weight into it, he kicked Aram hard to let him know how much he'd been thinking of him. The Arab let out an involuntary cough upon the impact of Jensen's boot. His gag slightly muffled the sound and stopped him from screaming as he sat there in the sand.

Jensen moved his hand away from his pistol and spun on the spot. He couldn't bring himself to look at Aram at that moment for fear of changing his mind. He took in a deep breath and composed himself. They'd done it. It was a success. He had to think of the positives. Their objective had been achieved. The hints of a smile formed on his face.

The trucks couldn't have been very far away as they were visible within a few minutes. They sped along the track toward the house, kicking up a plume of dust trailing behind them like an ostrich tail. A group of the prince's eager minions, waiting to load the newly acquired pallets onto the wagons. Jensen's heartrate slowed, and then the rush hit him. The smile cracked. He chuckled at first, his contagious laugh spreading to Marshall and Darius. The phenomenon known as a "Battle High" ran through him as the adrenaline still flowed in his body. The overwhelming post-fire fight feeling of excitement and the relief at staying alive circulated through him, displayed in his eyes. Darius saw an ideal window of opportunity.

"Come on, Jensen, what did Dwayn say? It's driving me crazy." Jensen was just about to answer when the bang from an unexpected shot caught them all off guard. Another of Aram's men had survived the carnage and ran at them, brandishing a pistol. Darius took a hit and dropped to the ground as the Syrian charged.

Jensen's mind instantly shot back to thoughts of James before he heard Marshall's shout.

"Contact left!" Marshall's yell caused Aram to scramble in the sand cowering in fear.

Jensen and Marshall's training kicked in, and they both raised their weapons before they even had time to think and, without hesitation, let a shower of 4.6 full metal jacket rounds rip into the attacker. The young guard aimlessly fired off a couple of rounds as he toppled face first into the sand. Marshall ran over, and a kick sent the pistol spinning clear to land around ten feet away. Jensen lay on top and carefully rolled the guard over, making sure no IEDs were a threat and that he was, in fact, dead. The man's wide-open eyes were lifeless, and the holes in his body were all seeping blood down his shirt front. His skin had paled, and the last of his life poured away into a big dark red puddle in the sand.

"Aaaaargh!" Darius was in serious pain.

Jensen cut away from his thoughts about the guard's body, and his mind filled with visions of James once again. The guilt haunted him, and he relived every moment of it. He ran over to his comrade, who lay in the sand with a now familiar pool of blood turning dark red around him.

"Hang on, mate!" Jensen checked the bullet wound in Darius's upper left thigh, praying it hadn't hit a major artery. He took his pocket knife and cut away the trousers from Darius's leg. The entry point was at the front, slightly to the left of center in the fleshy part of the leg. Jensen was relieved to note that the bullet appeared to have gone straight through without contacting bone. He took the shemagh from around his neck and wrapped it around Darius's leg. He then ripped open the side pocket of his trousers and pulled out a tourniquet, which he strapped above the wound on Darius's leg, and then looking up at him, he said, "This is gonna hurt." Darius looked back and gave him a nod.

Jensen turned the handle, and the tourniquet tightened, cutting off the blood supply to the seeping wound. Darius winced in pain, and a small grunt escaped his mouth, but he gritted his teeth and kept still. Jensen grabbed some more kit from his pocket and cleaned the wound. He then took a sachet of Celox quick-clot granules, ripped the top open with his teeth, and poured the contents of the sachet into and all over the wound, covering it again with the shemagh. Finally, he took an Israeli field dressing from his pocket and, using his teeth, rapidly ripped the plastic from around it. Jensen then removed the shemagh and applied the bandage to the wound. Using the plastic tension lever to tighten it and the plastic clip to keep it in place, the field dressing was good to go. Very slowly, Jensen loosened the tourniquet handle and removed it from Darius's leg, allowing the blood to flow again. With the wound packed and dressed, the bleeding seemed to have stopped. He checked Darius for any other injuries. He wasn't showing any signs of shock, and it looked like he'd only acquired the one hole.

"Here, you can keep that." Jensen threw his blood-soaked shemagh at Darius and stood. He hadn't even noticed that during the commotion, Marshall had gone and dragged Aram over to them and kept him in place. Darius looked up at Jensen.

"I was hoping for something a little better, like something for the pain." Darius's words were in jest, but he meant every one of them.

Jensen had a couple of morphine auto-injectors in his trauma kit back home but decided not to bring anything with him that could have caused an issue while they crossed borders. He was now questioning that decision. Jensen looked over at Marshall.

"Only a couple of codeine tablets. Nothing better, I'm afraid." Marshall took them from his pocket and threw them to Jensen.

"Here." Passing them over to Darius, he helped him to get his canteen and unscrew the lid. "It's the best we got for the moment."

"Oh, they'll do, believe me!" Darius was shaking as he desperately threw the pain relief into his mouth and started gulping at his water bottle.

"Change of plan. Forget the taliwagon. We all go together in the trucks." Jensen hadn't been comfortable about the team splitting up in the first place, so this was the perfect excuse to all ride in the same truck together with the money.

The sounds of a truck engine roaring toward them filled the air. Just one truck? That can't be right.

Jensen looked up to see which direction it was coming from.

"We got trouble incoming!" Jensen roared. "The second explosive didn't blow!"

Marshall looked up at the mountain track where the truck he'd placed the IED on was thundering toward the compound. Panic filled him—what had happened? Had he not attached the device properly? Maybe he pulled one of the wires away from the detonator when the dirt had gone in his eye. Either way, they were about to be outgunned. The truck stopped randomly on its way back from the mountain. It seemed to be an unusual stop, but then it continued on its way toward the compound.

"Maybe they're picking someone up?" Marshall said.

"I'm not bothered about that right now. Try and get Darius to cover and I'll go and get whatever guns and ammo I can find from the compound."

They'd both heard the whistle of an RPG before, but for some reason, neither of them seemed to react until the impact of it hitting the wall sent them tumbling to the ground. The huge boom as it detonated sent bricks and shrapnel flying in every direction.

The truck was getting closer.

Jensen ran for supplies, and Aram saw his chance and made a run for it. The slippery sheikh darted for the inner rooms of the compound before Marshall had even seen him.

"Jensen!" Marshall called.

Another boom echoed throughout the area. Not like the ones before—this wasn't an explosion.

The sound of a bullet coming toward you can actually be heard. It's a bit like a wasp or mosquito. It makes a vibrating buzzing sound. It's similar to when you fold a piece of paper over a comb and place it between your lips and blow.

That unique zipping sound of a bullet shooting toward him was what Jensen was hearing now. Time stood still for a second. That was why the truck had stopped, not to pick someone up but to drop someone off. A sniper. The round hit Jensen center mass and sent him tumbling over a small inner wall that crumbled as he fell backward over it. Only the bottoms of his combat boots could be seen, motionless, his body on top of the rubble.

"No!" Marshall cried. It had all been for nothing. All the way here, and Jensen had died after coming this far. Gunfire sounded around him.

Rounds chipped away at the wall where Jensen's body lay.

More rebels were closing in.

Chapter 37

Another RPG hit the cinderblock wall where Darius was. Marshall had just enough time to look over and see the explosion, but Darius was gone. What had happened? What had he missed? Maybe it was all too much, and Darius had made a run for it. Even with his leg injury? Perhaps he'd limped away to get out of here.

Marshall felt alone, lost. He looked around, and there was nobody. Nobody but himself to face what was coming. More trucks were approaching from the other direction. Four or five of them coming up the track toward the compound. Within minutes the whole place would be filled with rebels shooting at him. He was seriously outnumbered and outgunned. He looked over at Jensen's body were it lay motionless. Marshall needed to decide what to do next. Should he make a run for it, too?

Tradecraft: *Unlike in the movies, when your friend gets shot, you don't abandon the firefight to go and hold his hand as he dies. Chances are, you'd get yourself shot, too, and your mate might have only twisted his ankle. You shoot back and win the firefight first, then, and only then do you attend to any casualties. That way, you can give injured personnel your full attention without risking getting shot yourself.*

The convoy of trucks roared into the compound. Marshall had braced himself to be attacked. This was going to be his last stand. His world went from a place where it was going to end and miraculously shifted in a fraction of a second to an answered prayer.

Damien dropped out of the lead truck as a mass of the prince's men jumped out and launched a full-scale attack on the other truck of rebels. Damien stooped as he ran for cover with Marshall.

"What's going on? You said you were ready for extraction, and it was all done!" Damien shrieked.

"Everything went to rat shit!" Marshall shouted above the gunfire. "Jensen's dead, Aram got away, and I've got no idea where Darius has gone!"

They huddled for cover behind the wall, but when a crack of gunfire smashed away at the bricks right beside them, Damien panicked and ran back toward the trucks.

Marshall cocked an AK47 he'd removed from one of the rebels and returned fire. He looked up as another couple of rounds tinged off the truck Damien was running toward. Damien freaked out and froze on the spot. He turned around, but in mid-turn, a shot sounded out, and blood sprayed from the side of his neck. Damien's hand grabbed his neck as he fell to the ground and lay there clutching the blood seeping out.

The gunfire ceased. Everything went quiet. Noises of talking in Arabic in the background were drowned out by the footsteps of one of the prince's men.

"Mr. Marshall? It is all over. The last few have run off into the mountains. We have taken control of the area and killed the sniper from the hills."

The man who seemed to be in charge of the prince's men walked away as Marshall nodded. It had gone so quiet. Like an ordinary peaceful day. It was almost impossible to imagine there was carnage and chaos only moments ago. Marshall's mind switched back to reality, back to the present. He got to his feet and ran over to Jensen's body.

Crumbled brick and rubble surrounded Jensen as he lay there, a huge concrete area that housed a drain was raised behind his head, pushing his neck forward slightly. Dust had settled all over him. Something didn't seem right, though. He wasn't sure what it was at first, but then he saw the sniper tape lapping the edge of his body armor. Jensen had taped something to the rear of it. Marshall pulled him up slightly and cut the body armor straps, then pulled it away.

"Phone books!" Marshall yelled. "You taped phone books to the back of this shitty armor!"

They had stopped the bullet. Jensen was still breathing!

As he'd fallen backward from the impact, he'd hit his head on the concrete drain, knocking him unconscious. Marshall poured water from his canteen over Jensen's face, waking him instantly. With a huge intake of breath, Jensen snapped awake, looking around him with a sense of dread.

"What happened?" he asked, rolling onto his side in an attempt to haul himself up to a standing position.

"You bumped your head." Before Marshall could go on, Darius's voice was heard. A couple of the prince's men were helping him along, with Aram as his captive next to him.

"Darius!" Marshall exclaimed. "Where did you go?"

"Aram was getting away, so I went after him. I wasn't going to let him go. No way do I want to do all this again."

The three of them let out a chuckle as Jensen attempted to get to his feet.

A groan from Damien, still lying on the floor, made all of them look over. Jensen and Marshall ran over to check the severity of the wound and give medical attention to it.

Jensen knelt beside Damien. "Don't worry, I'm going to get you sorted." Jensen pulled Damien's hand back and stopped in his tracks. Both Marshall and Jensen just looked down for a moment at Damien.

"What is it? Am I going to die?" Damien asked, filled with fear. Marshall and Jensen burst into fits of laughter at the tiniest nick on the side of Damien's neck. It was barely a scratch from a tiny piece of stray shrapnel flying through the air.

"What, guys? Tell me!" Damien shrieked, his voice filled with fear.

"You'll more than likely survive," Marshall said with a chuckle. "I've cut myself shaving worse than that."

Damien stood, holding his neck, and moved over to the truck to try to see the wound in the side mirror on the door.

Jensen moved closer to Damien, where the prince's team leader had joined him.

"Load this truck up first, and then we can get the fuck out of here. The rest of the pallets can go on the other three trucks, and you and the myrmidons can go back to Prince Charming and tell him we've done what we agreed."

While the trucks were being loaded, Jensen went back inside the house. He took a carrier bag from his day sack and placed it on the table. Sliding out the contents of the bag, he arranged them.

There was a large Tupperware container with two wires trailing to a paper bag. The Tupperware container was about three-quarters filled with rice. Two lengths of laminate flooring had been cut down to fit inside with a block at each end, keeping them about a quarter of an inch apart. In the middle of the flex boards, a nut and bolt were going through a hole in the middle with a wire attached to each one. Jensen poured water all over the rice until it almost reached the surface. He wrapped the boards in a plastic rubble sack and put them back into the Tupperware container, clipping the lid tightly and wrapping duct tape around it. The two wires led to a paper bag connected to a nine-volt battery part way down and both with crocodile clips on end. The crocodile clips were gripping onto a bundle of fine-grade steel wool, all stuffed into the paper bag filled with cotton waste … like the lint from a tumble dryer. As the rice absorbed the water, it would expand, pushing upward and bending the flex boards, causing them to touch in the middle. The two bolts would make contact, completing the circuit powered by the nine-volt battery and making the steel wool instantly burst into flames. The flames would spread rapidly as the cotton waste acted as tinder, and the bag would be on fire in no time.

Jensen strategically placed the bag where it would cause maximum damage and loosely piled furniture around it from anywhere in the room, using whatever he could scrounge to add as kindling. A few other bottles of flammable stuff were thrown in for good measure. He emerged from the house to find that the second truck had almost completed loading.

When he passed Damien, who was fidgeting and looking extremely nervous as he paced impatiently back and forth at the truck's rear, he said, "You got about half an hour before the whole place will be a fireball, so I'm glad your guys are moving quickly." Jensen's words didn't seem to soothe Damien, and the color drained from his already pale face.

Patting him on the shoulder, Jensen walked toward the driver's door of the truck where Marshall, a patched-up Darius, a tied-up Aram, and a few extra procured weapons all waited to depart, leaving Damien standing at the back looking like a virgin in a whorehouse.

"You'll be fine!" Jensen shouted back as he pulled open the truck door. The hinges creaked as he pulled himself into the cab, started the engine, and pulled away.

"That's easy for you to say. I'm here alone in Shit Street if more of Aram's men arrive." Damien's words were said out loud, but nobody was there to hear him.

They weren't driving long before Jensen looked back in the rearview mirror and saw plumes of black smoke from the direction of Aram's house. A wry smile showed on his face, but he kept quiet.

Chapter 38

The agreed area for the handover wasn't far from Antalya Airport, which worked out satisfactorily for all concerned. Jensen drove the truck straight into a loading area where the truck was unloaded and the pallets stowed safely in the prince's private jet. Marshall and Darius watched the operation with interest while Jensen went, with a wad of US dollars, to get his hands on a suitable vehicle. In record time, he was back with a bright yellow Renault, complete with the obligatory furry dice.

"You couldn't have bought anything more conspicuous?" Marshall asked.

"It's the best I could do on short notice," Jensen replied somewhat sheepishly.

"Remind me to call ahead next time." Marshall laughed.

Even Darius laughed, momentarily forgetting about the throbbing pain in his leg.

"I'll need to take Darius with me to provide cover," Jensen said.

"He's not in the right state to fight, mate," Marshall said.

"He only has to sit in the passenger seat with a rifle and look mean. It's more of a bluff, really, and let's face it, it's not like he could do much guarding the money if a mob were to show up. No, you stay here and keep an eye on the cash, he can watch me through the scope."

Marshall was concerned about Jensen's choice of tactics, but after thinking about it for a second or two, he realized Jensen was right. And if it meant he got to stay with the money and not get killed, that option definitely had its merits.

Marshall piled the captive into the trunk of car while Jensen helped Darius to hobble over to the passenger side.

"Just keep the rifle up and look like you're ready to shoot anybody who tries to pull anything," Jensen instructed.

"I got shot in the leg, not the brain. It's walking I'm struggling with, not thinking." Darius's words came in between grunts of pain as they got him into the car.

Jensen ran around to the driver's side and clambered in. Marshall stood by the open window on the passenger side, and Jensen watched him as he started the engine.

"Now, you know what to do if this all goes to rat shit, right?" Jensen knew he did but wanted one last verbal reassurance from Marshall.

"Yep. Vegas, baby!" Marshall yelled with just a little too much enthusiasm.

Jensen rolled his eyes at Marshall. "See you when we get back," he said as they drove off to deliver the package.

"Do you trust him with all of that money?" Darius sounded genuinely concerned.

"No." The reply was short and to the point. Darius looked concerned, unsure if he'd heard Jensen correctly. "But he knows if he did fuck off with the money, I'd find him, and he certainly knows it's not worth it. So don't worry, he'll still be there when we get back."

Darius breathed out a sigh of relief and, knowing that his share of the money was safe, returned to contemplating his most immediate issue, the throbbing pain in his thigh.

When they pulled up at the appointed meeting place, Silver Top wandered over to the car. Jensen wound down the window and the cantankerous major poked his head through.

"You took your sweet time, twinkle tits. You only had to acquire one target, for fuck's sake. We've already shut down the London branch of his operation. Your nemesis, who gave you all the grief and sliced your partner's girlfriend, has been made to disappear, and we are in the process of clearing out the relatives in Europe. Have you got that sniveling sack of repulsive waste for me?" Silver Top's tone had hardly changed.

"Are you always this friendly, Major Jackson?" Jensen asked.

"Well, ain't you just the regular Sherlock Homo? And I see Jessica over there, where's Roger?"

"Actually, it was me that found out who you are," Darius added.

"Well, ain't you just a multi-talented commie faggot then? I bet you can lick shit and suck cum from the same ass at the same time, can't you?"

"He's from Lithuania!" Jensen realized too late that his attempt to defend Darius was futile.

"Oh, so you're from that shitty little bit of Russia that even Russia didn't want? No wonder you're such a reject, commie. Now, enough foreplay, you shit-shoving fairies, where's my package?"

"In the trunk." Jensen pulled a lever and the trunk lid popped open. He went to the back and, not too gently, manhandled the Arab out.

Aram groaned as he was being dragged from the rear of the car but didn't put up any kind of a struggle. Two Marines came over and grabbed him, one on either side, his feet barely touching the ground. Without so much as a second thought, Jensen plowed his right fist into Aram's face, splattering his nose and knocking him out of the grip of the Marines to fall flat on his back in the sand. The two Marines instantly picked him up and dragged him away to a waiting military truck.

"I said I wanted him in one piece," the major growled, trying desperately to hide the hint of a smirk of approval.

"Pucker up!" Jensen replied as he walked back to the car's driver's side door.

Jackson looked at him quizzically. "What the fuck d'ya mean by that?"

"So you can kiss my ass!" Jensen smiled as he got back in the vehicle, started the engine, and hastily drove away. Major Jackson took a drag of a barely lit cigar.

"I like that boy. He's an ignorant fuckwit panty wedge who needs some manners shoved so far up his ass they come out his mouth, but I like him." The major was talking to himself now. His face creased in a grin as the Renault drove off and he took another pull on his cigar.

***

Jensen and Darius were still laughing as they turned into the airfield to see Marshall and the jet waiting there.

"See, I told you. Now let's get you somewhere we can get that leg properly treated."

Jensen pulled the vehicle up alongside the plane. Marshall had already opened the passenger door, and Jensen got out and moved quickly around to the other side to help get their wounded comrade out. Darius winced with every move, the pain evident on his face, but his sense of humor still intact.

"I don't think we should do this too often," he joked as they lifted him from the passenger seat.

They all laughed as they loaded Darius onto the jet. Once settled, everyone made themselves comfortable. The interior of the prince's private jet was so lush that without thinking, they all took off their boots so as not to stain the thick pile of the cream carpet. They had deposited Darius in one of the deep and comfortable leather chairs, and Marshall moved forward, grabbing a decanter and one of the crystal glasses.

"Something for the pain, sir?" he asked, tilting the glass in Darius's direction.

"Oh yes, please." Darius mustered the strength to sit forward and was literally licking his lips.

"Good old Ginge has arranged for three vans from six's usual rental company to meet us on the tarmac when we land at Farnborough Airport. We split the money, get unloaded, and head for home." Jensen told the other two. "Darius, he arranged for some morphine to be waiting for you. Are you going to be okay to drive?"

Darius held up the bottle and checked the level of the liquor. "As long as this stuff is all gone and worn off by the time we touch down," he chuckled, looking into the glass and draining it in one swallow.

Chapter 39

Darius had ignored the advice of the Harley Street doctor and checked out of the top London private hospital. He was on his way to see Olivia, and nothing was going to stop him. Not even a bullet wound. Marshall made his way to an undisclosed location where Gucci was being prepared to be shipped out.

"Fifteen minutes." A serious voice snarled as he palmed the envelope of dollar bills. Marshall walked into the dingy room where al-Salah was restrained with handcuffs over a high pipe that ran the room's length. The cuffs kept his hands above his head and his bare feet just about able to touch the ground. The designer suit had been replaced with a pair of ill-fitting overalls.

"Orange really suits you," Marshall quipped. "I was going to bring you some water, but I figured you'd probably be sick of the stuff soon with where you're going." Marshall taunted al-Salah, but he remained defiant with that look of disdain still present in his eyes. Marshall pulled a ceramic razor from his pocket and proceeded to flick it onto his other hand. He slowly pulled a long strip of duct tape that had been discreetly stuck on the inside of his jacket.

"So they can't hear you screaming and begging."

"You can hurt me all you want. It will make no difference." Through gritted teeth, al-Salah's words were spoken in preparation for the pain he was gearing himself up for.

"Hurt you? Ha! Hell no. I've just come to have a chat." Marshall wrapped the tape around

Gucci's head, covering his mouth, and scruffing up his hair. "Sandy was an innocent in all this. She did nothing other than fall in love. She didn't deserve to die for that. That's what really hurt me more than anything. Hurting me? I can deal with that but not her. So that got me thinking, what would make you feel the same way? I decided to take the time to think about what I could possibly do to hurt you the most." He put the razor away and pulled a chair from the corner.

Marshall retrieved a manila file that was shoved down the waistband inside the back of his jeans. "Quite the student, your boy." Marshall flicked through the file as he spoke. The look in al-Salah's eyes changed. "He'll be out of surgery about now." Marshall paused, smiling as he watched Gucci's mind working overtime. "Don't worry, we've got the best team of people working on him. I've even met his new parents. Lovely people. I can already tell he's going to make a devout Christian! I've even enrolled him in Sunday school already."

Marshall's grin had become even broader as he spoke. The fear showed all over al-Salah's face. "Don't worry, though, he won't be in that situation for long. I want him treated worse than an Afghan prison goat!" Tears were forming in al-Salah's eyes with every word Marshall spoke. "I had to call in a bunch of favors and bribe a few people to get what I wanted. But hey, it's not my money, so what do I care? Ironic, really, isn't it? Your money is going to be funding your own misery. Ha, you're paying for your own torture. Well, while you're suffering in the cell of whatever hell hole you end up in, just think of your son gripping the Holy Bible and praying to God as he cries himself to sleep after being passed around the prison showers in a worse hell hole than the one you're in."

Marshall took a Polaroid picture from his pocket and slotted it into al-Salah's overalls. "A little keepsake to take with you. A lovely picture of your lad showing off his new crucifix." Marshall patted Gucci on the back. "Ha, glad we had this chat." He walked over and knocked on the cell door. "Oh. You're probably wondering what I meant when I mentioned his surgery?" Marshall had extended the index and middle fingers on his hand, making a snipping motion. "Wouldn't want the little fucker breeding now, would we? He's the last of your bloodline." Tears poured from al-Salah's eyes, and Marshall turned to look at him before the door was shut—a broken man, the look of defiance extinguished without a trace. The door slammed shut, and Marshall walked away satisfied, finally having closure.

"Make sure the kid's taken care of, and that piece of shit never gets to see him again," Marshall said to one of the team leaders at the black site.

Marshall walked back outside and sat in the driver's seat of the rented van. He unscrewed the cap from a fifth-size bottle of whiskey, raising it up in front of him. "Rest in peace, Sandy." He looked upward with both a tear and a smile. He stopped just short of taking a swig, then stared at the bottle. He didn't need it. Re-screwing the cap back on, he got out of the van and dropped it into the trash.

Chapter 40

The hotel parking garage was almost empty, and Jensen picked a spot as close to the elevator as he could. The lights illuminated the entire level as they flashed to say the doors on the van had been remotely locked. Jensen's footsteps echoed as he walked over and pressed the call button.

When the doors slid open, he inserted the room card he had and pushed the "floor" button and "close doors" button simultaneously until the doors had fully closed and the elevator had moved, then released them as he went up.

Tradecraft: *This little trick meant he would go straight up to the floor he wanted unimpeded and didn't have to worry about picking up extra passengers from the lobby, or any other floor for that matter. A snazzy little hack, especially if you're trying to get a VIP under close protection to their room without the risk of the doors flying open on any random floor.*

When he stepped out of the elevator, the corridor seemed to be so much longer than he remembered. The doors slid shut again, and he walked to the room where he'd left MJ and Elena. He got butterflies, and his pulse was racing again but this time for all good reasons. His hair stood on end as he turned, cleared his throat, and knocked on the door.

"MJ, it's me!" he said, his voice filled with excitement.

"What's the safe word?" Her voice came back playful and excited.

Shit, what was it? he thought. "*It was something Latin, no a Greek god. No a planet.*"

Before he'd recalled it, the hotel door flung open, and MJ sprung out, wrapping her arms around him.

"Oh, thank you. I love you!" She was laughing and crying simultaneously. Jensen wasn't even sure what he was being thanked for but wasn't going to argue.

"Daddy!" The little voice came from inside the room, the pattering of Elena's feet sounding out as she too ran to hug him.

"Daddy, Daddy." Elena was so excited her voice was filled with joy. "Daddy, I need the toilet!"

Jensen laughed and picked her up, taking her to the hotel bathroom, where he plonked her on the toilet. Turning a little red-faced, she strained.

"I'm not trained for this!" he yelled, then laughed out loud.